The Führer Must Die

The Führer Must Die

A Novel

Victoria Andre King

YUCCA

Yucca Publishing books may be purchased in bulk at special discounts for sales promotion, corporate gifts, fund-raising, or educational purposes. Special editions can also be created to specifications. For details, contact the Special Sales Department, Yucca Publishing, 307 West 36th Street, 11th Floor, New York, NY 10018 or yucca@skyhorsepublishing.com.

Yucca Publishing® is an imprint of Skyhorse Publishing, Inc.®, a Delaware corporation. Visit our website at www.yuccapub.com.

10 9 8 7 6 5 4 3 2 1

Library of Congress Cataloging-in-Publication Data is available on file.

Jacket photo: Dreamstime/Fernando Gregory

Print ISBN: 978-1-63158-104-5
Ebook ISBN: 978-1-63158-110-6

Printed in the United States of America

To Don,

I owe you a tombstone and I wish you were here.

Author's Note

A storyteller is under a different kind of obligation than a historian. Usually, history expresses the folly of the victors.

Politics, on the other hand, expresses the unrequited desires of the insatiable.

A historian is supposed to tell what they can prove actually happened. A storyteller tells what should have happened or what might have happened. But, a story is a story nonetheless an inevitably subjective account of what happened to somebody sometime...

I hope you enjoy it, but cannot guarantee any particular outcome or conclusion.

—Victoria

Acknowledgments

Some stories just get under your skin. Some individuals are remarkable precisely because, although they appear quite ordinary, they prove to be capable of extraordinary things. Georg Elser was just such an extraordinary, ordinary, man. . . as was Donald Schwarz.

I would like to extend special thanks to the librarians at the East 67th Street and Webster (York Ave.) branches of the New York Public Library (Don's home away from home where the lion's share of the research was done). They had the patience and tenacity to deal with my dear friend's changeable demeanor.

Also I extend many thanks to Peter & Sandra Riva for their valuable assistance throughout the arduous process of editing tweaking and finally getting this work out there.

I owe so much to my husband, Aristophanes Kondos. Not only did he understand and encourage Don's and my inexplicable yet bizarrely creative friendship, he also encouraged me when my confidence was at its nadir and supported my insanity even when that resulted in privations.

Lastly two great books by two great historians:

THE FUHRER AND THE PEOPLE
by
J. P. Stern.
and
HITLER'S PERSONAL SECURITY
by
Peter Hoffmann

The Führer Must Die

NOVEMBER 8TH, 1939

THE STIFF SUSPENSION OF THE R-35 motorbike jolted the spine of the Corporal astride it at every rut along the empty Munich streets. The dense fog caused the light to bubble around the street lamps and had filled the Corporal's goggles with sooty smears. He had tried negotiating his way without them but the gooey air had caused his eyes to sting. The limited visibility had made his progress frustratingly slow so he perked up a bit when the illuminated entrance of the BürgerBräuKeller came into view . . . that was until he recalled why he was going there.

Meanwhile, at a forlorn border crossing, two guards sat playing cards and taking turns glancing out the windows while they waited for the Führer's speech to begin. The particular crossing was on the outskirts of a sleepy berg called Konstanz located at the tip of a promontory, which, if seen from the air, resembled the scrotum of Germany nudging the northern border of Switzerland. It was banked on either side by two bodies of water: the smaller Untersee to the west, and the Obersee Bodensee to the east and south. It was never quite clear to which country the bodies of water rightfully belonged and as such was one of those unnatural borders that should have led to war long before as had happened in Danzig, the problem with Konstanz was that no one was interested. That inevitably made it the best possible place to sneak out of Germany.

The city's economic ties were with Switzerland and most of the locals had been commuting across the border for the greater part of their adult lives. In the '20s Konstanz had been a tourist trap, but by 1939 the tourists were gone and the only available jobs were in the towns that ringed Basel and Zurich. People commuted to work during the day or to their lovers at night or smuggled undisturbed. The traffic was too heavy for customs checks to be more than random. Even the border police had lost interest.

The night of November 8th however was unusually cold and traffic had died off before 9:00 p.m. The night was very black and white. No snow had fallen yet, but the moon was close to full and the pine and fir trees on the hills stood out blacker than the sky, sucking up the light around them. The thin wind off the lakes had given up once the temperature had shifted and the branches of the fir trees hung down heavily in the cold, wet air waiting to freeze.

Back in Munich SS officer Christian Weber, the Führer's chief of security for the event, listened without expression as the Corporal relayed the message. Yet another change in the program . . . this particular appearance had come to resemble one of those British drawing room comedies, the sort of theatre that was utterly incomprehensible to a practical people like the Germans. Weber was secretly elated at the prospect of the evening's activities winding down early and thus the weight of the entourage leaving his shoulders and returning to Berlin, but he had a solemn duty to show his underling that he was inconvenienced, lest the chain of command be threatened. Personally he found the "Old Guard" a tiresome "pride" of toothless lions, to whom the only pleasure that remained was hearing themselves roar. There were times when the amount of sentimentality that permeated the Reich baffled him, but alas. . . orders were orders.

Outside Konstanz the night was almost dead. The only movement was a solitary man walking through the trees moving relentlessly toward the Swiss border. Georg Elser was so completely ordinary that he was difficult to describe. There was no feature or gesture that summed him up. There was a strange lack of anything personal; even his women had always had trouble remembering what he looked like. Men rarely ever noticed him at all and that was the only reason he was still alive. He was of less than average height and very thin, swallowed up in a cheap black overcoat. With the moonlight full in his face his eyes shimmered like silver.

One hundred meters from the border he gave up any attempt at concealment and walked dreamily toward Switzerland. He was unarmed. He'd heard that in America every worker carried a weapon, but that was because in America work had a quality of adventure to it, a sense that all possibilities were open. In Germany they weren't; work was just boring and hopeless and you lived your life without interest, like it was a dead-end civil service job.

Back in Munich, Weber approached the entourage. He scanned the faces, searching for the next appropriate link in the chain of command, and speculated as to who they would finally appoint to inform the Führer at the podium. The din seemed to be nearing crescendo, that shrill voice reaching a feverish pitch while enthusiastic bellows emitted from the hall below. Weber dutifully singled out his immediate superior and passed the "hot potato" on.

Georg flexed his hands in his pockets, the thick tendons creaking in the cold; he was reminded of his strength and comforted by it. In the thin coat he hunched his shoulders against the cold and the darkness gave him the deformed shape of a factory worker: shoulders narrow, face unnaturally large, torso scrawny yet muscular as a chimpanzee's with the thick overdeveloped forearms of a carpenter. When he worked they swelled up to twice their size and the thick blue rubbery veins stood out hard as bone. Inside pockets, his hands were clenched against the cold, the fingers pressed to the palms and the hands pressed against his body the way a young child would hold them. Outside of the childish awkwardness there wasn't much to him, he was hardly there at all—the reason women had often found him attractive. He was like the faceless, strictly functional male figure in a feminine fantasy and women were able fit him into their current daydream without the slightest difficulty.

The sound of Hitler's voice pummeled its way into his consciousness. The Führer was working himself into a rage fit and somewhere in his subconscious Georg realised that he wasn't imagining it . . . he was actually hearing it, but he still didn't pay any notice.

At the border crossing the two guards were now smoking and watching the checkpoint from the open window of their post which, as the sign said, had once been a school for "Defective Children." They listened to the insect drone of Hitler's voice coming from their radio and the Austrian accent was murderous, you had to listen carefully to understand what was being said and the radio was turned up so loud that you couldn't tell the static from that screaming, scratchy voice. Georg heard it as clearly as the guards saw him, but it didn't register; it was indistinguishable from the other voices raging inside his head.

So, as he reached the checkpoint, the two guards seemed to appear out of nowhere and cut off his escape front and back. . . .

"*Papiere, bitte!*"

Papers, please . . . the one essential German phrase. The guards seemed more disgruntled than anything else, aggravated at having had to leave the comparative warmth of their post. Georg handed his papers over and smiled.

"Johann Georg Elser . . .," said the guard who was holding his papers, ". . . your travel permit is five years out of date."

"My apologies, I should have had it renewed."

He smiled again as he said it and the guards, not being complicated men, thought as clearly as if it had been written in cartoon balloons over their heads. . . . "*He's harmless so we should just let him pass.*" The best way to deal with a breach of routine since the dawn of time has always been to ignore it, and Georg was helping them with his innocent smile. But the guards were annoyed by the need to make a decision. Clearly, he was not a deserter so the simplest thing would be to let him go. He'd be let go anyway and there would be a stack of paperwork to make out in quintuplicate and all for nothing. . . .

But then, they noticed that he had no luggage. You do not travel to a foreign country, even one so close, without luggage, without even a tooth brush or a tool box. Again the balloons as they thought: "*He's a young man so perhaps he's visiting his girlfriend!*" So, one of the guards gave him a meaningful look.

"Purpose of visit?"

But Georg remained silent. He had never actually given it any thought so he actually had no idea. Spontaneous improvisation was not in his nature, and it had never occurred to him to rehearse something he had done so many times in the past.

"This is a routine inquiry. . ." said the guard holding his papers, ". . . but since your papers are not in order, we must conduct a body search."

Georg put his hands on top of his head and smiled again, but the guards had stopped watching his face. Their search was as slovenly as his attempt to cross the border. They were violating standard procedure. One searched him while the other stood looking over his colleague's shoulder with polite interest. That man should have been at a distance of five meters, covering Georg with a pistol in case he attempted to run, but they seemed to be inviting him to try or, maybe they were just sure he wouldn't.

The guards found nothing sinister, but what they did find was irritatingly pointless: some finely machined pieces of shiny metal, a dog-eared copy of Brecht's *Die Dreigroschenoper* or "*The Threepenny Opera*" with the name *Celia Peachum* scribbled across the top and a souvenir postcard from the BürgerBräuKeller, a beer hall in Munich. To complicate things further, the postcard showed the Führer speaking in the ballroom, face contorted, sawing at the air with fists clenched in rage between two rapt looking nerds with Hitler mustaches; a strange thing for a man trying to slink his way out of the country to be carrying. Clearly, as noted, the man was not a deserter. But no luggage and no girlfriend, that was very irregular and the guards did not like irregularities. Finally, they walked back into the school house for *defective children* and called for a *Polizei-Kubelwagen* to take him back to Konstanz, five kilometers from their post. They didn't say what to charge him with, that was never a problem as there were plenty of unsolved crimes in search of culprits.

Georg was driven back to Konstanz by one tired, old cop who kept him handcuffed in the front seat and didn't ask any questions. Being a police car, the kubelwagen had a radio. It was tuned to the Führer's broadcast; it had to be, it was on every station and the Führer raved on and on, chanting himself into a trance. He'd been talking for almost an hour and by now the stac-cato delivery was so fast that the words were unintelligible. It didn't matter, the bright giddy meaning was clear and the crowd clapped and stamped and shouted.

The Führer was still at it when the cop put Georg in a detention cell and began to itemize his belongings on a wooden table of an indeterminate color. The cop noted them down carefully as if he were signing a peace treaty, bearing down on the pencil to mark his way through all four carbons. The radio was still tuned to the Führer's speech, but it wasn't clear if it was Hitler or some party hack, they all sounded alike anymore. The same kind of hoarse grating voice straining beyond its range, the voice breaking then coughing itself clear and then starting again with a whoop and a shriek, rampant.

The cop's brows furrowed as he read the title of the play and he hissed between his teeth, "*Entartete kunst . . .*"—degenerate art. Then he came to the postcard from the BürgerBräuKeller. His shoulder badge announced that he was an *Anwarter*, an apprentice patrolman, though he looked like he was over seventy. All the able-bodied men were in the SS, preparing to defend the world from civilization. The "leftover" Anwarter glared at Georg suspiciously.

"Right now, at this very moment we are listening to the Führer speak from the BürgerBräuKeller."

The radio made a bang and a shrieking whistle and then went dead silent. The Anwarter looked at Georg with his face out of gear, as if he were asking himself a vague question. Georg gave him his most beautiful smile and said, "The applause sounded almost like an explosion."

The BürgerBräuKeller in Munich was a 300-year-old structure that had been built to last 100 years. It half supported the buildings leaning against it like a group of drunks that somehow managed to prop each other up. Under the force of the explosion the building swayed and shifted, trying to find a new point of balance. The gas lines to the kitchen had ruptured and were blowing flames into the ballroom. The ancient wood, dry as paper, was burning out of control and the stamped tin ceiling had come down like a massive fly swatter.

Within minutes the street outside was crawling with firemen and police. Access should have been easy because parts of the walls had blown out, but the tin ceiling was too big and wedged too tightly to be moved and they had no tools except the usual fire brigade axes and pry bars. An acetylene torch was suggested but, even if one could have been found, it would have cooked the wounded trapped underneath. Tin snips were suggested, but it would have taken hours to cut the ceiling into manageable pieces and they had minutes at best. Those who had thought to bring the manual rapidly thumbed through it to make sure they were following the authorized procedure for the situation, only to find that the manual did not cover such a situation. There were no rules to guide them, they were entirely on their own and would be judged by the success or failure of their decisions. It was completely unfair and absolutely terrifying. Someone suggested propping up the ceiling, but that would have required heavy machinery and they didn't have that either. Police, SS, SD, Gestapo, and Nazi party officials were in tight groups and shouting at each other. No one was listening, not even to themselves; it wasn't communication. The shouting seemed to serve some other utterly egoistic function for self preservation.

Each of the distinct interest groups represented had its own hierarchy. Distinguished-looking gentlemen were clinging desperately to procedure in an attempt to disguise their own terror while simultaneously trying to bully their underlings into taking as much responsibility as possible. It could be said that the stiffer the upper lip, the greater the sense of imminent doom. By far the stiffest upper lip on site belonged to Baron Karl von Eberstein, Munich Polizei Prasident, whose unenviable responsibility it had been to oversee security—albeit unofficially—for the Führer's appearance. The "official" responsibility had belonged to SS officer Christian Weber, who no one could locate at the moment and who, as such things usually went, would probably never be seen or heard from again.

Over the years, von Eberstein's title had afforded him certain privileges and a diverse social circle; however, it could by no means shield him from political fallout. To keep himself from becoming the Gestapo poster boy, he had to provide them another alternative immediately, and the shoe would have to fit more perfectly than Cinderella's. He scanned the various huddles of authority seeking out an ally; if not an actual ally then at least someone he could intimidate or manipulate sufficiently to save himself. The chosen would have to be high enough on the food chain to be effective, yet not high enough to sell Eberstein out to save their own future.

Artur Nebe had initially chosen a career in criminal investigation because he found it pleasantly diverting. It was one of few fields in which you could work as an individual, yet have access to functionaries who could relieve you of tedious errands. The political changes of the last few years had become more and more troubling. Anytime you looked over your shoulder somebody was always staring back, somebody who of course also had somebody else looking over their shoulder and so on. Personal loyalty and professional loyalty had given way to party loyalty, which basically meant you couldn't trust anybody anymore. Nebe gazed over the beer hall wreckage grimly. Whatever the motive had been, the result was purely political and would be exploited as such, serving the perfect pretext for nervous party climbers—people whose only insurance was the obliteration of all competence in the ranks below them. In five days, he would be forty-five years old; too old and too poor to enjoy life in exile, yet too young for any hope of retirement. Amidst the rubble he spotted his personal functionaries dutifully collecting physical evidence, photographs, and measurements, and he wondered for how long they could be counted on even for that.

A voice like shaved ice, the timbre almost but not quite effeminate, whispered in his ear.

"Herr Obersturmbannführer."

Nebe turned to gaze directly at the man's Adam's apple; he had to look up to meet the eyes. Von Eberstein had intentionally stood upon a section of broken wall to gain a height advantage. However ridiculous that might have made von Eberstein appear, Nebe responded formally, he was after all a civilized man.

"Baron! How might I be of service?"

The use of his civilian title as opposed to his SS rank caused von Eberstein's rib cage to expand noticeably and an expression of benevolence to soften his upper lip.

"Artur, I consider you to be among the very few members of the Polizei possessed of intelligence, imagination, and integrity".

Nebe's given name followed by three flattering epithets all beginning with the same vowel. . . . The situation was far worse than he could have possibly imagined. A sudden vision of Pontius Pilate caused him to struggle somewhere between mirth and dread.

"Rest assured, Baron, that you will be the first to learn of any and every development."

"I greatly appreciate your dedication. Herr Mueller has suddenly expressed an unusually personal interest in the outcome of this particular investigation. I'm sure you understand."

The steel gray eyes were most adept at conveying the abyss awaiting both men in the event that the outcome should disappoint.

Nebe remembered Heinrich Mueller, he had abandoned the ranks of the regular police in order to accept an appointment to some Gestapo Special Department, aside from being an obvious example of extreme bad taste, it was a sign of insane ambition—nothing sacred and no-holds-barred ambition.

"No sense in wasting time then. Am I to contact you directly?"

"Day or night, without exception."

Von Eberstein proceeded with as much dignity as one possibly could while stepping over corpses. Nebe watched him go with grim stoicism, comforted only by the affirmation seeking glances he received from his functionaries.

In the ballroom, the dead lay in awkward positions with their hair burnt away. Normally, the dead are so relaxed that they seem to be suffering only from sexual exhaustion. But the increased heat had caused muscles to tighten; the dead had shifted and crouched, faces hardened, and they slowly extended their arms toward each other. The movement was so gradual that it was impossible to say when it stopped. The firemen tried to pull the victims from the wreckage, but all they got were pieces that came off in their hands. At either end of that horrific tableau, transfixed and appalled, were Baron von Eberstein and Artur Nebe. Like a lot of people that night they had taken to wondering exactly how far it was to the Swiss border. The smell of roast meat was in the air. Many realized they were hungry.

November 9th, 1939

Back in Konstanz, Georg Elser was dreaming.

In his dream, Georg was back in that dingily furnished room that had been grimly scrubbed clean. He was in bed twitching in his sleep like a cat dreaming of mice. He'd been sleeping with the girl he'd met the night before; A tall, ugly girl with a bad face but good legs.

It was her room and she was already up. Her name was Hannah and although it sounded Jewish, it was short for Hannahlehr, an ultimately German name. Still there was something Jewish in the angular face and sorrowful eyes. She watched the man in her bed with a motherly expression that had nothing to do with her feelings. She was determined to save the situation, no matter what, and she forced the expression onto her face to reassure herself that there was nothing wrong. It was her room and that gave her an animal confidence, but that situation had gotten her scared. She had always enjoyed feeling vulnerable as long as it had to do with sex, but this was sickness. The man jerked and twisted in her bed, arms and legs twitching all at the same time, a sure sign of a first-rate nightmare, if it wasn't epilepsy.

Then he jerked himself awake and snapped into a sitting position, wide-eyed and staring, he shouted. . . .

"I didn't do it!"

She reached for him professionally with the frank confidence of a nurse in her hard, narrow hands. She sat down beside him, took him by the wrists and pulled herself forward, leaning over him nose to nose.

"Of course you didn't . . ."

She said it carefully.

"You didn't do anything."

Georg didn't answer. He squinted into space, seeing something happen somewhere else. He seemed likely to remain that way for the moment and, while she waited for him to snap out of it, she walked to the window and looked at the dawn sky. It was dingy too, gray over the town of Heidenheim.

Like every small German town, it looked like a fairy tale gone wrong. In the easy days of the republic, arson had been popular among the landlords. In the 1850s, everything had been declared a national monument. To put up a new building, you had to first burn down the old one. It was the only way to get rid of it.

Hannah glanced back at the man in her bed, another fairy tale gone wrong.

"Bad dreams?"

Her question was conclusive, like a doctor delivering a prognosis. Georg didn't answer.

"That bad!?"

He was still silent so she stomped over to the closet and threw it open. There were three white uniforms, a black worsted suit for funerals, and a cheap print dress. She reached behind them all to pull out a negligee that had cost her three months' salary. She put it on and Georg woke up a little. It was much too frilly for her, very sad, but kind of sweet.

"Morning after horrors?"

It wasn't actually a question but when Georg didn't respond she spat out, "I'm not that ugly!"

Her voice had risen to a shriek but Georg had only heard the last part of it.

"What are you talking about?"

He had said it very quietly.

"I asked if you've ever been kicked down a flight of stairs before."

"I'd better go . . ."

He started to get dressed but it was a complicated process. He had his pants under the mattress to maintain the crease. His coat and shirt were on the back of a chair. His shorts and under shirt were on a hanger in front of a partially open window. His shoes were lined up under the bed with the socks tucked inside. His shoes had been lined up under the bed every night of his life.

The inexplicable pressure he felt made him wildly uncomfortable. He scrambled out of bed and began skipping from one part of the room to another. Hannah turned on a hot plate and put on an Italian espresso pot.

She intervened gracefully.

"I think you had better sit down and have some coffee. A man is never responsible for anything he says in the morning before he's had coffee."

Georg was sitting on the bed with his right shoe on and the left one in both hands. To remove the right one would have insinuated a level of intimacy well beyond his emotional range. Being the sort of person who, having initiated an action found it impossible not to complete it, he really had no alternative but to put on his left shoe as well before tucking in his shirt.

"Did your mother tell you that?"

He sounded like he felt compassion and that annoyed him.

"As a matter of fact, yes!"

Her enthusiasm was not as comforting as he had hoped it would be. Georg fastened his belt and walked over to the small breakfast table. He sat down.

"You're very hard not to like."

Even as he said it, he simultaneously wondered if he should have.

He simply wasn't equipped with the social filters most of us take for granted, perhaps that was another reason women were drawn to him, it gave him an inexplicable vulnerability that made them feel empowered.

"Good."

Hannah's tone was imperious. . . . Check and mate. Georg smiled competently and his eyes checked the distance to the door. She decided to push her luck.

"What did you dream?"

She still seemed worried that it might concern her.

"I really don't remember."

He examined the tabletop while Hannah smiled shyly and ducked her head, watching him through her false eyelashes. She had made a decision as to what the dream must have been about: something sexual, something shameful.

"I do things too . . . like leaving with you. Yesterday, I was ashamed. But today I've reached the giggling stage. What about you?"

Her giddiness was obvious enough but Georg couldn't think of anything to say and it was his turn to speak. He still had the taste of her on his tongue. She had perfumed her bush in preparation for love. That had been a mistake, but he couldn't tell her. Her confidence was shaky enough as it was. She had told him she had finally found something she couldn't do without. Now he had her, but what was he going to do with her? It was only complicated because he liked her for some unfathomable reason.

"Coffee ready?"

He had asked politely, and that had seemed to reassure her.

Georg woke up back in the detention cell in the two-room jail in Konstanz. He knew he'd been dreaming, if only it could have all been a dream. As an escape attempt, it hadn't worked and it had finally occurred to him that he had given no thought whatsoever to what would happen next. He has simply resorted to a routine he had followed time and again—walking away from responsibility.

There was operatic shouting around him. A cop was holding a telex report and reading from it in a steady scream.

"A terrorist attack in Munich . . . the BürgerBräuKeller. The border is closed."

Another cop opened his mouth and worked his jaw, but no words came. "Why?"

"It doesn't say. . ." screamed the cop with the telex report and then stared at Georg with speculation. "I'll get you some coffee."

He said it and strode out, having found a purpose. Meanwhile another picked up a new string of news and shouted, "Any and all suspicious individuals are to be sent to Munich!"

After that, things were a blur for what seemed like a very long time. First Georg was in a car, then he was in a black Mariah and then he was in Munich, in the Marienplatz jail, in a long line of prisoners being processed. A turnkey was shouting:

"Criminals to the right, political criminals to the left, relatives of political criminals 2nd floor to the right. Administrative detainees: 2nd floor to the left. Anonymous denunciations: straight ahead to the door at the end of the hall. Repeat: Criminals to the right. . . ."

Georg stopped, holding up the line. He seemed uncertain which way to go. A turnkey grabbed him and threw him into the cage of political prisoners on the left. In the opposite cell block, in the common prisoners' cage, the wall was covered by a poster: "*Join the Reicharbeitdienst*" it said. It was a public works program, but mostly they spent a lot of time marching up and down. The poster showed a worker of heroic proportions carrying a shovel, his face lit with deadpan rapture. He was wedged between SS and Wehrmacht privates carrying slick art deco weapons. They were shown from a low angle looking up and they appeared to be over seventeen meters tall. As Georg was looking at it, a hand reached up and tore off a corner of the poster. A fat man who was squatting on the pot used it to wipe his ass. A political discussion about that ensued, but the fat man took a single-edged razor blade from under his tongue while a lean tattooed man pulled a sharpened bicycle spoke out of the hem of his coat. As they proceeded to murder each other, Georg looked away.

The political cage was full, the bunks and even the corners were taken. Georg lay down in the middle of the floor. In the dim light he started to fondle himself because that at least helped pass the time, but he couldn't stay awake. He curled asleep like a cat.

There was the sound of booted feet running and everyone was yelling, but he didn't seem to notice.

NOVEMBER 10TH, 1939

CHIEF DETECTIVE INSPECTOR NEBE SAT down behind his cigarette-scarred walnut desk—the Führer's picture looming above—and made a show of studying an 8x10 matte photograph of the wreckage of the BürgerBräuKeller. There wasn't much to it, just the burnt-out ballroom. The print showed the two pillars behind the Führer's podium. The one on the right had been blown half away but it had held. Not much of a bomb, so it was surprising how much damage it had caused.

"Talented . . ."

Nebe said and looked around for a reaction. Inspectors Brandt and Nolte were displaying worry in their usual ways. Nolte sat with his elbows on his knees feeling sorry for himself; he'd been handsome once and still used his face theatrically. Brandt was standing, chin-up and looking dedicated. Nebe hated both of them quite cordially. They had known each other too long and, like most old friends, had too much to get even for. He envied the easy friendships of American gangster movies where no one seemed to have any memories. He summoned his authority and drew an X on the hole in the right hand pillar. He held up the print and asked:

"What's the scale on this?"

"The pillars are one meter thick."

Brandt answered, but Nolte didn't want to be outdone.

"Some of them . . . The building was put up at different times. The ball-room was added in the 1850s."

He was trying to impress as usual, but if Brandt said that it was one meter thick, then he had actually measured it.

"Just so . . ."

Nebe took out a pair of calipers and began measuring. He slid a drafts-man's rule out of the middle drawer of his desk and held the calipers against it, writing down the numbers on a yellow pad.

"You want to go back down there and take another look?" asked Brandt.

"Evidence you have to get that way isn't worth the trouble." Nebe picked up the slide rule and did a quick calculation, then came out from behind the desk, holding the ruler and scowling triumphantly. He measured a height from the floor against the desk and marked it with a stub of chalk.

"Kneel down."

He said it to Brandt as he wiggled the ruler and smiled.

"What for?" asked Brandt in high voice.

"You are chiseling a hole in the side of a brick and concrete pillar."

Brandt knelt down and began to pantomime hammer and chisel. Nebe crossed his arms and waited. Brandt was genuinely stupid, which made him a pleasure to command. Nebe thought about Heinrich Mueller; that brilliant yet crude man, so brutal and tasteless that he had left the police and was now head of some Gestapo department or other. This should have been a Gestapo case; it was political and yet the Gestapo wouldn't touch it. Something was wrong and if they knew that when the case was but hours old then they had known about it in advance. Meaning what? The men gathered there had been *Alte Kampfer*, old fighters who had been with the Führer since the beginning, men to whom he owed an enormous debt but who were no longer useful.

Killing them off would have been an elegant solution . . . But, were that the case, then why then had the Führer bothered to show up at all? He had originally cancelled and then changed his mind, why? Again the answer came: so he could have one more miraculous escape. Goebbels was already claiming divine intervention. However, it still didn't make sense. The Führer was a brave man, certainly, but to trust his life to an infernal machine ticking away in the pillar behind him, that was an insane and pointless risk; unless there had been no risk.

Nebe shrugged it off, analysis wasn't getting him anywhere. If it were a Gestapo plot, that would be the best reason for keeping the investigation to themselves. A Gestapo plot would have the fall guy ready and waiting, as they had done at the Reichstag fire. Yet again an answer came to him: so that whoever might try to actually solve it could be brought down. He and his colleagues were middle-aged police inspectors and as apolitical as hedgehogs. Discrediting the police to the benefit of the SS? The police were now part of the SS. He himself was now *Sturmbannführer*. Having received his commission in the mail, he'd even had to go out and buy a new uniform. Having his measurements taken had been humiliating. He hadn't realized that his waist had crept up to 40 inches; his old pants were conveniently stretched out.

He shook his head. Discrediting the police to the benefit of the Gestapo? The police would fail, the case would be handed to the Gestapo and they would solve it. The case was obviously political so it rightfully belonged to them anyway. Why wouldn't they touch it? He needed a drink. He needed a bottle. He needed to stay drunk for three days. Perhaps he was trying to get more information out of this than there was in it. The investigation manuals specifically warned against that: stick to the facts, don't try to make sense out of human motivation or you'll drive yourself crazy. One thing was clear: he had to get out of this fast. Perhaps he could find a doctor under indictment for insurance fraud who could recommend a drug that would mimic the symptoms of a heart attack. Insurance fraud was which department? Bunko squad? At least that would be a place to start. It would require some tact and if he moved fast he might actually get out of this alive and with his pension, which was basically the same thing.

He was panicking, which was perfectly fine so long as he was the first one to do so. He would, of course, have to convince Brandt and Nolte that they were in no danger; that would be the only way to remain above suspicion. That could be a problem though because Nolte wasn't stupid. Nebe peered out the window at the moon. It wasn't there.

"Almost full, what is it. . . . Two days past?"

Brandt reached for a pocket calendar but Nebe stopped him.

"No, you keep digging."

Nolte got up and went to check the wall calendar.

"It's November 10th."

Nolte tore off two sheets and squinted at the phases of the moon in the upper right hand corner.

"No. A week past, full moon was on the third."

"Shame. Less to explain if it had happened on a full moon," Nebe said.

Nolte's face was indignant, which gave him a dowager's prissiness . . .

"This wasn't a loon."

Nebe murmured evasively . . .

"Even so, there was that attempt last year, that Swiss theology student."

The Gestapo had asked him his name and then cut off his head. No one had needed any theories about it. Nebe expounded.

"No one had been interested because he was just another ditsy amateur who had waded into a crowd with a little shit pistol. This attempt however is too good, too scary to live with. So, there must be some ironic trick interpretation that says that in some sense it doesn't really count."

"You read too much."

Nolte was pushing, but Nebe was feeling philosophical.

"Those might be the truest words you've ever said."

Brandt had no idea what they were talking about. Nolte, though, always felt the need to flaunt. . . .

"Was that. . . Hegel?"

Nebe shook his head. . . .

"Kierkegaard's *The Concept of Irony*."

Nolte conceded.

"So, why are you a cop?"

Nebe smiled,

"Because I'm a sadist."

At least that part was true. He had all of the classic German books on flagellation: thousands and thousands of pages just classifying different kinds of asses. It was the most boring shit imaginable. Nebe turned to watch Brandt playing hammer and chisel. He'd keep at it until he hemorrhaged or someone told him to stop.

"How're you doing?"

"My knees hurt. . . ."

There was a childlike whine in Brant's voice, brought on by the childish game. The man was pathetic. Nebe smiled at him.

"Good."

Brandt continued to dig away at the empty air then asked hopefully:

"Can I try this sitting down?"

Nebe was magnanimous.

"Of course you can."

Brandt's face lifted.

"May I?"

Nebe nodded. . . .

"Yes, actually it's an order."

Brandt sat down and began to claw the air double time.

"Much more comfortable; I'd have done it this way."

"Shit! He wouldn't have!"

Nolte said and he stood up and paced the center of the room intent on imposing his deductive superiority.

"Yeah? Why not?"

Brandt breathed out heavily. Nolte elaborated. . . .

"He would've had to hold his arms out straight, and they'd have tired far more quickly. If he had worked on his knees, he'd have been able to use some of the strength of his legs. We are talking about long, hard work, even for a strong man. Days, weeks . . . He could only work a few hours a night while the place was closed."

Nebe gave Nolte a paternal smile he had theretofore been unable to find a use for. He flicked his eyes to Brandt. The man was still hammering at the air; teeth gritted and sweat dribbling off the end of his nose.

"You can stop now."

Brandt got up, brushing himself off and looking peeved. Nebe inspected his two assistants.

"Either of you ever seen a scrubwoman's knees?"

"No, thank God!" Nolte said.

"What if he had used a pillow?" Brandt asked.

Nebe pulled up Brandt's pant leg demonstratively; Nolte raised an eyebrow noting the redness even after such a short time. Nebe smiled.

"They'd still be calloused, and if not, they'd be scarred. Come on gentlemen, maybe we'll get lucky."

And they set off for the holding pens in the second subbasement.

They got the political prisoners out of the tank and into a ragged formation in the corridor; lining them up against the bars of the cages. These were faces out of a political cartoon: Lenin beards and Bakunin haircuts, watery pleading eyes and chinless quivering mouths. There were a surprising number of round-lensed spectacles with gold-wire frames. These were men who knew what they were and they were trying hard to look like it. Nebe smiled at them; he liked stupid people. There was one demented character in a WWI cavalry uniform. He was standing stiffly erect, which couldn't have been easy; the heels of his boots were so worn they were almost perpendicular to the floor. There were also several normal-looking people, either pros or there by mistake. Nebe held up his hands.

"Everybody drop your pants. Yeah, I think I'm in love. Drop your pants!"

He said that doing his best Jimmy Cagney imitation. He loved American gangster movies.

They all dropped their trousers, shuffling and humiliated as his eyes ran along the line of knees. Knees like eggs, knees like goat skulls, knees scalloped with knobs of tendon. There was one without a kneecap. The leg was stiff. That let him off. Then Nebe's eyes stopped on a set of knees that were heavily scabbed. He looked up slowly to meet the wonderful smile of Georg Elser. Nebe found himself smiling too.

"Nothing personal . . ."

After having said that he wondered what he had meant by it.

"Alright . . . Solitary, suicide watch, continuous surveillance."

Two turnkeys shooed the other prisoners back into the pens and then lifted Georg by the elbows and carried him away.

"Don't you want to question him now?"

Brandt suggested, tactfully. How could he possibly realise that, no, obviously Nebe did not want to question him at that moment.

"Let the day crew get the background. They need the experience."

"But if he confesses, they'll take the credit."

Brandt was trying too hard to be helpful. Nebe would have loved nothing more than for someone else to come along and take the glory! He could even protest over the head of the Gruppenführer and, maybe, be forced into early retirement. That would be beautiful. He didn't say any of that, of course.

"We caught him, it's our case. At ease. You're dismissed, momentarily. We'll meet you upstairs."

Then Nebe and Nolte went up the narrow backstairs to the property room. It had a window like a post office, facing the corridor, and the clerk was as nondescript as any postal employee. Nebe was feeling his oats.

"What did he have on him?"

"Who?"

The clerk's question was stoically non-judgmental and Nebe suddenly realized he had forgotten to get the name, but Nolte magically produced the identification. The property clerk handed over a large manila envelope with Georg's belongings inside. They dumped them on the ledge in front of the window and Nebe poked through them, scowling professionally. There were some lovingly machined little metal parts, one that looked very much like a trigger; the inevitable family pictures, too retouched and faded even to be used as identification, nothing more than the echo of a life trying valiantly to be forgotten. Nolte picked up the dog-eared play with a haughty scoff.

"What do you bet he's a communist?"

But Nebe's attention was drawn to the postcard of Hitler orating at the BürgerBräuKeller. In the picture, there were the two pillars behind the podium, almost obscured by a huge Nazi flag. The pillars went up through both floors, though the balcony to the roof. On the right-hand pillar, just above the floor of the balcony, a circle had been drawn in pencil. The pencil mark had faded; it had been drawn months, maybe years before. He showed it to Nolte and they both smirked. It was over. Extracting the names of accomplices was simply a matter of technique and it was a technique that always worked.

"And that is that . . ."

Nebe said it with almost with post-coital languor and turned to begin a triumphant saunter back to the squad room. Nolte hadn't moved. Nebe noticed and took it as an invitation for a lecture.

"Just routine police work,"

Nebe was waving the postcard.

"Not like the movies. Filmmakers love ingenuity because they want to believe that there is an easier way to solve a problem than hard work."

Nolte was looking embarrassed and patient, so Nebe stopped talking.

"Von Eberstein will be delighted."

Nolte was suggesting, with the low cunning that defined him, that they call the Munich Polizei Prasident immediately. Nolte was playing the same role as Brandt: trying to wheedle him away from making obvious mistakes.

Clearly they had no idea just how useful such obvious mistakes could be when manipulated properly. Normally, they were never that interested. They both must have been very scared.

"When we're ready; when we can actually answer the questions obvious enough even for him to have thought of."

Insulting a mutual superior was supposed to imply camaraderie, but Nolte still looked worried in a motherly way. Nebe turned and started walking with Nolte one step to the right and two steps behind.

Von Eberstein was a political appointee, always undesirable. Worse, the man was married to a Jewess, but being of the nobility he was absolutely untouchable. It was in the worst possible bad taste to even mention it. Still, it did indicate a chronic other-worldliness. The man could not be relied upon for anything, except of course that he wouldn't take responsibility for the case unless he was convinced that it had already been solved. Perhaps that was the answer: convince him that the case was solved, have him take full credit, and then watch it blow up in his face. Entertaining!

November 11th, 1939

They assembled in Nebe's office. Nebe sat down behind his desk and began to reorganize his paperwork, reassuring himself with a familiar ritual. Brandt was standing at attention again and Nolte was playing with his brass knuckles. As with all such tools, the Nazis had made improvements. These were made of aluminum so your pocket wouldn't sag and had spiked teeth like a cross-cut saw. Nolte fondled them with his fingertips. He looked back and forth between the Führer's portrait and a mug shot of Georg Elser that had been tacked to the corkboard. His intentions were easy to recognize. Nebe actually considered slapping his hands with the ruler.

"I know how you feel; but I don't care," Nebe said. "I want to see some self-control around here."

Nolte slipped the brass knuckles into his pocket with a practiced gesture, screwed up his mouth, and squeezed it shut. He lowered his chin to look up at Nebe from under his eyebrows, as sad and vulnerable as a woman who had just made a sexual decision. The man wasn't homosexual, at least not exactly, just narcissistic to the point of insanity. Clearly he had had an idea that he was impressed with. Nebe sighed and looked bored.

"It's a British conspiracy," said Nolte. Nebe started to ask a question but Nolte was still talking. "On the radio . . . just this morning . . . the attempt was exposed as a British conspiracy. The problem is that we have no information on that. Even if he could give us precise descriptions of British agents we wouldn't be able to recognize them. We can't ask him to identify faces from photographs in a file because we don't have any. This case must be given to the Gestapo!" It made perfect sense. As usual, Nolte was showing off his intelligence in a situation where the only real defense was to act stupid. "Unless, of course, the Führer believes the Gestapo is somehow involved."

Nebe nodded slightly, very slightly. It was a viable attempt to maintain plausible deniability. He meant agreement but could insist that it was just acknowledgment that he had understood what had been said. "Why don't you use that imagination in trying to do your job instead of trying to get out of it?"

Nolte nodded back, his face closed; he was mentally consulting train schedules to Switzerland. Nebe wasn't the only one trying to discover a way out while it was still a possibility.

Brandt began to read aloud from a small manual the size of a pocket date book. It was titled *Physical Methods of Interrogation*. "If you are going to gouge an eye, do it slowly, taking care not to damage the optic nerve. Then you can leave the eyeball dangling down the cheek still functioning. The brain will be unable to make sense out of the contradictory images."

"It's a common problem," said Nebe. "In fact, you may have just described the human condition." He reached for a manual of his own, its authority only slightly impaired by having his place marked with a beer coaster. He flapped it open and began to read: "The interrogation of the guilty party is of great importance for the uncovering of wide spread conspiracies." He closed the book gently. "I don't want to have to call Berlin to tell them that we killed our only source of information in an excess of enthusiasm. Heil Hitler!" He had spoken slowly and carefully as though he were testing the mental clarity of a man suffering from a nasty head wound.

"Heil Hitler, Herr OberStürmbannFüher." Nolte had used Nebe's SS rank, even more bad taste.

Nebe pointed an accusatory finger. "If I believe that you are endangering the prisoner's life, I will personally put a bullet through your head. Are there any questions?"

"No, not really," said Nolte.

"Strange that he hasn't tried to commit suicide," said Brandt, cheerfully.

"The investigation is still young!" said Nolte and they were all smiling, they were a team again and Nebe beamed a Christmassy approval to his apprentices.

Several hours had passed while background info was sought out and sifted through. The men's faces had the studied inscrutability that can only be cultivated by years of routine.

"So now," said Nebe, "what do we have?"

Brandt was eager to please. "I called the Gestapo. It turns out that they do have a file on Georg Elser. He voted communist in 1933."

Brandt stopped talking but Nebe peered at him expectantly. "And?"

Brandt shrugged. "And nothing . . . He's a worker; a carpenter. Our contact at Gestapo said that they couldn't have had anything interesting on him or he would have gone in the purification of 1936. They're sending the file by telex. There are some snap shots and things, miscellaneous documents. They're being sent by courier. They won't get here till tomorrow around noon."

"Their office is ten blocks away," Nolte said, helpfully.

Nebe shook his head, "If they were eager to help, then I'd be worried, or at least more worried. It means there's nothing more we can do tonight. Change of orders: No one else is to talk to him. Let him sweat, wondering how much we know." Nebe stood up and pulled down his vest. It had a tendency to ride up.

"You want to call von Eberstein?" Nolte persisted.

"Yes, I suppose." He picked up the phone and called the Munich police chief. It was late but the Polizei Prasident answered at once and listened for only a few moments before interrupting Nebe's summary of the police work. Nebe listened in silence, not answering the Prasident's rhetorical questions, waiting for the opportunity to offer his resignation, but there was nothing specific to object to. The Prasident claimed to know everything, but what he knew was unclear. It was almost like Nebe was hearing a playback of his own thoughts, dominant amongst them was the underlying dread—why wouldn't the Gestapo take it out of their hands? Von Eberstein's ranting had the tone of a proclamation, recounting events so momentous that the details were irrelevant; there was no pretext for a reply. The Prasident raved on and on; he seemed to be able to keep talking on the inhale. There was a pause for effect before the next rhetorical question and Nebe leapt into it, offering his resignation. The Prasident ignored him.

The Prasident was still talking; the investigation had degenerated into a romantic search for extenuating complications. Nebe was ignoring the obvious and looking for subtleties where there weren't any in an attempt to make the obvious mean something different than it did. It was impossible to know what he was talking about; he didn't say, but his intentions were clear: in case anything went wrong, he wanted it on record that he had objected to the conduct of the investigation from the start. Incredibly, the Prasident had paused for a breath.

"I'm scared too," said Nebe and it was the stupidest thing he could have said. The entire theory of interrogation was based upon the premise of keeping the man talking. It didn't matter where you started or how many digressions were made, sooner or later he had to talk about the one thing on his mind. But now the Prasident was on guard and his language became truly evasive, relying heavily on the rhetorical device known as invited inference, as though the truth were so obvious that it would be embarrassing to state it clearly. Everything was suggested, but if anything had actually been said, Nebe had missed it. The only clear message was that when the Prasident had finally stopped talking, he hung up without waiting for a reply.

Nebe jiggled the receiver until he got the switchboard and called Heinrich Mueller in Berlin. The line was busy. Nebe told the operator to keep trying.

"And what do we do now?" Brandt asked. Nebe shot the phone with a forefinger but it refused to ring on cue.

Fifteen minutes later the phone rang and the switchboard girl told him that his call was ready.

"I was only just now talking to von Eberstein," said Nebe into the phone, "and I agree completely. It is unthinkable that a German worker would try to kill the Führer. Obviously, it's the English again. They planted the evidence on him, trying to embarrass us, paying us back for van der Lubbe."

Lubbe was the feeble-minded Dutchman who had been framed for the Reichstag fire. The voice on the phone said something that sent Nebe into a coughing fit. It was thirty seconds before he could catch his breath.

"We were not taken in by it," he said. "He is being detained only to establish the connection with the Englishmen who entrapped him so that we can track them down. There is one problem," Nebe managed to say before Mueller could hang up. "This case rightfully belongs to the Gestapo. I am concerned that certain departments may feel that we have taken it away from them by intrigue and that we are attempting to set ourselves up as rivals in some sense."

Heinrich Mueller's office was appointed with a rococo touch, and with the dim lighting and long shadows that one would almost expect Bella Lugosi, Lon Chaney, or Christopher Lee to make an entrance at any moment.

"They are supposed to," Mueller's voice deepened. "We have so many police forces and they all have overlapping and contradictory fields of authority, exactly like the army and the SS. The Führer has deliberately fostered this confusion so that none of them will have the power base to replace him. This is simply a continuation of existing policy but," there was a pointless menace in the phrase, "in police work there is a limit to the amount of useful confusion. For that reason it is essential that we maintain a clear line of responsibility on this. No one is to talk to him but you. I have already given orders to that effect. Good to see that you're making progress but try to keep him alive. Brutality is, after all, only another form of sentimentality. Neither have any place in police work."

"So I have told my men," said Nebe, but Mueller had already hung up. Nebe put down the phone. . . . *A coup d'état by the police?* It might have been a possibility in Luxembourg, but never in Germany.

Nolte and Brandt were on their feet and watching him. He sighed gutturally and looked away. He rubbed his chin like Lionel Barrymore, trying to remember what movie that was from. He covered his face with his hands. Then he put them on the table. Nolte and Brandt were still watching him, rigid as figures in an Easter crib. Nebe smiled at them. "You hear any of that?"

"Enough," said Nolte. "He's innocent. He was framed. He's going to go free." Nolte started to reach for his gun then thought better of it. "You . . ." Nolte searched for a word, "are . . ." he searched for another. His stomach swayed on its moorings. "It was an English plot. He will say that."

Brandt was standing, watching them with his mouth open; he'd had his tonsils out. Nolte's face twitched through a series of expressions that were like title cards in a silent movie. Clearly the man kept thinking of questions and finding them unacceptable.

"In answer to your question, the investigation is being conducted by the police, so there can be no question of political involvement." Listening to himself, Nebe was amazed at how smoothly he lied. If this kept on going he might just manage to cheer himself up.

"Oh," said Nolte. "Oh?" he said it again.

"Meanwhile, we'll find out what actually happened, just in case that question comes up."

Brandt was smiling at Nebe with a devotion that would embarrass the average dog and Nolte suddenly relaxed. The Chief Inspector stood up, his pants slid down past the bulge. Seven days on a fast and he still didn't have a waist. Well, such things take time. For the first time in a week, he realized he was hungry. "Let's take a break," he said.

Nebe invited Nolte for a drink. It was an honor and Nolte was properly appreciative. Nolte would want coffee, as usual. Nebe preferred beer to free his subconscious associations, but beer would imply an informality that would defeat the purpose of the occasion.

They walked into a working-class bar that had the brownish glow of an old master with too many coats of shellac. Conversation died around them as they passed, which was nice, and they walked through the scrape of chairs and the rattle of beer stein lids to find a table at the back.

Nebe looked around for the barmaid. Across the room, over-decorated beer steins were stacked to the ceiling like pieces in a three-dimensional chess game. The barmaid appeared in the center of his vision. She had no waist and no neck. Her hair was cut short and brushed straight up like that of a student with a taste for dueling. She had arms like a circus strongman. Her upper arms may have been just fat, but the forearms were real: she was holding ten *maßkrugs*—one-liter beer steins. Nebe briefly considered suicide. He nodded to her and she smiled back. She had all her teeth, which was a mercy. He turned back to Nolte, who was sitting with his eyes down.

The table was set with blue tiles showing the coat of arms of something of historical importance. The barmaid slammed two glasses and a bottle of schnapps on the table, meaning that Nebe was known there. Nolte didn't react to that, which was promising, but it was one more argument against moderation.

Nebe poured each of them a double shot. The noise level was rising again. It was getting a little loud for an intimate conversation. Shouting, belching, spitting, and banging on the table might not be good manners elsewhere, but this was Bavaria. Nebe leaned forward conspiratorially. "Do you think I drink too much?" he asked, undermining his authority to see what Nolte would do with the opening.

"What I think is of no importance," replied Nolte.

Nebe looked up from the glass, regarding Nolte with the beginnings of professional interest. He gave him a smile that didn't quite reach up to his nose. They were investigating a plot against the Führer and suspected a plot against the police, but perhaps, it was a plot against Nebe by his junior officers led by Nolte. Nebe thought of telling him that the schnapps was poisoned and that he wouldn't give him the antidote unless he confessed. Heydrich had played those games with Schellenberg, who had promptly poured himself a double, toasted Heydrich's health, and then drank it down.

"Excuse me a minute," said Nebe, standing up. He had suddenly remembered an abortionist. In the Third Reich, abortion was murder and, if you measured the severity of the act by the number of years you took away from the victim, then abortion was the ultimate crime. The man had been headed straight for a colorful public beheading but there had been some political connection and they'd been forced to let him go. Nebe found a phone by the W.C. and called him.

The doctor's office was sterile in every sense, much like the balding middle-aged surgeon himself. He had just donned his coat and hat as the telephone rang. He considered ignoring it but times were lean, even for those on the dark side of the medical profession. Upon hearing Nebe's voice he rolled his eyes, irritatingly not intimidated by his name or rank.

"How would a man fake a heart attack?" Nebe asked.

"Why ask me?"

"Because you're a criminal, you know how these things are done." Nebe's tone wasn't actually accusatory.

The doctor thought a moment, "Digitalis, possibly strychnine . . ."

Nebe became snappy, "Those cause heart attacks. This man is interested in faking one."

"The extract of pig's pituitary gland, it causes arrhythmia—irregular heart beat."

"Would that be grounds for a man to take an early retirement?"

The doctor could no longer contain his exasperation, "If he had a physically strenuous job, yes. This is the third call of this nature I've had this month, tell 'this man' to mount a younger woman and the heart attack might come naturally."

Nebe's voice became sinister, "There has to be something else."

"Try blutwurst and red cabbage. Nothing looks like a heart attack more than a good case of heartburn." His ironic tone was belligerently insubordinate.

Nebe seethed, "What did you mean by 'try it'?"

"I meant consider the possibility," the doctor said.

Nebe hung up without replying. It was his turn. When he got back to the table, Nolte was watching him with a serene reptilian alertness, eyes wired directly into the spinal cord. He could catch flies out of the air with either hand. He looked like he could catch them with his tongue too.

"So," said Nolte, "how do we get out of this?"

"We don't. . . ." said Nebe.

November 12th, 1939

When Nebe got to his office the next morning the door was locked. When he unlocked it he saw that his desk was gone. Then he remembered than no one had spoken to him as he crossed the squad room. He stood staring into the empty room for what seemed a very long time, though it must have been less than a second. He wanted to turn around and shout but he knew the result in advance as clearly as if he were remembering it. He would demand to know what was going on but no one would answer. They wouldn't know either. They would know that Nebe had become a dangerous man to know. Then he noticed a note taped to the door. When he unfolded it, it said that his office had been moved to the fifth floor so that he wouldn't be disturbed. With a sigh that was more resignation than relief he recalled Muller's statement: *I have already given orders to that effect. . . .*

Nebe had worked in the building for 25 years but still he had to ask directions twice to find his new office. Brandt and Nolte were already there, so were his desk and filing cabinets. Was there a phone? There was a phone on the desk. Brandt and Nolte were as morosely industrious as condemned men trying to demonstrate their rehabilitation. Nolte was smoothing out the telex file and snipping it into pages. Brandt was tucking them into a brown cardboard folder.

Nolte looked up, frightened as a child. How quickly they regress. "We're under quarantine," said Nolte, still snipping away. "Does that make sense?"

Nebe sat down behind his desk. "This is what Muller ordered. They're taking precautions so that they can control the attention the case receives. You were there. By questioning our orders you gave the impression that our cooperation had to be enforced. Before that the responsibility for the case had been mine alone, now you will share it."

Nolte looked down and chewed his lower lip, still smoothing and snipping. Good. Nebe patted his desk with both hands, as if he were calming an unruly steed. "So, what do we have?" he asked.

"Lutheran, pure Aryan. . . . That's embarrassing," said Nolte. "There's a lot of personal junk: got a girl in trouble when he was eighteen; father's an alcoholic."

Nebe gestured for them to get moving. "So, read it."

"Do we really need to go through all this?" asked Brandt, incredibly.

"Oh, yes. It will be useful in making him uncomfortable later on." Nebe nodded his chin upward at Nolte, who shuffled the pages out of the file but didn't refer to them.

"The father ran a sawmill and a logging camp. Wanted Georg to enter the business but the little fellow didn't like the way the horses were treated."

"I've always wondered why so many cold killers are animal lovers. It's ironic." Nebe tended his fingertips and smiled.

Nolte gave him a school teacher's frown, "No it isn't. That's the side they're on. If that's the only place they have found love and loyalty, then they're on the side of the animals against man." Nolte had an answer for everything. It was infuriating but it was his value. It was foolish to hate him for it.

Nebe smiled and nodded, and Nolte went on, "Business declined, father became an alcoholic then sold the house out from under his family, except for one small room in the attic where he moved in alone."

They looked at each other in disgust. "So, he hates his father," said Brandt. "He has an Oedipus complex." This reference to the Jew science was yet another exercise in bad taste.

Nolte resented Brandt seeking attention, "An authoritarian society like ours cranks them out like link sausages," Nolte replied.

"So what?" Brandt had apparently had similar experiences.

Nolte was not in the mood. "So, this is getting a little obvious."

"It's supposed to be," said Nebe, reining them in as he nodded again.

Nolte picked up the telex pages and began to read in the singsong voice of a court clerk. "Johann Georg Elser: passed his journeyman's exam as a cabinet maker with the highest marks in his class in the spring of 1922.

Unable to find work, he walked 215 kilometers in the middle of winter to the Dornier Aircraft Company in Friedrichshafen. Obtained work in the propeller department but was terminated without prejudice when wooden propellers were discontinued. It's all like that." His questioning glance at Nebe was met by a nod to continue. "Mastered the difficult art of making cuckoo clocks with hand-carved wooden gears till the company went bankrupt three months later. The man is a joke. He kept learning a trade just when it became obsolete. Another clock factory, then he went door to door offering to repair furniture. He was very successful at it, widows and landladies loved him. Then . . . something . . . I can't find it."

"But he kept looking for a job. So he had to have believed that things would change." Brandt was always the optimist.

Nolte ignored him. "He learned to play the zither and joined the band in a dance club."

Nebe chuckled, but Brandt was wide-eyed. "Why do all women want to sleep with musicians? I've never understood that."

Nolte opened his mouth. He had the answer, he always did. "They're not around much."

"Never mind!" said Nebe. "Try to stick to the point. Police record? Politics? Foreign contacts? Subversive organizations?"

"None." Nolte twisted his mouth; he didn't like the answer either. "Not a political fanatic. Not an embittered loser. Not even an attention seeker or he would have signed his name to it and wouldn't have tried to escape. So, what was his motive?"

Nebe shrugged as though it were easy. "His life was a disaster. He thought he could change all that in the last reel. Like any assassin, he wanted to commit some gigantic melodramatic act that was supposed to change the meaning of everything that had come before it." He spread his hands to show that there was nothing up either sleeve. "They promised money to his family if he'd take the fall for this. Maybe they even paid it. But we'll promise him even more if he just tells the truth."

"Precisely," said Nolte, as though it had been his idea. Nolte didn't change expression at first but Nebe and Brandt were smiling and he began to smile too. They were still smiling at each other when two patrolmen with gigantic shoulders and little heads came in the door carrying Georg Elser by the elbows. They all gave the Nazi salute, the patrolmen missing Georg's face by inches as they held him. After letting Georg go, the patrolmen left.

Nebe and Nolte sat Georg down in front of the desk, wedging him in from either side. They spread out their files, photographs and evidence and Brandt sat down in front of the typewriter. They glared at Elser, waiting for him to look ashamed. Nothing happened. He looked awestruck—as the working class always did with the police—and eager to help. But he didn't look guilty. It was a face from the Depression, lean and worn down, reduced to a mechanism by grinding routine. The eyes were alive, alert like a cat watching you with terrible innocence. It was going to be a very long night.

Nebe picked up the photo of the wreckage with one hand and the postcard with the other. He held them next to each other in front of Georg's nose.

"Cause and effect are easy to put together," Nebe said. Georg didn't look away, but neither did he look like he was seeing what was in front of him. Nebe rattled the postcard at him to get his attention. "You shouldn't have kept this, Georg. You shouldn't have been quite so proud of it." And it sounded wrong to Nebe as he said it. Brandt began to type.

"He should be proud," said Nolte. "He almost changed history single-handedly. Like Napoleon at Waterloo, he staked everything on timing. And it went wrong only by seconds."

Georg looked puzzled; he was good at that. He had tried; he had failed. They were going to kill him, so why were they making it so complicated?

"I didn't do it," he said obligingly.

Nebe groaned. This part of the interrogation could be conducted by a player piano. "What were you doing in Munich, Georg?"

"I was looking for a job . . . at The BürgerBräuKeller."

Nebe smiled. "Of course, that's how you got the postcard. Is that also where you got the scars on your knees?"

Georg tried to appear nonchalant, "I was scrubbing floors for my landlady to pay rent."

Nolte interjected, "The only work you did for her was in bed. I bet she was fat and ugly, wasn't she, Georg?"

"Maybe he just likes women." Brandt's Candide-like romanticism caused them all an involuntary shudder.

Georg smiled at him. "I like women who read."

All three men looked at him as if he had suddenly fallen from the sky. Nolte was aghast. "What difference does that make?"

Georg shrugged. "They're more interesting than women who don't."

Nebe struggled to keep a straight face as he let the play drop on the desk in front of Georg. "So is this a souvenir, or do you make a habit of reading subversive propaganda?"

Georg didn't seem to understand what he meant. "Reading just makes it easier to forget that I'm hungry."

On seeing the title, Brandt practically shrieked, "I thought they had burnt all that trash!"

"Speaking of burning," said Nebe, "one of the people you killed was a waitress, sixteen years old. Would you like to see her picture?" He handed the photograph to Georg. Georg took it.

In the background, Brandt clattered away at the typewriter like a centipede with lead shoes. The hand holding the photograph began to tremble. Georg handed it back.

"Doesn't leave a whole lot to be said," said Nebe.

Nolte looked like he had just invented the wheel. "You have it exactly wrong. That's all it leaves. What can be said is the only thing that can change what it means."

Nebe gazed at Nolte with the same sinister benevolence with which one regards a precocious child that insists on interrupting adult conversation to show how clever they are.

"Yes, if he cooperates, if he tells us who paid him to do it. That could change it. Then he wouldn't be an enemy." Nebe tried the same look out on Elser. "Isn't that right?"

Georg was suddenly lost. "I didn't . . ."

Nebe moved in. "Of course you didn't, but you know who did."

"Johann Georg Elser: Born 4th January 1903 in Hermaningen, out of wedlock. Parents married a year later. One brother, three sisters, only one of which he's still talking to. Alcoholic father. Is very close to his mother." Nolte did have a splendid sense of timing.

Georg shuddered. "Leave my mother out of this."

"If we can, Georg. If we can." Fear at last. Nebe smiled.

Elser gazed ahead of him pathetically. "My family has nothing to do with this."

Nebe's smile hardened. "Then tell us who does?"

Georg wet his lips. If he couldn't talk, at least he could do something with his mouth. There was nothing to say, nothing at all.

Nebe pressed on, "I like it, Georg. Lying is not natural to you and that's a pleasure. You wouldn't believe the people we get in here. You having a good time? If you are, this might just go on forever."

Nolte started to probe through Georg's wallet. He found the photographs and held them up. There was one of a puckered, bitter old woman, lines around her mouth cut deep into her face. She was trying to smile but couldn't raise the line of her lips past the horizontal. There was a picture of a woman, about thirty, with a strong resemblance to Georg, especially in the sharp angle of the jaw. Both pictures had been hand-tinted in ghastly pastels, confectioner's pinks, blues, and yellows. They weren't pictures; they were icons, something to be worshipped. "Your sister, Georg? Fine-looking woman."

"Write it out, whatever it is, and I'll sign it." Georg's tone was matter-of-fact.

"But Georg, you didn't do anything. We need the names of the Englishmen who framed you. It was a beautiful job, but you couldn't have done it alone." Nolte seemed almost empathetic.

"Amateurs don't plan things that well. Amateurs wade into a crowd with a little shit pistol, they're very proud of what they've done. They don't even try to escape. This was planned, by a pro, Georg, and that isn't you."

Georg looked baffled, not as though he didn't understand the words in question, but as though he didn't understand language, period. Nebe began to wonder if the man were some type of autistic savant.

"He may keep this up forever." The centipede came to a halt and Brandt swiveled in his seat. "Shall we get on with . . ." He pantomimed breaking a pencil but Nebe held up a pawnbroker's gently negating hand.

He turned his attention back to Georg, "Just tell us about it. Start anywhere."

His eyes flashed from Nebe to the others and back again. "My mother, my sister, they've got nothing to do with this."

Nebe nodded. "So you've told us, Georg."

Georg's face was anxious. "Then you'll leave them out of it?"

Nebe smiled in encouragement. "As long as you cooperate."

Georg sighed. "So what is it you want to know?"

"Please, God, let this be a dream. Has he got brain damage or what?" Even Brandt had passed the point of exasperation.

Nolte dutifully consulted the arrest report. "It doesn't say so. The doctor looked at him last night."

Nebe shrugged. "So, that means he's drugged."

Nolte twisted his face like a radio dial. "Only 25 milligrams of Methedrine to get him talking. But, I think this is natural. No fixed stare. He's not even sweating."

"Then what the hell is going on here?" Nebe asked.

For once Nolte had nothing to say, so he stood up and pulled a blackjack out of his back pocket, the one where he usually carried the brass knuckles, and thumped Georg across the shin with it. When Georg doubled up to clutch at his leg, Nolte cracked him behind the elbow and Georg fell face forward on the floor. He didn't make a sound, they never did; the pain was too strong and they couldn't get enough distance from it to comment on it.

Nebe didn't feel compassion, he didn't feel pity, but he did sometimes get disgusted. He stood up and pushed Nolte hard enough to stagger him back into his chair. He turned to Georg and said, "My colleague was just trying to get your attention. Now, get up and sit down." He turned to the others. "Maybe, just maybe, we're asking the wrong questions, questions so wrong that he doesn't know what to say."

The three detective inspectors waited for an answer to present itself, hands folded and faces twisted into configurations of attentiveness. Nebe wasn't about to say anything and every time that Brandt or Nolte adopted a posture that indicated that they were about to speak, he cut them off with a gesture. Nebe scowled so hard that he was looking at Georg through his eyebrows.

Then, in a gesture he had learned from the movies, Nebe tapped his right forefinger to the side of his nose and then pointed to Georg. "Tell us, when was the exact moment you knew that you were going to do it?"

Georg looked up. It was a question he could answer and the Methedrine was making it easier for him to talk than not to.

"I was on the receiving dock of the Waldenmaier armament factory at Heidenheim. Ulrich and I were rolling crates on a dolly heading for the storeroom. Ulrich was tall and thin and uselessly fine featured. He was aging badly. At 27, he already had three-dimensional bags under his eyes and his skin was curdling. It wasn't the thickened terracotta skin of a drinking man; he was going fish-belly white. He was clearly dying of something else. He unlocked the four-meter-high steel doors of the storeroom and I wheeled the dolly inside. Ulrich yanked on the hanging naked bulb. It put out a thick yellow light that made the pine shelves look like cake. He heaved the door shut. Then he leaned against it and said, 'You almost got me killed last night.' There was a strange lack of emotion in this, as though it were a minor breach of good taste that he had mentioned only because he was a friend.

"We had been drinking in a bar where we'd hoped to be safely ignored. There was a doddering old waitress whose breasts hung down below her belt and no one cared to look up from their beer. That was September 28, 1938, the day before the Munich Agreement was signed, and everyone was locked into some internal calculation and waiting for the signal that would tell them to stop being afraid. A group in Nazi uniforms were having a jubilantly obnoxious conversation at the end of the bar, tearing at the air like it was a piece of meat. Then the bartender waved and shouted for silence. He turned on the radio and the voice of Josef Goebbels announced that Adolf Hitler was about to speak from the Sportpalast in Berlin. Goebbels sounded crazier than usual, or maybe just happier; with him it's the same thing. He had written a novel he couldn't sell, but suddenly . . . Here he is with an audience that has no choice, happy at last. I listened to the frantic skirling voice for a while; it gibbered and squeaked. Then I got up and walked out. I hadn't thought about what would happen next, but Ulrich filled me in of course, considering he survived the standoff.

"The Nazis at the end of the bar couldn't believe what they were seeing. My disrespect was unthinkable and while they were unthinking it, I was already out the door and gone, peddling away on my bike. They did a slow take on Ulrich, spreading out in the defensive formation known as 'the hedgehog.'

"They were all either gawkily thin or fat and egg shaped and their faces were as malformed as illustrations in a poorly drawn comic book, but there were a lot of them. Then the bartender intervened. There was a roll-down grate over the bar like it was a store window. The bartender slammed it down, locking himself in with the beer kegs and schnapps bottles. He peered out with one eye and poked his nose through the grill work.

"'Hurry up and get it over with,' he had said it helpfully, 'the Führer is about to speak.' Ulrich jumped up and gave the Nazi salute. 'Heil Hitler!' And he must have said it as though it were the answer to every problem because the point man on the formation returned the salute quite casually and said, 'Heil Hitler?' as though he'd never heard it before. 'Who was your friend?' he asked.

"'Who? Him? I really don't know.' Ulrich said it holding up his empty hands to demonstrate his innocence, he did that quite often as I recall.

"'He seemed to know you.' That was the Nazi behind the one in front, peering over his shoulder.

"'I'm just friendly, you know how people take advantage of that.'

"'Quiet!' the bartender shouted from behind the barricade. Then Adolf Hitler began to speak. The Nazis turned around to face the radio as if the speaker were in the same room and poor Ulrich stood there, stiffly at attention with eyes misting over with what he hoped was the appropriate emotion, all the while he listened to the Führer slowly and plausibly work himself into a rage fit. Ulrich told me that he had thought: *Hitler is scared, this time he is actually scared, so he can't be completely crazy.*"

Nebe took a deep breath and raised his left palm like he were about to take an oath. Elser paused, sensing that was what he was meant to do while Nolte's head swiveled Nebe's direction as Brandt's plodding fingers clambered to a halt and he did the same. All three men looked at Nebe with curious speculation.

"Georg, though your enthusiasm is almost inspiring, I am finding it extraordinarily difficult to believe that Ulrich, at least as you've described him thus far, actually related this tale to you in such vivid detail." At which both Brandt and Nolte nodded in mute unison. Georg looked from face to face not comprehending what their problem was. He spoke when his gaze settled back on Nebe.

"But I always remember things as pictures. I mean, I was there, at least until I left, so I had all of their faces and the layout of the bar already in my head. When Ulrich told me what had happened I saw it, that's how I can remember it to tell it to you now."

Brandt glanced at Nolte for some confirmation that Elser was talking nonsense, he dreaded having to type up Georg's staggering narrative, but Nolte had opted to put on his 'not now, I'm in contemplation' expression. Only Nebe had felt the full impact of Elser's statement and registered its possible implications in regard to the investigation and all of their, now common, futures.

"My apologies for interrupting you Georg, I appreciate your having shared that with us. Now, by all means please continue." And with that he rapped his knuckles firmly upon his desk to bring Brandt and Nolte back to the here and now. Georg nodded to each of them before resuming his tale of their woe.

"In the shipping and receiving office, Ulrich and I were counting the packets in a crate of cordite, or maybe picric acid. There was a ritual to it. If you kept your movements strictly mechanical, each motion an exact duplicate of the one before until only the spirit were free, the time passed pleasantly.

"Fritz, the 'supreme supervisor' of inventory, was bending over the books jerking his finger in time to some internal music. A roll of fat hung over the back of his collar. He was a devout Nazi, but since he was too old for the SS or even the army, it looked like a free ride. He looked forward to the war as though it were a movie: after all, Goebbles advertised it very much the same way.

"I turned to Ulrich and whispered, 'You should have left too.' We were having the same conversation for the third time and he just looked at me and smiled, 'When among wolves, howl!'

"Then Fritz started yelling. 'Gentlemen, perhaps I haven't given you enough to do.'

"We stopped talking and kept counting. Fritz looked back and forth between us and watched with satisfaction. He smiled, 'Procrastination was possible under the republic, but not now.' He waited for a reply but we had none. That was the way it was going to be from then on: small-time sadists, dead-end menial jobs, and fat landladies suggesting ways to save on the rent. There were no other possibilities so there was nothing to think about. The days passed: the same deadly routine, again and again and again.

"That night I was drinking beer with Franz and Ulrich. It was a different bar than the night before, which was elementary caution. Franz had arms as thick as my legs and covered with wiry red hair. He was talking about opening his own carpentry shop. It was impossible to save that much money, but he had elaborate plans for getting it from his wife's relatives. No one was listening.

"'I'd kill him,' said Ulrich. 'I really would. But can you kill an adding machine? You can break it, you can turn it off, but can you kill it?'

"I asked 'Who?' and Franz said, 'Do we have enough money for another pitcher of beer?'

"I told him 'No,' so he leered at me bitterly.

"'Maybe, you could play your zither and we could pass the hat.' I let my face go blank and Ulrich said to Franz, 'Maybe, you could murder a prostitute and steal her money. Then we could drink all night.'

"Franz thought that over but ruled it out. 'You have too much ambition,' he said.

"'Come on, work tomorrow.' I had tired of them.

"Ulrich was getting maudlin. And the day after that. . . . And the day after that.'

"'Let's go,' I repeated, and me and Franz got up and started to walk out. Ulrich lagged behind to steal the tip. We pretended not to notice. A fat man in a Nazi uniform walked by then, he had a pretty girl on his arm. She turned her head and gave me an imploring look. In profile she looked like a Neanderthal angel, the bright blonde hair was heartbreakingly sincere. Franz stuck a grapefruit-sized elbow in my ribs and gave me a stern parental glare. I nodded, but I had stopped walking. Franz frowned some more, then nodded too. When Ulrich caught up with us, Franz took him by the arm and steered him out the door with Ulrich complaining that no one ever told him what was going on.

"The girl's room smelled of cockroaches and incense—a brown room with dim yellow light. I squatted in front of the huge Telefunken radio listening to the BBC German broadcast on the short wave band. The girl was standing behind me in silk stockings and a garter belt. She looked as though she were trying to appear patient. The BBC wasn't much help.

"'And we tender a very relieved set of thanks to Prime Minister Chamberlin who, with the Munich agreement, has secured peace in our time.'

"I looked at the window. It was covered with heavy drapes to keep the smell in, but it was almost dawn. I tried radio Moscow.

"'We applaud Germany's reorganization of Czechoslovakia. These small nations crowded between Germany and Soviet Union can survive only by pitting these two giants against each other. They must not be allowed to start a great war as they did in 1914....'

"They would do nothing. They congratulated themselves on doing nothing; so they would continue to do nothing. Germany would continue to make demands on other countries to incorporate them. They would talk of complications and how each side had so much to be said for it that they couldn't decide which side had more to be said for it and that, no matter what catastrophe fell down on top of them, they would muddle through untouched so it had nothing to do with them. It would end in war. It simply had to.

"I felt anger and disgust and anticipation and something else.... I had to stop it, even if the reason was still rather vague, I didn't know the word for what I felt, at least not then. Actually I didn't even know if there was a word for it. It felt like my life had become a song that someone else was singing. Putting a name to your emotions could be a useful skill, but it's not really in our repertoire yet. Anger and disgust are easy, people explain them to you, they recognize the symptoms and they tell you what you're feeling. But those are forms of desire and desire makes sense, desire has reasons, desire can be bought off, and most times eventually wears out on its own. Passion, on the other hand does not. Passion doesn't need reasons; it just keeps getting stronger until it kills you. That is usually depicted as something melodramatic; lots of facial grimaces, large arm movements, and emphatic conversation. But it isn't like that at all. Passion is untroubled and serene. An alley cat standing her ground against a Rottweiler to protect her kittens would understand it perfectly. The word is passion. Up till then I had felt passion about only one thing: not letting anything get too close. But war penetrates every aspect of life, there is no safe distance, you can't keep it away unless you stop it. So that's what I had to do.

"Then the blonde got between me and the radio, turned it off, and pushed me backward until I fell across the bed. There were noises in the night, coal down a chute, crowds running through the streets, and they were shouting things out of a nightmare.

"I was getting dressed sometime before dawn when her bookshelf caught my eye. I had just finished Hesse's *Beneath the Wheel* so I swapped it for Kafka's *Metamorphosis*, it looked like she had read it so I figured she wouldn't miss it."

Nebe leaned his chin on his fist. Nolte looked at him with his eyebrows semaphoring a signal. Nebe gave him a sleepy half smile. Georg wondered whether he was afraid, and was only half surprised to find he wasn't. Seeing as he was going to be killed no matter what he did or said; in essence, there was nothing to worry about.

"A first sign of the beginning of understanding is the wish to die." Nebe's tone was strangely nostalgic and Brandt and Nolte looked at him as if waiting for some form of explanation. He ignored them and addressed Georg. "It doesn't surprise me you chose Kafka, you two have a few things in common: he sired a child with his fiancée's best friend."

"You sure you want to hear all this?" asked Georg.

Nebe sighed. "You're going to hurt my feelings, Georg. Are you suggesting I'm not giving you enough attention?"

Georg made faces that made Nebe think of someone fiddling with a radio dial trying to bring in a weak station.

"No, Georg, we decide what's important. Tell us. We're very interested in all of it. We're very interested in everything you have to say, so please go on." Georg shrugged and went on.

"Ulrich was filing while Fritz and I were going through the requisition slips and entering them into a ledger. I pulled the last one off the bill file. I told him, 'This one says twelve dozen number 18 hexagonal nuts . . .'

"'One gross,' Fritz said and wrote it down. I looked at him to be sure he had heard me correctly.

"'But we only have ten dozen number 18 hexagonal bolts.'

"Fritz was annoyed. He opened and closed his mouth mimicking stupidity. 'Yeah? That's their problem. They know what they want. That the end of it?'

"'Yes.' I had reached automatically for the broom but put it back against the wall. The floor was immaculate.

"Fritz needed to flex his authority. 'We're three days ahead on everything. Sit down!'

"I sat down and took some shiny machine parts out of my pocket and began to play with them. They were steel and vanadium alloy and beautifully machined. But of course you know that, you have them now. But Fritz didn't know, 'What the hell are you doing now?' and there was a mother's desperation in his voice.

"I smiled at him. 'Seeing how they fit together. It's like a puzzle.'

"'How do you even know they're parts of the same machine?' Fritz said it to keep the conversation going.

"'They all go to the special department. They only make one thing.' . . . Timing devices for artillery shells.

"Then a girl came into the office. She was pretty, almost, but the lower half of her face was too big and her brow sloped back. She was all mouth and Fritz jumped up smiling, 'May I help you? Just tell me what you want.'

"The girl leaned her eyes heavily on me and smiled, her mouth seemed three inches too wide. 'Georg knows what I want.' I retreated among the shelves then came back and handed her a cellophane package as she handed me the requisition slip.

"I called it out because that was expected. 'Two typewriter ribbons, number three.' Morosely Fritz wrote it down, impaled the slip on the bill file, then pulled it back off. The girl retreated, smiling over her shoulder, but I was ignoring her.

"Ulrich had been watching all of us and he smiled at Fritz. 'She's a little young for you.'

"'I'm not old,' said Fritz, 'just ugly, and not wealthy enough to compensate.' But that was not only funny, it was self-deprecating, undermining his authority in two ways at once, so he scowled at the machine parts and shouted, 'Those parts are stolen from the company.'

"My tone was matter-of-fact, 'How can they be stolen, they haven't been removed from the office.'

"Fritz looked baffled. He took a deep breath and started again. 'You know your problem, Georg?'

"'No, sir.' I scooped up the machine parts and put them back in my pocket.

"'I don't know either,' Fritz sighed. 'The Nazi party was supposedly designed to serve the interests of craftsmen like you.'

"'But I'm no longer a craftsman.' I turned over my empty hands. The calluses were gone and the palms soft for the first time in a decade. Both hands looked smaller, but that wasn't possible.

"He insisted. 'But you are. The Führer said at the Nuremberg Rally: We can make no distinction between skilled and unskilled labor.' Fritz was not about to be dissuaded from his belief system.

"'Then what's the difference from not working at all?' asked Ulrich, muttering as he filed. 'I mean if it doesn't matter how well you do it.'

"Fritz scolded, 'Ulrich, think with your hands.' So Ulrich went back to filing the onion skin carbons that had a tendency to stick to his fingers and come apart in his hands.

"Fritz continued to talk. 'Georg, you walked out on the Führer's speech. Yes, I do know about that. And, yes, you are becoming an embarrassment to the company. Is that what you want?'

"'I lowered my eyes appropriately. 'No, sir. . . .'

"'History,' said Fritz, looking over his bifocals in an almost grandfatherly manner, 'is no longer a game from which you can walk away.'

"I repeated the words to myself internally. 'Yes.'

"Fritz cocked an eyebrow. 'Yes what?'

"I pulled myself erect. 'Yes, sir!'

"Fritz was almost amused. 'I mean, what did you say yes to?'

"That could have gone on for some time, but a sawed-off stump of a man walked in. He looked like Rumpelstiltskin without the cap and bells. His name was Eisner and he carried a medium-sized box covered with warning signs and swastikas in red and black. It bore the stamps and seals of all the departments it had passed through. Eisner was trying to make a delivery. Fritz told him to come back in the morning, and then they were shouting at each other. I ignored them, watching Ulrich trying to file the onion skin flimsies. It was like trying to file wisps of smoke. He started wadding them up and throwing them into the drawer behind the metal divider.

"Fritz and Eisner were still shouting. I tried to continue ignoring them, but the noise level was becoming painful. Eisner called Fritz a traitor and a Communist. Fritz called Eisner a Jew and an Anarchist.

"'I will report this to the plant manager,' said Eisner.

"'We will go together,' said Fritz.

"Then I walked up between them, took the box out of Eisner's hands, and walked away with it. Fritz and Eisner stared at each other, baffled then they turned jerkily and haltingly walked away. Ulrich had a dreamy half smile and there was a question in his eyes. Even after they were gone, Ulrich kept staring as I lit a cigarette. I offered him one but he grabbed the lit one from my mouth, took a quick drag then stamped it out with an exasperated gesture at the high explosive signs. 'You weren't the center of attention for 30 seconds and you went berserk.'

"I laughed. 'I stopped it, didn't I?'

"He shot me peeved glances. 'That's only because they weren't arguing with you. If they had been, you would have let it go on forever.'

"I shrugged and reached for the broom but save for the cigarette the floor was still immaculately clean.

Nebe smiled at Georg—at least he showed some teeth—and Georg smiled back. Nolte tented his eyebrows and sighed wetly. "I've never heard of an office like that; all so crazy."

Nebe would have agreed with him, but he said, "That's why it sounds true. He wouldn't make up a story like that, but . . ."

Nolte wouldn't shut up. "Someone did. It's coming out too neat. It's like a parable in a sermon to illustrate some moral point that no one asks you to believe actually happened."

"He's telling it the way he remembers it!" said Nebe. He would have kicked Nolte under the table, but he wasn't within reach.

The cocky SOB continued, "He can't be. Memories aren't that organized, not unless he thought it through for a long time and, if he did, he'd have some answers. They'd be lies, but they'd be answers."

That was almost interesting, thought Nebe. "Meaning what?"

Nolte looked a bit smug. "He's telling a story that someone else made him memorize."

Nebe shook his head. "I don't really give a shit as long as he keeps talking. Sooner or later, he has to talk about the one thing on his mind."

"Right now I'm thinking about food. . . ." The childlike candor in the tone of Georg's comment made Nebe chuckle involuntarily and drove Nolte to crack his knuckles. Brandt merely licked his lips, a reflex at the mention of food, while his fingers clomped along the keys of the typewriter.

Nebe straightened his back and gazed at Georg like a British headmaster. "Well then we must push on to the point of our business mustn't we? No victuals until you tell us the whole story." Georg lowered his eyes and swallowed, then the gears began to turn in his mind once more. . . .

"I was with Franz and Ulrich, again. We'd gone out for beer and it was a different bar, again. We were using up bars fast because it was a small town and there really wasn't anything else to do. They were all pretty much the same: dim light, worn dark wood, and gray mirrors with the liver spots of age. There was a jukebox and someone kept playing the same record, a polka band doing their version Preussen's 'Gloria'. Franz looked at me strangely before turning to Ulrich. 'Isn't Georg almost hard to see? You think he's handsome, but he isn't. If you look away from his eyes, you can see that his ears are too big and his chin too narrow and pointed. His nose is too long. It should be a rat-like face, but it isn't so, he is a handsome man in an entirely nondescript sort of way. It makes about as much sense as anything else.'

"Ulrich was paying no attention to anything Frantz, he complained, 'Anyone got any money?' Franz threw some coins on the bar and pulled out a picture of his son in a Nazi Youth uniform. The color was lousy. The face looked like an orange gumdrop with buck teeth. The mother stood primly behind the boy wearing a gray face to match her gray dress. She looked like a fireplug with eyes.

"Franz flapped the picture at us. 'Look,' said Franz was saying, 'I don't like everything that's going on either. They're giving anti-Semitism a bad name. I feel like I live in a conquered country, a country conquered by midgets.'

"What he said made me think about my family too but I threw the images away as fast as they came to mind.

"'More beer, now that's a cure for conquering midgets.' Ulrich grunted and signaled to the waiter.

"'What the hell are you doing now?' asked Franz. I had split a beer coaster and was sketching on the blank side with a charcoal pencil. I showed them. I was drawing a cuckoo clock. It looked good, too good.

"Ulrich looked at it. 'Yeah, you've got talent. That's a problem. Makes you think you're better than everyone else. If you didn't have talent, you'd know you were an asshole.'

"I was only half listening because I was watching a panhandler working his way through the bar until he was chased out by the waiters. 'You guys ever look at derelicts?' I asked.

"'I try not to,' said Ulrich.

"'It's surprising how many of them were once handsome men. How many men are good looking? One in ten? One in twenty? But if you look at derelicts, at least half of them were once handsome men.'

"'What's he talking about now?' Franz interjected. The beer hadn't arrived yet.

"'He's telling his fortune,' Ulrich explained. 'They were like you, Georg, visibly better than the people around them, so they expected more. When they didn't get it, they refused to compromise. They're your heroes.'

"I smiled at him. 'You sound like Fritz.'

"Ulrich had been leaning over me almost perched on my shoulder. 'Not surprising,' he said, 'sometimes I think he's inside my head.' I had finished the sketch of the cuckoo clock, but instead of a bird popping out it was a very puzzled Christmas tree angel. Franz decided to ignore us but Ulrich went on. 'Now you see, that's clever and you're not like me, always trying to prove how clever I am. You only use it when it's vitally necessary, or entirely unnecessary. You're always so calm and in control, I can't understand why you're such a bum?'

"I looked him full in the face. 'I don't like anyone either. Maybe that's why, lack of motivation.'

"'What about that 'anyone' over there?' Franz interceded gracefully and he nodded across the room to a tall, skinny girl with good legs and a bad face. She was wearing a tight shiny dress that ended above her knees. It looked at least ten years old. She looked about thirty or, maybe, twenty-five and bitter. Then she saw Franz and I looking at her and she looked away. 'She's not much, but she knows it so she tries extra hard, at least that's what I hear.'

"'That's all you'll do is hear,' said Ulrich. 'She's a dental assistant. She wouldn't go out with a factory worker.'

"That suddenly made me take interest in the sport. 'I'm a cabinet maker.' I said it like it had just come to me.

"'You could have been a lot of things,' said Ulrich, 'but what you are right now is an asshole just like us.' But Hannah and I were already smiling at each other across the room. I got up and walked over to her. She seemed to be alone. There was a lot of smiling and whispered conversation, but I wasn't listening to what either of us said. I had the impression she wasn't either and then we left together. Franz and Ulrich watched us go.

"The next morning I woke up screaming in her bed, shouting from out of a nightmare. Somehow I got dressed and was sitting at the table. She had on a night gown. It was all ruffles and lace but with an eye to function, closed only at the neck. I wanted to say something, but there was nothing to say except, 'Coffee ready?'

"I had considered running but she had tactfully recommended I have some coffee before I do or say anything regrettable. She had an authentic Italian espresso pot so I decided to be patient when she said: 'In a minute . . .'

"I got up and paced around the room while she fussed with the coffee paraphernalia. I spotted her lone shelf, mostly novellas, so I slipped Mann's *Professor Unrat* in my coat pocket and left her Kafka. Funny but I don't think she ever noticed.

"She served the coffee and sat down, pulling up her negligee and crossing her legs to draw attention away from her face. 'Tell me about your dream.'

"I sat across from her. 'Nothing to tell.' I lowered my eyes and breathed in the aroma of the coffee. It was good, all things considered.

"'It's all new to me. I'm interested.' She raised one knee higher to flash me a little, but I looked away so she clasped her thighs together.

"'I can't think of anything to say.' I really couldn't.

"She grabbed both sides of the table and leaned towards me. 'You mean there's one thing on your mind and you're afraid to say it. Say it!'

"Then I smiled, it's a defense mechanism really, and she sat back down. 'You're too damn smart.'

She drilled her eyes into me. 'I'd better be, since I'm ugly. But my legs aren't bad.' She uncrossed them and held one out for appraisal.

"I had to agree matter-of-factly. 'Your legs are beautiful.'"

"Hannah hummed to herself, almost purring. She stood up to show off her legs one more time and poured more espresso into my cup. 'You were saying?'."

"You were saying?" asked Nebe. Georg said nothing. "So, what did you dream, Georg?" Georg pointed to the photograph of the wreckage. The detectives looked at each other. None of them believed it.

"Sounds almost true. Sort of," Nolte said soothingly.

Brandt looked up from the typewriter, "Do you believe that shit? Coming to him in a dream? Isn't that a little too melodramatic? I mean too cute and stupid to be real."

"It's embarrassing," said Nebe, "but dreams often can be. Real motives aren't clever. They're dumb and bestial," he searched for a word, "at times humiliating. No, what he said was all right. What bother me are the things he left out." He lit a cigarette to give himself time to think. After it was lit, he didn't know what to do with it. He put it in the ashtray and watched it burn. "How you thought of it doesn't matter. It's fascinating and I'm glad you told me but . . . Let me illustrate: one time I thought of poisoning my wife, but all I did was to think about it. She had the decency to die of pneumonia before I could work myself up to the act." He lied smoothly. "Thinking of doing it is different than actually doing it. Something always happens in between."

"Not when you have nothing to lose."

"Don't answer for him," Nebe snapped at Nolte, but he hadn't actually said anything. The voice was emanating from inside his head so Nebe leaned forward and smeared out the cigarette.

"Like grinding out that cigarette," said the voice, *". . .between thinking of it and doing it, what had happened?"* Nothing conscious . . . That didn't help.

"Perhaps," said Nebe, "if you stopped trying to prove how clever you are and just did your job. . . ." Nolte looked uneasy and Nebe left the sentence unfinished. He recomposed his features and smiled at Georg. "I understand. You had the skill and the opportunity and nothing to lose, but those aren't reasons. They were circumstances that made it easier, but aren't reasons. So, why did you do it?"

Nebe momentarily considered feeding him a cyanide pill, could say it hadn't shown up on the body search; that would mean disgrace, maybe demotion, but he'd still be alive. "Georg, if you hadn't thought of it, you wouldn't have done it. If you had anything to lose you wouldn't have done it. But why did you do it?"

Georg woke up a bit. "I was trying to stop the war." Nebe nodded to Brandt at the typewriter, but Brandt widened his eyes and gave a tiny shake of his head in warning. Again, he signaled to Brandt to type and again Brandt looked scared and froze.

"Doesn't make sense, Georg," said Nebe.

"What time is it?" asked Brandt.

"Same as it was an hour ago," said Nebe.

Nolte was looking pleased with himself. He licked his lips and smiled like a wolf pursuing a troika; meaning: another smart ass remark was coming.

Nebe didn't give him the chance. "Georg, your girlfriend . . . the ugly one, is she what happened in between? Are you in love with her?"

"That's none of your damn business!" All three men noted the emotion behind Elser's response.

"Might be the only true words he's spoken tonight," said Nolte.

Nebe chose to ignore that line for the moment. "But the way he tells it, this was a message from God."

"I didn't say that." Georg's indignation seemed genuine.

Nebe laughed. "You said it came to you in a dream like Joan of Arc. Georg, we don't mean to be rude, but we don't believe you. Why did you do it? We know you did it, so what difference does it make? Tell us why."

And at that moment the answer occurred to Georg. It was an idea that would certainly get him killed. It had been an extraordinary crime and, therefore, all had assumed that it must have an extraordinary motive. But it didn't. The only extraordinary part about the whole business was how easy it had been for him to execute. He'd spent seven years making cuckoo clocks, ideal training for making a mechanical time bomb. Then an inept management structure put him in charge of inventory at a munitions plant with access to all the explosives he could possibly use. . . . The obvious had happened. That was all. Even had there been no motive but the craftsman's itch, the overwhelming drive to exhibit skill and precision, the orbs had aligned placing Georg's frustrations and skills in the right place at the right time. Have you ever thought about doing something, then become obsessed with doing it just so you could prove that, even if it seemed impossible, it could be done by you?

Nolte picked up a dossier and flicked through it. "January 1937 you walked 215 km to get a job at the Dornier Aircraft Company at Friedrichshafen. 215 km in the middle of winter, Joan of Arc couldn't have done it better."

Something about that seemed to amuse Nebe. "What happened just before you took that long walk, Georg? Another woman?"

Georg raised his eyebrows in surprise. "Well, yes, actually that's why I needed a job."

Nebe stifled a chuckle. "And you said you'd send for her, but you never did, am I right?"

Georg shrugged and swiveled his head violently. "Pretty soon, you're going to torture me. Can we do it now?"

"No, Georg, thinking about it is much worse, that's why we save it for last." Nebe was smiling sadly, but Nolte was on his feet and shouting. It was so sudden it took seconds to understand what he was talking about.

"Did you hear that? He's a hero. At some point we allowed him to play the role of The Hero. This is totally fucked." That part sounded true.

Nebe took a slow, careful breath. "That was your idea. You told him he was a hero, tried to get him to brag about it, Napoleon and Waterloo and all that, remember?"

"It was your fucking idea, and it's your fucking responsibility!" Nolte was having a Führer-style rage fit.

Nebe's tone held more menace than he may have intended, then again maybe not: "Those words aren't necessary for expression, you gibbering bucket of shit."

Georg's eyes went wide, something was happening, something that made him extremely nervous. "It was two Englishmen," Georg said. "They offered me 40,000 Swiss francs to assassinate the Führer."

Silence. No one was breathing.

Then Nebe said, very quietly, "What were their names?"

Georg's eyes widened. "The Lion and the Unicorn." The words hung in the air like smoke.

More silence.

Everyone was waiting for something, but nothing happened. Nebe leaned forward speaking softly, not kind, not unkind, not anything. "Those were their code names, fine. That's all you would know. What did they look like?"

Georg looked from one detective to another then stared into the middle distance. Even the noise in the street seemed to have stopped. The entire world was still, waiting for Georg Elser to speak. He shook his head sadly and said, "This isn't going to work. Why don't you just write out what you want me to say and I'll sign it."

Nebe got up and started walking around his desk in a circle, gave up, and collapsed back into his chair. "I wish. But it isn't that easy. It would satisfy the court, but not the Gestapo. They'd know. They'd say it was a frame up to protect the real conspirators and then we'd all be executed. Do you want to kill us, Georg? Aside from this *Untermensch*," he pointed to Nolte, "we've treated you with every courtesy. Do you really want to kill us?"

Georg looked embarrassed. "No," said Georg, "you're harmless."

Nebe was transfixed. His world was ending, but if Georg thought they were harmless, that meant he'd open up. It was a new and better line of attack. Nebe heaved himself out of his chair and walked to the door of the interrogation room. He threw the door open and looked out the window at the end of the corridor. It was dawn and the gray light was coming in like fog around the tweaked medieval rooftops. The light was still too faint to be colored by the roof tiles and the city was as black and white as a photograph. There was the gigantic baby carriage shape of the Frauenkirche and the intricate gothic wedding cake of the Rathaus-Glockenspiel, the new town hall trying hard to look like a cathedral. There were rows of fake gothic apartment blocks, boring as any other dormitory suburb except that this was in the center of the old city and the pattern of the streets made no sense. All the Hansel and Gretel gingerbread offended him. He preferred fascist architecture, it was an idea made real. But the silence was beautiful. He thought of a black-booted, black-corseted prostitute, her hair sleek and shiny as her boots. He owed himself a treat. All he had to do was dance his way out of this.

"It's dawn . . .," said Nebe, "or is it sunset?" He looked at his watch. He had forgotten to wind it again. He looked at the clocks set into the twin towers of the Frauenkirsche. "6:30, it could be either one." He closed the door and walked back. "What time is sunrise?"

"I don't know," said Georg.

"Torture him until he confesses," Nolte said helpfully.

"That's all right, Georg, don't pay him any attention," said Nebe.

"Yeah," said Nolte, "I was just bullshitting a little."

Nebe looked at Nolte. He looked at Brandt at the typewriter. They all looked at each other. Nobody had any ideas. They looked at Georg. He didn't have any ideas either. Nebe reached under his desk and pressed the buzzer. Nothing happened.

"The entire floor is empty," said Nolte. "They're all downstairs."

Nebe needed a break. Going to the men's room would be a perfect excuse, but he couldn't do that. It would look like he had ordered a Wachtmeister to take a dump for him and, if that were possible, it would be mandatory. And that would be bad. Driving to work and shitting were the only times of the day he got to be alone. He needed to be alone right now. He started pacing, the next best thing.

"All right, you had just realized that you were going to kill the Führer. What happened next?"

The confession jerked along like a hand-cranked silent movie. He was obviously lying, but why was it obvious? There was more office politics in the storeroom.

Georg continued. . . .

"Ulrich and I were rearranging shelves in the storeroom trying to create more space. I was preoccupied and Ulrich seemed to have a bad hangover. He turned his head slowly, squinting against the pain and said, 'You have a good time last night?' I ignored him but he went on. 'I shouldn't have asked, though I don't know why not. I was pretty drunk. Did I say anything stupid?'

"'I was too drunk to remember,' I said and that seemed to relax him. 'Good.' It was noon and we quit for lunch. Ulrich smiled shyly as he walked away, he never came back from lunch.

"About 3 p.m. I was with Fritz at the loading gate. We were rolling in a hand truck loaded with cartons labeled: DONORIT/ DANGER HIGH EXPLOSIVE/ 12 GROSS. I was pushing and Fritz was steering, we followed with two hand trucks of cordite. I just had to ask, 'Where's Ulrich, did he go home sick?'

"Fritz smiled like a camel. 'I persuaded him to join the Reicharbeitdienst.' I was hurt, but Fritz seemed to find that threatening. 'I'm sorry about Ulrich, but you must know it was necessary.'

"'It's digging ditches,' I said. 'He's a clerk, he can't handle the work.' Fritz drew himself up, pointing his Adam's apple at my left eye. 'The discipline will do him a world of good. And it was his choice. The alternative was to be fired without a letter of recommendation; that would have made him unemployable, an indigent and an honorary Jew. It would have meant forced labor in a detention camp—a death sentence.' Fritz was proud of himself. When among wolves, howl! I didn't trust my voice so I just nodded emphatically.

"Fritz quickly stepped off, leaving me with a quarter ton of explosive. I rolled the dolly to the storeroom, unlocked the door, turned on the light and rolled the dolly in. I relocked the door before I began to unpack the cordite and put it on the selves. It was slow work. The explosives themselves were safe enough, but the air seals were bad. Sometimes the explosives would form nitrates from metal particles in the air and then the slightest jar would set them off.

"I didn't really know about cordite, it was gunpowder and supposed to be stable. I willed myself to relax and slow down with no sharp corners on my movements. When my muscle memory told me that I had the routine I sped up and had the cordite shelved in under an hour.

"Fritz was at the desk playing some game with the numbers in the ledgers. I wondered if the only function of it was to look busy. I walked up and stood at attention with my thighs pressed against the desk. 'The cordite shipment is eight units short.'

"'That's their problem,' said Fritz and returned to his ledgers. Time passed and he noticed that I was still standing there. Fritz looked up. 'Look, we reorder when we're down to three gross, *verstanden*? The shortage won't be noticed unless you call attention to it. Don't create problems.'

"'Yes, sir, but what if there's an inventory check?' The tension was out of my throat and my voice was an octave lower, but Fritz just didn't seem to get it.

"'There hasn't been one in 12 years.'

"I persisted. 'But what if there is?'

"Fritz was getting annoyed. 'Then tell them that I told you to ignore the shortages. Now, do something useful.'

"'Yes . . . sir!' And I actually found myself bowing. It was like he was slowly fading before my eyes. A sacrificial victim is always slightly holy."

Brandt suddenly stood up from the typewriter. "Sir, am I expected to type this metaphysical tripe?"

Nebe stood as well, his ass was getting numb and his head heavy. He picked up his cigarettes and nodded to Nolte. "Let's all take five, except for you of course, Georg. You just stay there and think your story through."

Nolte and Nebe went out to smoke in defiance of the Führer's regulations. Brandt cracked his fingers and stretched his neck while Georg glanced at him apologetically.

In the corridor Nolte leaned against the wall. "I love detective stories because the motives never make sense, just like in reality."

Nebe released a cloud of smoke, swirling from his nostrils. "You're complaining that his story makes sense?"

"This isn't a confession, it is sedation!" Nolte wasn't known for his delicate sense of aesthetics, but he had a point. Nebe could grant him that much.

"So, what do you suggest?"

Nolte's face lit up. "How about I shoot myself in the foot practicing fast draw? It's a PPK and the safety doesn't hold. It would be a legitimate accident."

Apparently this case was going to drive them all round the bend. Nebe had to scold. "Hush, I was serious."

Nolte snubbed out his cigarette in exasperation. "You know the worst part? He's the only man I've ever met with no talent for telling a story. Everyone's got some talent at it, everyone except him. He's the only completely untalented man on earth and we're begging him to tell us a story!"

"Let's get back to it." Nebe dropped his cigarette on the floor, grinding it out with a pivot of his toe. He nodded to Nolte to pick up the butts.

They entered to find Georg dozing, chin nearly on his chest, while Brandt seemed to be contemplating the ceiling. Nebe clapped, jarring both guard and captive back to alertness. "Naptime's over, boys. Georg, you've got a confession to finish." Georg nodded dutifully, it was his only chance of ever getting anything to eat.

"The next day on our half-hour lunch break I finished assembling the artillery fuse. Fritz had watched me sourly, munching on his sandwich and drinking a beer. 'Alright, you solved it. Now take it apart and put the pieces back.'

"'Of course,' I said, but I put the fuse in my pocket instead.

"That night I took the wooden chest out from under my bed. I'd built it years earlier, and it included a false bottom to protect my valuables in the event I ever had any. It had been an ambitious project for an apprentice cabinet maker. The joins were undetectable even to my finger tips. There was a button near the right front corner that looked like merely a whirl in the wood, it popped open the lid of the secret compartment. I took the artillery fuse out of my pocket and placed it inside next to the eight packets of cordite. That's the way things went for weeks, it had become a routine so I no longer needed to think about it.

"The next thing I remember was that Schulz, the office manager, had walked in unexpectedly one day. Schulz gave the Nazi salute and Fritz and I Heil Hitlered with enthusiasm. Then Fritz put his arm around me and started talking energetically. A fork lift rumbled by, it was carrying a turret lathe and under the strain it made a noise like mountains walking. It drowned out the words but Fritz was obviously praising me and Schulz was smiling proudly. I tried to look shy and grateful. The pose came with an ease that surprised me.

"That afternoon I stole the percussion caps for the artillery fuse out of a box labeled: MERCURY FULMINATE/ DETONATORS/ DANGER: HIGH EXPLOSIVE. I'd put off taking them for weeks. It was dangerous stuff to have around and I treated it with respect, wrapping each one in a separate cotton rag so they wouldn't knock against each other. I now had over a hundred packets of cordite inside the chest, along with three 155 mm artillery fuses. I put the fulminate caps at the opposite end of the chest from the cordite, each cap tucked inside a neatly rolled pair of socks. Then I wedged a pillow between them and the cordite and hoped for the best. The lid of the compartment wouldn't quite close, but I had stopped worrying about it. Any serious search would have found them anyway."

"And when was that?" Nebe knew that time continuity would be essential to appease the Gestapo. Not surprisingly Georg's reply was vague.

"It could have been months later. I don't remember exactly".

Nebe wasn't satisfied, something just didn't fit. "OK, let's go back a minute. Why were you working as a shipping clerk?"

"I had started out on the assembly floor, sandblasting rough castings and within a few months I was moved up to a responsible position."

"But still not one where you could use your skills; that was 1937, yes? The country had recovered. You could have earned more as a carpenter."

"Anything I make over 24 marks per week goes for child support anyway, so it doesn't matter. The important thing for me is that the job be interesting."

Nebe thought: if this had been a movie, he'd have walked out. "Interesting. Sandblasting? It's a dirty job, a disgusting job. You get sand and metal particles in your lungs. You spend all your time coughing up black phlegm and then you die. Coughing up your lungs is not interesting. It fully occupies the mind, but it is not interesting. You're lying, Georg."

Georg had no reply. Nebe wondered why he was asking these questions. No one would read it. When the record of the interrogation was finally read this nonsense would be skipped over. Georg still had no reply.

"You're lying, Georg. You took the job because you knew it would give you the opportunity to steal high explosives. You had already decided to assassinate the Führer, a year before the Munich Agreement."

Georg still had no reply. This wasn't working even as intimidation. It was completely pointless. Nebe was getting edgy. "Well go on, Georg!"

"From there?"

"Yes, from there."

So he continued.

"I remember that I had gone into work early, like I always did, but this time Fritz was already there. He was wide-eyed and breathing in gulps. He jumped up and Heil Hitlered like it was the answer to a question. 'Heil Hitler! There was an inventory check. We're a gross of cordite short among other things. . . . I don't know either. Twelve years. . . . New rules have been imposed on high explosives. They checked the inventory. Why now?'

"'But who? What are we going to do?' I tried to act baffled. It was easier than it should have been. My mother had always told me that I was a lousy liar, but the situation had changed lots of things.

"'What could I do? I changed the numbers on the requisition slips.' Fritz was becoming even dimmer and I found nothing to say. I knew that he had just killed himself, actually he was already dead, but he still kept talking, extenuating. 'I talked to my wife. She told me to blame you, to say you stole it. She said they'd believe me but I told her, no. I couldn't blame you because you were the one who told me about it but she kept on. She screeched at me to think of my family. I tried to explain that you didn't do it so it wouldn't stop the thefts, it would only make things worse, but she didn't listen.'"

"Fritz fell silent a moment before continuing. 'My son, he's in the Hitler Youth. I hadn't thought of that. He must have told them. My own son turned me in.' His face slipped out of gear, not like he was trying to think of something to say, but like he was trying to remember it differently, as though that would change something. He looked at me questioningly, his eyes asking if it were true that he was dead. I nodded slowly.

"'Thank you.' Fritz jumped up, straightened his tie and buttoned his coat. 'Herr Schulz has asked me to his office,' he said it and walked out, stiff legged and fast. The corridor lights weren't on yet and in the gloom the metal taps on his heels struck sparks from the concrete floor. I watched him go, trying to memorize him. I knew I'd probably never see him again. When Fritz went out of sight around a corner of the building I picked up the broom and began to sweep the floor. I'd be having visitors soon.

"They didn't come though until after lunch. Schulz walked in with a Hitler Youth type. Their faces were set. I gave the Nazi salute casually, as though it were an old habit. 'Heil Hitler, Herr Schulz.'

"'Heil Hitler, Georg. This is your new assistant, Herr Dieter Boltzmann. You've been promoted. You are now the new supervisor of inventory.' I don't know if I was supposed to be surprised. I just sort of responded automatically.

"'I am honored, Herr Schulz. I am grateful for your trust, but what about Fritz?' I should have used his last name, but discovered that I didn't remember it.

"'He has been detained. By . . . the police.' The pause meant it was really the Gestapo, but no one liked to mention them by name. 'It seems he was stealing explosives.' My expression must have passed for astonishment, I can't be sure, but apparently whatever my face was registering Schulz considered appropriate.

"'How can you know?' I said. 'It might have been me. Maybe I took it.' He gave me a pseudo-paternal look, like a middle school principal might give the class clown in a private moment.

"'No. I understand your loyalty, but he's already confessed to forging the requisition slips. And, that you called his attention to the shortages which he told you to ignore. It was his own son who denounced him.'

"'But why?' I then quickly corrected myself. 'Why did he steal it?'

"Schulz raised his hands. 'To sell it to the Communists, I suppose, or to Beppo Römer's men. I assume they will find out. Now . . .'

"Schulz kept talking. I watched his lips without listening to the words. The gestures told it clearly enough. He was telling me to show Boltzmann his duties. I bowed as Schulz left and Boltzmann bowed deeper. Boltzmann said something, but I didn't hear it, I just nodded mechanically and walked off. 'We'll start in the storeroom,' I said over my shoulder. Boltzmann followed me neatly, one step to the right and two steps back, the right-hand man.

"Later I discovered that Fritz had left his briefcase, so I emptied it out. Fritz had carried a briefcase so I could too, right? I could steal explosives a box at a time. I thought of Fritz, but didn't feel guilty, just a little sick to my stomach. I knew what would happen to him and that there was no way to avoid it.

"Have any of you ever attended a German civil execution?" Georg gazed from one to the other but there was no response. He elaborated,

"They are done by decapitation, but with a local flavor. My father had taken me to one as a boy, said it would do me good even though my mother screamed and cried. In Fritz's case the beheading was done by a large butcher with a large meat cleaver who was wearing a silk top hat, white tie, and tails. The executioner was an enormously fat and powerful man with the curling mustache of an Old West bad man. A number of guards were standing around to make the thing look orderly and two bored men in rubber boots, aprons, and wearing derbies were standing by with mops and buckets.

"There was also the usual audience of reporters and police, Nazi bureaucrats and Gestapo men watching faces and people who just happened to like that sort of thing. Fritz didn't have anything to say, men rarely do in that circumstance. Schulz had insisted that we go to witness, that it would be inspirational. He turned to me and smiled then we both looked on as Fritz was led up onto the block and fastened.

"The fat butcher in the top hat picked up the cleaver and tested its weight and then beheaded Fritz with one soggy crunch. Fritz's head tumbled into the basket, bounced up and almost out, only clinging to the rim of the basket by its teeth, the eyes rolling and blinking. There was an enormous whoop of laughter and applause and then the head fell back into the basket. I was not able to think of anything, my mind just sort of temporarily shut off.

"Schultz and I took the train back to Heidenheim and though I can't remember the trip back, I do remember that while walking home from the station I saw a church and went in. It was a Catholic church so I knelt. I recited the Lord's Prayer; recited it several times.

"'I have never prayed to God in a personal way, that is, freely and in my own words. And I have never made my action—I mean the wish that it succeed—the object of my prayer. When I was a child, my parents took me to church; later I went alone a few times, but less often as the years went by. Only in the past year have I visited churches more often, even on work days, even Catholic churches when there wasn't a Lutheran close by. I don't really think the denomination matters. I admit that my prayers were connected with what I was going to do but in an abstract way, I couldn't think of anything else and I'm sure I wouldn't have prayed so much if I hadn't been planning this. It's not that I thought that what I was planning to do was sinful. I was trying to prevent even worse bloodshed."

"*You were trying to PREVENT bloodshed?* Bet you love dogs too. All murderers love dogs," said Brandt, ever the sentimentalist.

"Yeah," said Nolte. "Yea though I walk through the shadow of the valley of death, I can always blame Fritz for it. Your best friend gets his head cut off and you're giving us a song and dance about being an altruist."

"Fritz wasn't my friend." Georg looked from one to the other as if this fact should have been clear to all.

"Maybe you weren't his friend," said Nebe, "but he was probably your only true friend, except maybe Ulrich but you very likely got him killed too."

"You're a monster," Nolte explained.

"I don't feel like a monster." Georg tried to feel guilty, but couldn't manage it. He just felt hollow.

"Monsters never think they're monsters. They think they're just stronger or cleverer than everyone else. Or, worse, they think that whatever they do isn't for them it's for their art, which entitles them do anything they want to anyone." Nolte was having an almost fatal moment of insight into himself, but he survived it.

"Enough." Nebe pointed to the typewriter and drew a finger across his throat. The noise of the typing died away. He turned back to Georg. "You are saying we killed the wrong man."

"Yes, sir." Elser's earnest expression was infuriating.

Nebe turned back to Brandt, who had his fingers in midair over the typewriter. "Strike that, all of it." Brandt looked puzzled. He was often puzzled. He was a good man in a gunfight, always followed order, and he didn't mind typing. "Take it all. All of it! Run it through the shredder, twice! Put it all in the wastebasket then swallow the wastebasket."

Brandt pulled the sheet out of the typewriter. He stared at it. He picked up the rest of the pages and wandered off looking humiliated yet not surprised about it. Nebe followed him out the door and shouted in his father's, the Sergeant Major's, voice. Before he could walk back to his desk, two uniformed Anwarters had double-timed up the stairs and run into the room. They turned their ponderously attentive faces to Nebe and waited for instructions. "Get him out of here!" he said. "Put him in the cage in the squad room and don't let anyone talk to him." Georg stood up and the Anwarters grabbed him by the elbows and wheeled him around so fast that Nebe felt a spurt of wind against his face. They heel and toed their way out and closed the door with slow motion delicacy.

There was the sound of someone falling down in the squad room. Nebe contemplated the ceiling and waited for another crash. Nolte gave him a look that said: *Who are you trying to impress with this shit? It's fucking embarrassing.* Nebe shrugged. "Well," he said, "we're supposed to be upset that we killed the wrong man, it gives it a moral tone."

"There is no conspiracy . . .," said Nolte, very quiet and very scared. "How can we be expected to handle this? The case itself is a time bomb."

"We'll get the truth out of him." Nebe fussed with some folders on his desk and tried to look professional.

Nolte was having yet another epiphany. "Obviously, he is telling the truth. So, if you want a conspiracy, we'll have to invent one. Pick some suspects at random and make them say they were in on it with him."

Nebe looked at him unhappily. "We've been all through that! Any thorough internal affairs investigation would make it appear to be a cover-up. Stop grasping at easy answers."

Nolte was not to be dissuaded. "Since it wasn't a conspiracy then it has to be something personal. A Brown Shirt kicked his dog, the SS raped his sister, he hated to brush his teeth as a child and the Führer's mustache reminds him of a toothbrush."

"There are probably at least 20 million men out there with something personal against the Führer, but Elser is the only one who acted on it. To reduce it to someone having kicked his dog trivializes the man without explaining anything. It says it didn't really happen or, if it did, it doesn't really matter. But we have to have a conspiracy, the party line demands it. The Führer has the unwavering support of every German worker; therefore, a German worker cannot have possibly plotted to kill the Führer, full stop!" The need to continually repeat the obvious was beginning to wear on Nebe's patience.

"The Gestapo arrested his brother, Manfred, put him in Dachau."

Nebe would have asked how Nolte knew that, but he would have an answer and it would give him a chance to go on talking even longer. "Manfred was a Communist, not a sympathizer like Georg. He was a marching, shouting Communist. He got taken off in '36 in the roundup before the Olympics. It isn't in the file but at least 300,000 were arrested and surely most of them had brothers."

"But few of them were Aryan Germans. Manfred was. There would have been a routine check to see if he had any relatives in sensitive jobs. Even the most casual check would have found that Elser had spent seven years making cuckoo clocks." Nolte suddenly seemed driven, like his life depended on making the square peg fit in the round hole.

"Seven years off and on and making cuckoo clocks would not have been considered a sensitive job." Nebe resigned himself to playing the straight man until Nolte got whatever this was out of his system.

"What about inventory at the munitions plant?" Nolte was almost pleading.

"That was after the purge, and he had started out sand blasting. By then he was no longer a person of interest anyway."

Nebe was just short of smug when Nolte suddenly had another revelation. "Heydrich is the only party leader who wasn't at the beer hall. It was a celebration for the old fighters, the veterans of the putsch of '23. Heydrich didn't join until 1930. He wasn't invited. He wouldn't have been welcome. He had the perfect excuse for not being there."

"So Heydrich made Elser a deal on the life of his brother who he hadn't spoken to in 22 years? Two decades of silence implies a certain amount of hard feeling."

Nolte would not be put off easily. "The Gestapo having him put in Dachau made it personal."

Nebe realized shooting him might be misunderstood so he tried to be gentle. "So, then get me the file on his brother."

"It's missing. The folder is there, but it's empty. The file was borrowed in '37 and not returned. 'By the Highest Authority,' but no names."

Nebe closed his eyes. "The intermediaries?"

"They're dead, they have to be. Heydrich wouldn't have left them alive."

Throughout this exchange Brandt looked on, head swiveling back and forth dumbfounded, like a child watching the Wimbledon finals: he was certain that it was important, but clueless as to why. Nebe was about to serve an ace.

"Then there's no evidence. We can't uncover a conspiracy, we can't invent one, and we can't deny that there is one. What do you suggest?"

"Shooting myself in the foot?" Nolte was actually serious.

Nebe considered the idea. "Hmm, we could crash the car and cripple ourselves just slightly. 70 km/hr, that's like falling off a three-story building. That could do it, except that I doubt we're competent to do that either. We'd either be killed or completely uninjured. You can get out of this anytime. Just walk out the door, take the train to Switzerland, and lose your pension."

That should have shut Nolte up. It didn't. "Why is he the only one? Where are the others?"

Nebe smiled and nodded. It was nice that Nolte had now found something else to worry about, even if he were exchanging one insoluble problem for another.

Nolte went on, "Other men could have had his skills. They could have learned to make explosive devices. Not all of them would have blown themselves up trying. But where are they?"

Nebe blinked and composed his features to mean patience. "The amateur assassin never goes back to school to learn how it's done. It's never happened. If they even practice with a pistol for an hour, that's more training than most of them ever put themselves through. For the amateur practice creates a crisis in confidence; they become overwhelmed by the practical difficulties of their mission and immediately give up."

"Maybe bombers are different than shooters?" Brandt's question was genuine, and got the attention of both Nebe and Nolte. "There aren't any ranges where they can go to practice. You can't just go into the woods and start letting off explosives without causing alarm, so it's all theory until the day that it either works, or it doesn't."

Nolte suddenly perked up a bit, "Perhaps in Elser's case the term *amateur* applies as the French use it, for those who lack professional expertise yet are nonetheless passionate about their art?"

Nebe pondered that a moment but then shook his head. "Ever the romantic, Nolte . . . Gentlemen, I appreciate your insights, the naked truth however is that it doesn't really matter whether Elser was passionate about what he did or not. The unthinkable has happened, an Aryan Lutheran German worker made an attempt on the life of the Führer, and we cannot plausibly explain it away." That was a mistake; he shouldn't have said that, the statement led to a dead end that led mystically and despairingly back to the first question.

"What's going to happen to us?" Nolte's lower lip was almost but not quite trembling.

Nebe was feeling romantic himself. He felt a rush of something he couldn't name, but it felt like being nineteen and awake at 3:00 a.m. "That doesn't depend on us," he said. He wanted desperately to see a movie, a gangster flick like *Public Enemy*. The detectives were always untouchable and in total control. It was more than that, a movie offered you refuge in a perfect world where the snow never turned black and the lovers never had to get up to piss and no one ever had trouble hailing a cab; where all motives were clear and all consequences were logical the way they never are in real life. And above all, everything was foreshadowed; everything was anticipated so that, in fact, there were no surprises. That was the best part because after forty, there were no good surprises.

It was pointless to argue that this was unrealistic, that kind sedative reassurance is what movies are about and, like any government-sanctioned use of narcotics, had to be considered a political act. When the Führer had conquered Poland he had made sure that alcohol and pornography were cheap and readily available. Nebe could do with some heavy-weight sedation himself, but he'd have to make do with schnapps. The detective with a bottle of schnapps in his bottom drawer was a cliché, but like most people he had made himself a caricature. Why did Georg do it? Ever ask a master craftsman why he does his thing? He won't know what the hell you're talking about.

NOVEMBER 13TH, 1939

ONCE AGAIN, GEORG WAS CARRIED into the interrogation room. He gazed from one to the other of his bearers and smiled up at them with what could almost be gratitude. Brandt flexed his fingers like a concert pianist before taking his seat at the typewriter, while Nolte made a face like someone had just passed a rotten herring under his nose. He glowered at Nebe with an expression that screamed "How much more of this will we be expected to endure?"

Nebe, ever the stalwart professional, said, "Sooner or later he has to talk about the one thing on his mind. Right, Georg? What do you have to tell us today?"

George continued from where he had left off the previous day, almost as if had been repeating it to himself so he wouldn't forget where he was.

"I took Hannah to a Konditorei with table cloths so white they looked like they glowed in the dark, with waitresses in white uniforms that looked like silk and with glass cases of cakes in bright comic-strip colors. There was nothing to celebrate but it was an occasion, or at least I knew it would be before it was over. Hannah was eating something with almonds and pink frosting. The smell of rum carried across the table. She ate with twittering little bites, rolling her eyes and washing down a pellet of cake with a mouthful of coffee. It didn't take much to make her happy. I started spooning my way through a slab of *Schwarzwalder Kirschtorte*. I couldn't taste it. I stopped and told her about my promotion, then about Fritz. She listened patiently.

"'You liked him a lot.' She had said it like she knew what she was talking about.

I couldn't help but object that I didn't like him at all. That he was just another vulgar mediocrity exploiting his little wand of authority. I could have hated him but actually I didn't. Even if I had . . . I was doing what I knew to be right. It was a surprise that I was going to get a lot of people killed. But of course I couldn't tell her about that.

"'He brought it on himself.' Her confident tone was so natural.

"I nodded. I was grateful she had completed the sentence. She stuck her tongue out at me, childlike and conspiratorial. 'He came in once to have his teeth cleaned.'

"My eyebrows shot up. 'Fritz?' I hadn't expected that.

"'Yes. He pinched my ass and I stabbed him through the gums with the dental pick. Then I giggled and said I didn't mean it, I was just startled.'

"I smiled in spite of myself. 'Alright, so you're an accomplice.' Of course she had no idea what I was talking about.

"'An accomplice to what? You didn't do anything.'

"I laughed. 'Maybe not, but I got a promotion out of it, so I feel guilty.'

"'That's silly.'

"We chewed in silence for a few moments, each a captive of our own musings. Hannah looked across at me from under her spider-leg lashes. 'Now that you have your promotion, we can get married.' Even though I had been expecting it, I still gulped; indelicate I know.

"'I still make only twenty four marks a week.' The rest is still going to reimburse that woman for having had my illegitimate child.

"'Well, I make fifty-five, I can work too. I always expected to.' She was such a sensible girl, always infuriatingly hard not to like, but I was old-fashioned.

"'I don't want that.'

"'I don't mind,' she went on, determinedly. 'Times change and we have to go with it. The Führer isn't wrong about everything. And then when we're married, we can get your son from that bitch and you won't have to pay child support.' It was an argument, a good one. 'What's his name?' she asked. 'You've never told me.'

"I had stopped listening though because her offer was considerable. I could have married well when I was younger. To marry for comfort was probably the last good offer I was ever going to get. I wondered if it would be different if I was in love with her. I've never been in love so I had no point of reference. People talk about love with the same hysteria as politics, so I don't really believe in either. It was the first time I felt unsure about the explosives under my bed, not sure that I wanted to go through with it. I wished I could tell her about it so she could talk me out of it. I had no doubt that she could have. But she had stopped talking. She was looking at me and waiting. I continued my thoughts aloud, which is always a mistake. 'I don't know, but as I grow older, I'm beginning to think that courage can't be separated from vanity, because the one essential to courage is to think that you're a little better than the people around you; so, if something's to be done, it's up to you to do it.'

"Her mouth fell open. 'What the hell are you talking about?' she said it loud enough for the cashier to turn at us and frown.

"I stage whispered, 'I'm not the stuff of which heroes are made.'

"Her brow furrowed, 'I'm not asking you to be a hero. Does it really take that much courage just to be seen with me?' She was speaking quietly but her voice kept breaking; I realized I was making the situation more complicated than it should have been.

"'I didn't say that.' I spoke in an unnaturally deep voice and it slowed her down. We sat looking at each other from out of the silence.

"Finally she said, 'I wanted to touch you but I was afraid. Why was I afraid to touch you?'

"My thoughts were still elsewhere. 'I don't want pity,' I said and she slapped my face, insulted. She had a wiry strength that caused my ear to hurt and my sinuses to fill. It felt like someone had stuffed a pillow up my nose but I didn't blink; I'd been expecting it ever since Fritz had been arrested.

"'You want to marry me or not?' Her voice jiggled the silverware. Everyone in the pastry shop was trying not to watch us. Even the cashier had turned his face away."

Brandt pressed his hands to his temples as if trying to hold the hemispheres of his brain together. Nolte had begun to pace in agitation. "OK, we get it, he had other plans."

Nebe closed and opened his eyes slowly, deliberately before turning back to the prisoner. "But, what did you say, Georg?"

"Ugly things; terrible things . . ." Under other circumstances such sensitivity might have been admirable in some way, but not here.

"What for? A simple 'No' would have been enough." Nebe's fingers traced the schnapps bottle in his drawer with longing.

Georg looked from one to the other as if seeking support. "It seemed better that she thought she was walking out on me."

Nebe's tone grew stern. "But there was no need to insult the girl. Couldn't you have claimed to be going queer?" Yet again he longed it were a bad movie so he could walk out. Walking out on a stage play would be even better. Someone actually might notice. He yearned for some way of drawing his superiors' attention to the fact that he was aware that the whole mess was a poorly staged farce from the very onset. That he knew it was an abomination with no solution. It was like one of those hideous dreams in which you are naked but all around you stubbornly refuse to even acknowledge that you are there.

Georg tilted his head. "I didn't think of that."

Nolte hissed, "No, you wouldn't have."

"So what did you say, Georg?" Nebe prompted, motioning with his hands. Georg looked down.

"I had to end it, to force her away. . . . I was grasping. So I said, 'It's not that. It really doesn't matter whether I do or don't. You're the best friend I've had in a while and we're good as lovers but, well, you're just not presentable.'"

"That is pretty ugly and terrible, Georg," said Nebe.

"And you said you were trying to be kind," Nolte guffawed. "Maybe you are queer."

Brandt was somehow offended by that. "Why does everyone feel competent to advise everyone else on their sex life?"

"Point noted, Brandt." Nebe was glaring at Nolte. "Please go on, Georg."

"Hannah, she was about to start screaming but settled on a penetrating stage whisper that carried to all corners of the room. The other customers were trying to do a three-quarter turn away from us.

"'You hate me.' Her whisper was like a wind tunnel. 'And you hate yourself for being with me because I'm not pretty enough.'

"'Maybe I love you. I said so . . .' I really had said that, or at least I thought I had.

"'No you didn't.' She was finally screaming, but no one heckled us, for a wonder.

"'I am saying it now. Maybe I love you. But that's not enough, is it? It's never enough, is it? That's why you should never even talk to an ugly girl. If you don't find out what nice people they are you don't have any conflicts.'

"'Why do I put up with you?' she said in a real whisper.

"'Because I'm from somewhere else and you don't know how you should act toward me and you feel a little nervous about that. You only think you're in love.'

"Hannah sat very still with a look in her eye that would scare an executioner and then she said very softly, 'You deserve everything that's going to happen to you.' Which was entirely true, then she marched out of the pastry shop, her long legs striding. The door slammed so hard behind her that the glass cracked, but no one looked up. They didn't want to mess with her and I didn't blame them.

"I don't know, Georg," said Nebe. "But when you found yourself acting like a pig in the name of honor, maybe, you should have rechecked your calculations."

Nolte put in by way of conciliation. "What happened to her?"

"Oh, she took up with the podiatrist she'd been seeing when I first met her."

"Good for her!" Nolte shouted and clapped his hands.

Georg nodded. "Yeah, I did at least one thing right."

Nebe raised an appraising eyebrow. "You actually believe that, Georg?" He waited a second, but wasn't really looking for an answer. "Now that that's over with, let's get back to building our bomb."

Georg's face contorted as if he were turning the reels of his memory to get to that part of the story. "I had started to dress differently, less like a manual laborer and more like a junior manager. I saw myself in a bakery store window one day, my reflected head sitting among the *kuchens*. I was wearing a black bowler instead of a worker's cap so it had to have been sometime after my promotion. I was passing a news stand when I saw a front-page photo of Hitler standing on a podium in front of two white-washed pillars. It was the *Völkischer Beobachter*, Hitler's official newspaper. I bought one and read it carefully, awkwardly; it wasn't a habit. I had never felt compelled to be informed in that way, the radio was more entertaining. I always liked to read books, in fact reading can be nearly as much fun as masturbation, but the language used in that paper was somehow high-flown yet sub-literate. I don't know how they did it but it was almost painful to read. The article went on and on, something about Hitler always speaking on November 8th, in commemoration of the Beer Hall Putsch.

"A platoon of Bunde deutscher Mädchen marched by. It was some national girls' club. They were marching in military formation but what they were up to was unclear. The uniforms were innocent enough: shapeless black suits with white gloves and pilgrim collars. They wore narrow-brimmed black fedoras. It took a second glance to see that it was a uniform. They looked dressed for a funeral and they marched in a trance. One of the girls in the last rank turned and gave me a quick look. When I smiled at her, the squad leader shouted, "Eyes front!" The girl snapped her eyes away and they marched off. I was walking slowly, holding the *Völkischer Beobachter* in front of me with both hands, studying the picture of Hitler chanting himself into comic strip rapture. I folded the paper and put it under my right arm, away from my heart. Abruptly, I started walking very fast.

"I'd gone into a library and a motherly woman in a dress like a priest's chasuble handed me bound volumes with back issues of the *Völkischer Beobachter*. I checked the front pages for the ninth of November for the previous years. On each one, there was a photo of Hitler speaking in the same place, at the same podium in between two pillars. And they weren't the same photograph. In each one, Hitler's face was contorted in a different twitch, his arm jerking in a different direction. 'But they all might have been taken the same night,' I had said it aloud and the librarian looked up. She asked if I had said something. I must have looked embarrassed and scared. The librarian smiled understandingly.

"'If it helps to move your lips when you read, you go right ahead,' she said, consolingly.

I went back to comparing the photos. Two of them showed part of the table in front of the podium. There was a flower arrangement on the table and the two arrangements were different. The pictures had been taken in different years. In 1933 and 1934 Hitler had been in front of the two pillars, speaking at the BürgerBräuKeller at precisely 8:00 p.m. on November 8th. My eyes fumbled through the texts, looking for confirmation, trying to untie the black knots of bureaucratic prose. I found it on the front page for November 9, 1935: 'The ceremonies of 8/9 November 1935, honoring those who had fallen in 1923'—in the Beer Hall Putsch—'have taken up the Eternal Watch creating the basis for the National Socialist Procession.' The thick, squat Gothic letters were blurring and I had to stop to rub my eyes. 'Therefore, ceremonies in all future years must be arranged exactly as in 1935.'

"'Exactly.' I said it out loud, almost like a reflex, because at precisely that moment I knew it could be done. With ponderous and creaky condescension, the librarian smiled in my direction so I returned the bound volumes and rushed out."

The pause was thunderous as Georg looked from one man to the other with the expectant anticipation of one sure they had just shared a great revelation. He could not understand his auditors' lack of enthusiasm.

Nebe's fingers wound themselves around the neck of the schnapps bottle slowly and Brandt's clackity clacked to halt as he finally caught up with the verbose narrative. Nolte's expression broadcast a nearly homicidal exasperation.

"Gentlemen, that will do for now. . . ." Nebe nodded to Nolte, who rushed to call the turnkeys while Brandt massaged his fingers with the expression of a child wondering why he's being sent to bed without supper. Georg sighed as he was airlifted from the room once more. Nebe knew that the longer this dragged on the harder it would become for them to suppress the urge to kill him.

Nebe waved his underlings out, lingering behind on some pretext. He desperately wanted a slug of that schnapps, but most importantly he didn't want his colleagues to see in which direction he opted to depart that evening. He craved release and desperately needed it in order to maintain his composure. This situation was testing them all and he certainly didn't want to have to explain having shot one of his colleagues or the prisoner. He had lived through this process hundreds of times but there had always been some point to it. At least it had been possible to convince oneself there was because the extenuating circumstances favored some conclusion. In this debacle there seemed to be nothing but extenuating circumstances, and they all appeared to be lethal.

This wasn't an interrogation, it was a penance, for what he wasn't sure but he would have preferred the Hail Marys and Our Fathers to this interminable nonsense. A smile crept over his lips as he thought about his plans for the evening and he actually licked them as he lifted the bottle from his drawer. Seeing as he was already paying penance he might as well enjoy the sin.

The reception at the brothel was cordial but not enthusiastic. He was law enforcement, which meant "pro bono" service, and he was too low in the hierarch to be an extravagant tipper. That night however he was looking for something particular to satiate his urge, so he pulled out all the stops and teasingly slid an unassuming yet respectable banknote along the madam's throat before tucking it into the snug crevice formed by her ample décolleté. For this "treatment" to be effective the girl would need to exhibit the same unnerving innocence as Elser. The ingénue that the madam presented was perfectly cast to type, the question was whether she could play the role convincingly.

Her initial choice, to play it reluctant, nearly ruined the whole thing but Nebe had been sufficiently stirred by her to wave an admonishing finger and she took the cue like a pro. She suddenly became wide-eyed and docile, completely trusting: just like Georg. She waited to be told, to be led, to be used as he wished.

The sting and tingle on the palms of his hands was restoring Nebe to jolly good humor and the girl's rosy buttocks were delightfully hot to the touch. Her lithe form squirming over his knees had inspired an insistent erection, which, despite his Lutheran ethics, he felt was a shame to waste. He decided to compromise: he would remove her gag and have her suck him off.

NOVEMBER 14TH, 1939

GEORG WAS DAYDREAMING WHEN HIS keepers came to collect him. The effects of hunger and sleep deprivation were beginning to show so he seemed to slip in and out of reality with considerable ease. He was still daydreaming as they led him out and down the hall. He was remembering a night with Hannah, having skipped the part of how he had gotten there, he was enjoying the feel of her deft slender fingers as they worked their way down either side of his spinal column. She was naked and as she leaned over him to work on the corded muscles in his lower back her muff was at eye level. She had done away with the perfume and he had marveled at how women often just pick things up instinctively. It seemed men needed to be told a thing flat out over and again and most times still didn't get it.

He was still enjoying his massage when he was placed in the familiar chair.

"Shall we start with what were you doing in Munich, Georg?" Nebe gazed at him, then at the guards. The shook their heads, indicating that he hadn't been given any more methedrine.

At that moment in his daydream Hannah's bush was suddenly replaced by Fritz's head teetering on the edge of the blood-soaked basket and Georg went rather pale. He wore no expression to speak of and Brandt looked almost concerned. "Has he had a stroke?"

Nebe shook his head while Nolte began to twirl his blackjack. "Can't we just torture him already; if we keep this up we'll all be catatonic before long."

Time had passed and Nebe sighed to indicate that he was being patient. "It's been three minutes since I asked the question, Georg. Perhaps, you don't remember it. The question was: Why did you go to Munich?"

Georg's eyes went wide as he suddenly emerged from his stupor like a drowned man revived. "The BürgerBräuKeller . . ."

Nebe urged him on. "Yes?"

"I wanted to go see it a week before. I mean, a week before a year ago, a week before the November 8, 1938 speech. I had read those newspapers but I wanted to see for myself, to be sure. There were SS men everywhere, like they were waiting for a parade, and police in every doorway. But . . ."

Nebe nodded. "But there were none inside, did that surprise you?"

Georg shook his head. "I didn't really think about it like that."

"You didn't think about it? Adolf Hitler was going to be giving a speech there in one week and the ballroom was completely unguarded. Why didn't you think about that?"

"Because it didn't pose a problem."

His answer caused Nebe alarm. "That's too logical. It's even kind of scary. . . . Perhaps I'm just getting tired of this."

Georg looked at him candidly. "What is it you want?"

He should have been near collapse. He wasn't. *Don't answer*, Nebe thought; let him drive himself crazy trying to figure it out.

Georg stared at him expectantly. "You keep asking questions about all these tiny details. Aren't you interested in the bombing."

Nebe smiled. "The bombing is the main course; I want to know how you decided to set the table. So, what if the room had been guarded?"

"Then I would have done it before they got there, a month before or even a year before. I knew that he had to be there." Georg's frustration almost looked like resolve.

Nebe smiled again. "You went alone?"

Georg answered without thinking. "No, I went with Hannah so we'd look like tourists."

Nolte stared at him. "I thought you'd stopped seeing her." Nolte's tone was almost prissy and Georg looked at them sheepishly.

"I thought I had too. We were walking down Ludwigstrasse across the Odeonsplatz during the Fohn, the south wind, and the air was full of minute particles of greasy junk. The square was full of sticky golden light and visibility was as bad as in a heavy fog. We passed under the statue of crazy King Ludwig II, who stared down with a stern look that said he wasn't going to put up with anymore nonsense. I nodded agreement. We walked along Theatinerstrasse, full of streetcars and department stores, button-hook street lamps and sidewalks too narrow for two people to walk side by side. Pompous, ponderously rococo buildings were wedged so close together that they had lost all dignity, like a costume party crammed into an elevator. I had to look away.

"Hannah was wearing spike heels and a long, overly fashionable raincoat. The result should have been disastrous but she was tall and leggy and it looked perfect on her. I turned to look at her. She was shockingly attractive. We passed Perusasstrase to Marienplatz and circled our way through Munich, following the parade markers, through Tal and Isartor, to the Isar. It used to be more of a river; it had once washed entire villages away. Now, it was turning on the Ludwigsbrücke to Rosenheimer Strasse and from there it was a straight line to the BürgerBräuKeller. I felt slightly groggy. I still had my fighting heart and all the best intentions but was about to lose on a TKO.

"Hannah smiled, very shyly, and asked me, 'Care to take back any of the horrible things you said?' I tried to make up for being such a louse the last time I saw her by saying, 'I never take back anything I have said, but sometimes I might really mean something I didn't say.'

"And she laughed. 'You are a bastard.' It was hard to keep a straight face, confronted as I was with my own bullshit. I told her that I don't have the kind of life I could ask anyone to share and she laughed even louder. 'Liar. You're so rotten! I just can't quite believe it.'

"I nodded emphatically. 'That's what I'm talking about.' I had intended to keep on talking, explaining, but she closed my mouth with a kiss. When I tried to speak a second time and was again kissed into silence I just gave up and Hannah, smiling with increasing confidence, took my arm as we walked across the Rosenheimer Platz. The walls had been white-washed but they had a sticky brown cigarette stained look and the slanted slate roof had turned a throbbing purple with its accumulation of oily smoke. Suddenly, I wanted to go home, I just wasn't quite sure exactly where that was.

"A wooden sign over a stone arch in a brick wall announced that we had reached the BürgerBräuKeller. There was a dispirited garden beyond the wall. We walked in and stopped, uncertain which way to turn. From out of nowhere, two SS men were walking toward us. They looked over eight feet tall and carried parachute model *Schmeissers*: Art Nouveau machine guns. The taller SS man reached us first. He could have been the Schreckgespenst that many parents use to torment their children into submission. He asked us, 'May I assist you?' with a bloodcurdling smile.

"Hannah wiggled and cocked her head, goofy and ingratiating. 'Heil Hitler!' and he seemed to grow even taller. 'Heil Hitler.'

"She was positively brimming with enthusiasm. 'We came to see where the Führer is going to speak.' I looked around, across the square. All the windows in all the buildings had their blinds down and the windows were closed, so I asked, 'Why are all the windows closed?'

"The tall SS man smiled at me like a werewolf. 'Security. For the Führer.' As I looked at the rooftops, SS men appeared on every roof abruptly, pointing their Schmeisser machine pistols at me. Hannah said, 'We are glad to see that the Führer is so well protected!' and the tension was gone. The rooftops were suddenly empty again.

"'Yes,' the tall SS man had said, doing a shy and boyish routine, 'we have a most important job.' He probed the air with his nose, like a cat, and straightened his back until his septum pointed at the sky.

"'Georg!' Hannah clapped her hands. 'Take his picture!'

"So I pulled out my worn Leica M1 and took a photograph while the SS men posed grotesquely. Behind them a troupe of Reicharbeitdienst schlepped by in broken formation, with shovels on their backs; they looked like refugees from the Thirty Years War.

"'Don't take a picture of that,' the other SS man had said. 'That's British propaganda.' Hannah and I gaped and then we were all laughing. I kept that picture pinned to the wall at the foot of my bed. Their blank jubilant expression, the features congealed into a mask of office, the eyes fixed stiffly with an insect's empty alertness. I looked at that photograph whenever I had doubts, studying it, thoughtfully, as though I could somehow understand it all if I could tease meaning out of that rigid empty face. The face told me that there was nothing to understand, there was no one there, that our country had been overrun by automatons."

"I know exactly what you mean," said Nebe. "The look in the eyes, that's where the criminal mentality always shows itself. It's not anything positive, it's a lack. You look into their eyes and there's no one there, just a pit where there was supposed to be someone. The problem is, I look into your eyes and there is someone there. It's obvious to me that you're not a criminal. How do you explain that?"

Georg could not answer, or perhaps thought he wasn't expected to.

"You thought of shooting him, didn't you?" said Nolte. "The Führer, I mean."

Georg shook his head bewildered. "No."

Nolte hated it when somebody refused to support his theories. "Sure you did. That's why you checked the windows and the roof. Why kill all the bystanders just to get to one man."

"I was never a marksman. One shot with no time to aim?" Georg continued to shake his head; the idea was just too absurd. "It never would have worked."

Nebe gazed indulgently at Nolte. "That is precisely the point at which most amateur assassins give up. I'm sorry I called you an assassin, Georg, but that's what you are, isn't it? That's the word for it: *assassin.*"

In German, the word for *assassination* is *attentät*, meaning literally, "the attempt." The word for *assassin* is *attentäter*, meaning "the attempter." That made it sound almost spiritual.

"Did you know a Swiss student named Maurice Bauvaud? No? He tried to shoot the Führer outside the BürgerBräuKeller in 1938. He was there the same time you were. You might have even seen him. No? Well go on then Georg, tell us about Munich."

". . . Outside the BürgerBräuKeller. It was a public restaurant but I didn't realize how big until we went inside; a gigantic place, a mass of interlocking dining rooms that took up a full city block. It was noon and all the dining rooms were crowded, the tables full of tradesmen, heads down and shoveling it in. No one even noticed as we checked the rooms, one by one until, by elimination, we found the ballroom where Hitler was going to speak. I took out my Leica and took pictures of the pillars from several angles. Hannah said nothing. Perhaps, she thought I was finally taking an interest in politics. I took out a tape measure and wrapped it around one of the pillars. Its circumference was 3.14 meters, the value of pi. The pillar was one meter thick.

"'What are you doing?' said Hannah.

"I smiled at her. 'Oh, these little details make it more real. There's more to remember.' She gave me her worried goofy smile and we walked back, working our way through the building until we found a dining room with an empty table. I had ordered *Königsberger Klopse*, meatballs in cream sauce. Capers had given it a green tinge and for a second after I saw the color I was frightened that I was going crazy. I looked across the table at Hannah. She had a lamb shin bone, a clump of brown-black meat, and she savaged it.

"We had to stand in line for the cashier and while we did, a thickset man with a walrus mustache walked in the front door and out of the back. The central hall ran the depth of the block. I handed over the money with the check. 'That man, he left without paying.'

"But the cashier smirked at us. 'Oh, no. The hall runs through to the next street. People use it as a shortcut.'

"I thought that over and nodded, then bought that souvenir postcard of Hitler speaking in the ballroom. Hannah started for the front door but I took her by the elbow and led her out the back way. The next street faced a set of brewery yards with windowless walls. We were completely unobserved. There was no place from which anyone could watch us. I grinned happily; delighted like a child on Christmas morning. Dutifully, Hannah decided that she was happy too and she leaned her head on my shoulder.

"We'd gone to the library and then taken the train back to Heidenheim. I was staring at the postcard with a carpenter's eye; Hannah was placidly looking out the window as the train rolled through the dense and dirty industrial suburbs. She turned to smile at me. 'I'm so glad you're taking an interest in the Party,' and turned back to the window.

"'Ah, yes.' She probably thought I agreed but my mind was elsewhere. I took out a pencil to draw a circle on the postcard, on the right-hand pillar just above the balcony.

"There was a delay outside of Augsburg, halfway to Heidenheim. We were alone in the compartment and the train wasn't moving. Hannah was doing an occasional wiggle of impatience, peering out the window then questioningly at me then back to the window again. There wasn't much to see, a ragged forest on a black night with only a sliver of moon. I was about to make a decision, something I did not enjoy, when she spoke. 'How long has the train been stopped?'

"I looked at my watch. 'Twenty-three minutes.' Then I deliberately and self-consciously lit a cigarette. Hannah pointed to sign in four languages. 'There's no smoking.'

"I inhaled deeply but kept the smoke in my mouth, then I blew a smoke ring, the first time I had ever tried it but it seemed to come naturally. 'I'm not supposed to be smoking, but the train is supposed to be moving so it's a breach of contract and all obligations are void.' Hannah looked at me in astonishment."

"Bible stories? The moral is always: If thy brother offends thee, then cut his throat. Are you going to pretend to believe this shit?" Nolte was adamant but Nebe maintained an otherworldly composure.

"Sooner or later, he has to talk about the one thing on his mind." Nebe said.

Brandt sighed, stretching his fingers and cracking his knuckles. "It's already later, isn't it?"

Nebe looked from one to the other with a curdling stare. "I seem to recall that I sign off on your payslips gentlemen, let's not waste any more of the tax-payers' money because you don't have the courtesy to do your jobs. Go on, Georg. What happened next?"

"In Heidenheim, Hannah and I were on our way to the cinema. We had passed a newsstand; the headlines announced that Germany had invaded Bohemia and Moravia, the rest of Czechoslovakia. That would have made it the end of March; six months after the beer hall reconnoiter with Hannah. I read her the cover story, 'It was clear to me from the first moment,' the Führer was quoted as saying to his generals, 'that I could not be satisfied with the Sudeten German territory. It was only a partial solution. My decision to march into Bohemia was made. Then came the establishment of the Protectorate over Czechoslovakia and with that the basis for the invasion of Poland was laid.'

"It hadn't happened yet, but the Führer was talking about it as if it were already in the past, it was that certain. The British didn't believe it; they thought he was trying to bluff his way into a better deal on the Polish Corridor. But I believed it and it meant I had to start soon, actually I should have started already.

"An alley cat was staring at me from out of a doorway: a scrawny black cat with a long horse face, a lumpy pink nose, and mournful yellow eyes. It had a big red scratch down the middle of its big pink nose and looked like the unhappiest cat in the world. It stared at me without hope or fear, just staring with its gold-leaf eyes asking me to look back. Ugly and soulful, it had the look of a Madonna in a country church. Hannah was shouting behind me that if I wanted to take the cat to the movie instead, she wouldn't stand in our way. In front of the movie theater Hannah had walked up to the ticket booth and paid for both of us, glancing at me over her shoulder. 'Do you mind?' But it wasn't a question. I took her arm as we went in.

"The film was a rerun of *Morgenrote*, a UFA film about the adventures of a submarine commander and his crew in the Great War. The climax was that the sub was sinking and there were only eight escape suits for ten men. The captain and the first officer offered to go down with the ship. The crew refused. 'Either everyone or no one,' they said.

"The captain replied, 'We Germans may not know much about living but we're great at dying.' I spat on the floor between my legs which wasn't like me at all. Then the newsreel started depicting the triumphs of the regime.

"THE NIGHT OF THE LONG KNIVES: The SA leadership was dragged out and killed in scenes of strange informality. One SA leader was thrown in front of a firing squad wearing a white satin corset. He was Heil Hitlering frantically, hopping from one foot to the other, the corset garters slapping against his thighs as the machine gun caught him in the stomach and his body exploded from internal pressure. The corset burst and the stays fluttered like eye lashes. The audience laughed and screamed; even I was smiling.

"KRISTALLNACHT: The windows of all the Jewish stores were being broken. Elderly shopkeepers were crying and pleading. One of them was beaten over the top of the head until his brains ran out his nose. I was the only one who stopped laughing. I began to watch the crowd right and left out of the corners of my eyes.

"ANSCHLUSS: The German Army marched into Vienna. All the pretty girls were waving Nazi flags and smiling but all the smiles were identical. It was a horrible movie but the crowd around me was cheering even louder.

"THE INVASION OF POLAND: But that couldn't have happened yet then, it was only March and the invasion of Poland didn't happen till September 1939. I must be combining the two memories; that had to have been a different night. . . . Yes, now I remember, the 4th of September. The newsreels had been back within 24 hours, and were in the theaters within three days. I can't remember whether Hannah was next to me that night. Polish cavalry charged against Mark I panzers with machine guns. The results were predictable. There was one Mark I with a mounted flame thrower. A white stallion was caught in the fire stream, leaping, reeling, every inch of its skin burning. I felt like my skin was burning too. For what? Invade Poland and what do you get? Polacks. The invasion of Poland made no sense unless the true intention was to invade Russia. The Führer had been talking about that for 20 years. Invade Russia and what do you get? The same thing that everyone had gotten who had ever invaded Russia: a round trip to Moscow. Come, take our famous walk! And the results of that were predictable too.

"I knew I had to start immediately. I'd put it off as long as I could, longer than I should have. I had to quit my job the following day and get on with the attempt. I'd only saved 400 DM but, if I had to, I could go without eating for up to a month. I'd been on a 30-day fast before, involuntary but it had been kind of interesting, especially toward the end. Meanwhile the horse was still burning. The crowd was delirious with joy, howling in a Maenadic frenzy. I looked around, then got up and walked out. Two men shouted insults and waved their fists at me.

"But I'm getting ahead of myself. Outside the cinema, with Hannah, it was still March 18th, memorial day for the dead of the Great War. A brass band was playing the 2nd movement of Beethoven's 3rd; there was a lot of crying with shrill shouts and marchers with oversize Nazi flags that wrapped around their bodies in an oddly sensual way, like a naked woman caught in the act of wrapping her body in a sheet."

Georg suddenly went silent. Nebe sighed heavily; Nolte and Brandt exchanged puzzled looks. Frozen in a momentary wave of panic, Georg thought to himself, *They are right, no matter how confused it is it's still too linear to be reality, but that's the way I remember it. Even if I tell them a hundred times, they still won't believe me.* The three men were staring at him as if he were challenged in some way. "Sorry, what was that?"

"Come on, Georg, it was a simple question. You have shed light on an age-old debate: that art imitates life which imitates art. We thank you, but now to the point! Your next step was?"

"I got fired. It was an argument with Office Manager Schulz. He said stupid things to me too many times." Georg was doing his best to be cooperative, however ineffectually, and that was driving Nolte round the bend.

"We talked to him. He said you were 'fired' by request."

Georg blushed. "Well, yes. I didn't want to involve him."

Nebe stifled a laugh and opened his arms in a sweeping magnanimous gesture. "Involve anyone you like. It's in your interest. Tell us all about it."

"Well, Schulz had walked me back around the great white shed of the munitions plant with the Bauhaus frosted glass walls. The milky light of the softly clouded sky gave it the glow of a hospital. Schulz had his arm around my shoulders, as though he were supporting a convalescent on his first day out of bed, and kept talking. I didn't listen. I knew Schulz was pleading but he gave up, dropped his arm, and walked ahead of me into the office. He sat down behind his desk and I stood in front of it, an established ritual. Schulz pulled a piece of letterhead stationary out of a drawer and picked up a pen. He sighed. 'Nothing I can do to change your mind? You're determined to leave?' I was silent and he went on. 'You know I can force you to stay. It's illegal for a worker to change jobs without permission.'

"His insistence was almost touching but I told him, 'I know that, sir.'

"'Yes, well, you were wasted in an office anyway.' He held up his hands and flexed them. 'I'd give you a skilled job here but there aren't any. This is all mass production.' Schulz sighed again and began to write me a letter of recommendation. He stopped and looked up. 'It's hard to give a convincing letter of recommendation when I'm supposed to have fired you. I'll have to say that you were fired for insubordination. That sounds bad but it isn't really. Employers will take a chance on a worker who showed a little too much spirit if he's capable.' He actually laughed at the idea of me ever showing too much spirit but he continued writing. I looked out the long windows at the sky. It was lead gray as usual.

"The next milestone in my employment record was most definitely a step backward, but for a purpose. The management office of the quarry was just a shack 100 yards from the artificial cliff that had been cut into the side of a granite mountain. The foreman was a foot taller than me. He had his face screwed up and his lips puckered in concentration as he tried to decipher the flowery language of Schulz's letter.

"'But why would you want to work in a quarry? You were a cabinet maker and a junior executive; you'll ruin your hands.' In the quarry beyond the window there was a juicy explosion followed by a rumpling cascade of rock. The foreman chuckled. 'You get used to it. After a while, you may even get to like it. You're not the only one you know. We've got a PhD in mathematics out there, 110 pounds and glad to have the job. Was a professor at Heidelberg, or used to be. But you're not Jewish or anything. It doesn't make sense.'

"'I just need a job.' I smiled and the foreman shrugged.

"'Alright, let's see what you can do.'

"An hour later, I was trying to make little rocks out of big ones with an eight-pound sledgehammer, but without much success. A small man, even smaller than me, walked by, stopped, took the sledge out of my hands and split the rock with one blow. He bowed and handed back the hammer. 'Your motion is inefficient. Swing the hammer in a circular arc and strike perpendicular to the rock surface.' He bowed again. I bowed back and watched him walk away. And, that's why mathematics is so important.

"That same night I was drinking beer with the other quarry workers. We weren't exactly drunk but we'd had enough to feel entitled to act like we were. The others were singing some hysterically self-pitying and sentimental song and I was accompanying them on the harmonica. They linked arms and began to rock back and forth in a paroxysm of nostalgia that could have gone on all night. I jumped up, bobbing and weaving explaining with gestures that I was about to throw up. There was general laughter as I wove a sinusoidal path across the floor and staggered out between the swinging doors. I kept lurching; hand over my mouth until I was out of sight of the front window. I was stone-cold sober and stood very still as I looked around, trying to act casual. The area was empty so I strode off fast toward the quarry.

"The night watchman was asleep in the shack so I walked straight into the unlit quarry pit, stumbling through the litter and darkness. The explosives chest was in plain sight with big red lettering to explain what it was. I knocked off the padlock with a sledgehammer, with one quick and efficient movement; it had been practiced many times in my head, in fact the entire theft had been over prepared to the point of boredom. When I opened the chest I closed my eyes in frozen reverence. I picked up a handful of dynamite cartridges, all in all I carried away twenty kilos of dynamite and plastic explosive called Donorit. That night, as I went to sleep, I started laughing at the thought of what was waiting under the bed. I was still giggling when I lost consciousness and found myself in a dream, the only man in a rooming house full of ballet girls."

Nolte put his head in his hands, Nebe was more magnanimous. "Maybe when the war is over and none of us are at risk of getting our heads lopped off you can buy us some beer and tell us about the ballet girls, Georg. For the moment, just tell us what you did with the explosives under the bed." Georg nodded obediently.

"The next day I withdrew my money from the bank. 400 DM was certainly not enough to evoke suspicion. I had sold my bicycle to Boltzman in the shipping yard at the Waldenmaier plant. He had given me five marks for it. That was the extent of my equity and I had nearly five months to support myself until November 8th.

"Monday I went to work at the quarry anxious to get it over with. I waited until nobody was looking before deliberately bringing the sledgehammer down in an overhand swing onto my left foot. I sat down howling, the pain seemed to explode through my body. Three gigantic quarry workers gathered around in a circle, watching and shaking their heads like farmers at the birth of a two-headed calf. The foreman walked up and said, 'Alright, everybody get back to work.' Then he saw me. 'Oh Christ. I told you, you couldn't handle the work.' He picked me up and carried me, like a bride, back to the shack-office.

"After having been treated, splinted, and crutched, I found a sporting goods store and bought a box of eight mm Mauser rifle ammunition. 'That's a heavy round,' the storekeeper had said. 'You could bring down a bear with it. You hunting bear?' I told him I was after elk. The storekeeper looked me over. 'I wish I had time to hunt.'

"I smiled wistfully. 'Ah, but you have to make time.'

"The following evening I pulled the bullets out of the cartridge cases and emptied out the powder. I sawed off the base of a brass cartridge case, the part that held the primer; I did it carefully, stopping to drip water onto the brass to cool if off, to keep the primer below flash point. It was like I was reinventing the Wheelock pistol, that overcomplicated weapon that was half flintlock and half cuckoo clock. In my version, the clockwork wound up the slack on a steel wire running through small pulleys, the kind that might be used on model boats, nailed to a board. The wire was strung to one of the detonators I'd stolen from the plant in Heidenheim. The wire wound slowly around the axle of the hour hand until it tripped the tier of the artillery fuse. There was a five-second wait and then the firing pin snapped out of the detonator with a nasty click.

"I walked up the basement stairs into the garden carrying my device, my pockets full of clockmaker's tools. It was summer and the bushes had turned black-green like the sea under a storm. A burly orange cat was grumpily stalking a bird that fluttered around the garden fountain. Unfortunately for the cat, it had a bell hung round its neck so the birds always had sufficient warning. It was an old game for all of them but the cat learned and the birds didn't. The cat was on his right side, holding the bell to his chest with his left paw to keep it from rattling. With his right paw he side stroked himself across the grass toward the fountain, his eyes wide with ancient innocence. I was still playing with my modular Wheelock, but this time I had a primer from a cartridge case in front of the firing pin. The clockwork wound the wire up slowly, with infinite patience, until the tension tripped the detonator and the firing pin exploded the primer with a startling pop. The birds scattered and the large orange cat stomped out of the shadows, hissing, the feline equivalent of *I simply can't work under these conditions*. It swatted the detonator with its right paw; the extended claws clattered off the smooth metal, then the indignant animal whirled around and clumped off, with his tail in the air like a middle finger extended out of a fist. I tried to fix the picture in my head, consciously designing the memory, watching it become a memory, impenetrable as an old movie. My glance kept switching back to my work and it took a deliberate choice to keep my eyes fixed on the cat.

"The memory of the cat swatting at the detonator was projected onto what I saw and the cat turning away was projected onto that. The image became a blur of memories in multiple exposures and I was losing the memory by trying to hold it. This one time, I could put a name to my emotion: I was sad. Simple enough but the emotion wasn't natural to me. It was strange, like something I remembered from out of a dream and that might have been the very essence of sadness, but like with love I had nothing to measure it against."

"Touching image, Georg, but what the hell does that have to do with anything? Where the hell is this basement you're coming out of into a garden all of a sudden?" Despite his well-deserved indulgence of the previous night, even Nebe was finally starting to lose his cool.

Nolte looked at him imploringly. "Just once more, a quick crack across the shins, it'll get him to focus."

Brandt simply sighed in resignation, he was once a religious man and if there was a purgatory, they were in it.

Nebe pressed. "Where are we, Georg?"

"Oh, Stuttgart . . . I only had 405 DM and had to make it last, so I went to my sister's."

Nolte sneered. "The freeloader who thinks he's an idealist."

Nebe couldn't afford enough prostitutes to deal with this shit. "Fill in the blanks, Georg, quickly, before we all face a firing squad."

"Anna-Sophie, my sister, and her husband, Werner, had a grim lower-middle-class house with a grim middle-class dining room crowded with Hummel figurines and brown fading photographs of dead relatives, the fetishism of the very poor. One of my cuckoo clocks hung on the wall, actually there was one in every room. The bleak despairing will to go on had worked itself into the walls. Hopelessness stiffened the air; it hung all around us, formless and pervasive as an odor or a moral concept. I looked out into the small living room. All the furniture was old and worn, hung onto for far too long and for no reason. But it was all dutifully slip covered with layer upon layer of antimacassar, as if to convince you that what was actually underneath was something different than what it appeared to be. My spoon made scraping blackboard noises against pink-flowered soup bowl. Then my twelve-year-old nephew marched through the dining room and into the kitchen, without speaking to anyone. My head swiveled to watch him go.

"Werner hissed, 'You behave yourself in my house or you will leave.' I was taken by surprise because I hadn't done anything. . . I searched Anna-Sophie's face but she kept her eyes on the table; Werner's eyes kept moving from my face to the kitchen door, he looked terrified, he whispered frantically. 'And watch how you talk in front of my son.'

"I tried to put him at ease. 'Werner, I appreciate your concerns but I didn't say anything.'

"My sister threw her spoon into her dish with a noise like a pistol shot and glared at him. 'You can't ask Georg to leave. He's out of work with a broken foot and he has nowhere to go.'

"Werner had stood up then, seeing an opportunity to exercise his spousal authority. 'So that means he can freeload off us?'

"Sophie's eyes took on the hue of glacial ice. 'Yes. That's exactly what it means. Now do sit down and shut up.' Werner considered his options then sat down and shut up. She turned to me tenderly. 'Does your foot hurt?'

"I didn't want her to fawn so I played it down, 'It's just some broken toes. I don't really need the cast. I could just tape them up.' She had squeezed my arm reassuringly then. 'Don't try to be a hero.' If I've ever loved anyone it is her, I mean of course without any sexual connotation. My mother was always sort of pathetic in her tenderness, but Sophie meant it. That's when my nephew came back out of the kitchen gnawing on a large clumsy sandwich and inspecting us all with careful eyes. I couldn't remember his name but I knew I had to say something so I pushed back from the table and folded my hands on my stomach. 'I'm moving to Munich.' I said it directly to him. 'I think it will be an inspiration to work near the birthplace of the Party.' The boy lowered his face shyly then turned and ran out. Werner and Anna-Sophie watched him go out the door, staring at the closed door for a long moment to make sure he was really gone then looked at each other in relief. They exhaled slowly in a low sigh; they'd both been holding their breath.

"'Jäger Schnitzel!' said Anna-Sophie, brightly, over her shoulder as she went to the kitchen. I sing-songed back, 'My favorite!' and took a deep breath. 'Yes,' even Werner nodded and grinned, even he was cheerful.

"Most of my tools were already stored in their basement, ever since I had left them in 1929. That was when the world went bang and I'd started a random tour of the small towns of Bavaria and Schleswig-Holstein, to wherever I thought I might find work. The tools had been used carelessly over the years, used and left un-oiled. They were speckled and caked with the rust of long neglect. I braced myself for the jolt of anger when I saw them but nothing came. It just didn't matter anymore. I had worked hard to collect them, yet there was no nostalgia or sentiment of any kind. Suddenly they belonged to my past. I lit a blowtorch with a pack of matches that said BürgerBräuKeller in black letters on the red flap, and took down the rack that held the wood chisels. They were stainless steel so it had taken devoted abuse to get them to rust. For the first time, I looked at rust without anger, without feeling betrayed, and its colors varied from pink to orange to black-red in patterns intricate as that of a snowflake. It was pretty if you didn't know what it meant. Then I started to make digging tools out of my cabinet maker's chisels, heating the hafts red-hot in the flame and bending them into shape. The metal was losing its temper but that didn't matter either. I used a brick for an anvil. I knew I should have been crying but felt nothing at all. The cellar door opened and Werner came down the stairs. His son, clearly in command, stood in the doorway and looked down at the two of us; his Hitler Youth uniform was a brown smear in the yellow light of the hall. Werner's pants were open and the tail of shirt stuck out of his fly. His son had gotten him out of bed. According to my watch, it was 3:00 a.m.

"Werner's voice was groggy, 'It's been a week, hasn't your foot healed yet?'

"My smile only reached halfway up my face. 'Werner, it doesn't pay to take chances with something like this.'

"'I suppose not,' then he saw the surgical steel of the chisels bent into crude claw like shapes. 'What are you doing?' His voice betrayed his alarm. I was numb. 'I'm making special tools to help me find a job in Munich.'

"His eyes met mine warily. 'Those don't look like carpentry tools.' There was a sudden certainty in his voice.

"I kept smiling steadily. 'I know my job and I can be trusted to do it.'

"Werner shuffled and scowled, he clearly wanted an excuse to go back to bed and apparently I wasn't giving it to him. 'Well, as long as you're here, you can repair some of the furniture. At least half of it is chipped or broken.' He retreated up the stairs, muttering reassurances to his son. I called after them saying how thoughtless I had been not to offer. When Werner slammed the door I set aside my best chisel to deal with their furniture then went back to work.

"I had managed to stretch my stay another month, conserving my funds, but the sixth week even my sister was giving me significant looks across the dinner table; it was time for me to go...."

The detectives were showing signs of boredom, showing it theatrically enough even for Georg to notice. They yawned and stretched, playing it crude and wide as though they were signaling to him from across a football stadium. Maybe they thought that he'd try harder if he thought they were losing interest.

Nolte yawned and sat up straight again. "Aw, let him talk, you can never tell what's going to turn out to be important."

"I can," said Brandt, looking at the typewriter with the expression of a man who just found a cockroach swimming in his beer.

Nebe sighed, leaned his elbows on the desk, and made a tent with his fingers. He smiled as comfortingly as a doctor in a laxative advert. "Georg," he said, "you're new at this. Getting caught, I mean. You clearly don't understand the function of interrogation. People do horrible things, but that's not so bad as long as they make sense. Of course, they usually don't make sense. Nothing really makes sense. People have jumped into bed or out the window together and they have never known why. But that doesn't change history so it doesn't matter. Georg, you're not a great man; you're not a political or economic force, yet you almost changed history. That's horrible. But, as long as there's a logical explanation, we can live with it. If we can put a name to it, we can control it, it can be categorized and the case neatly closed. If it's pure random horror, that's unbearable. You're going to drive a lot of people crazy or to execution and you don't want to do that, do you, Georg?"

"No sir," said Georg, more than a little lost. "I never meant to hurt innocent people."

Nebe leaned a bit closer. "All you wanted to do was kill the Führer. Tell us about that."

Georg thought that over. "Maybe I should start from the beginning," he said.

"No!" All three men shouted in unison.

Nebe shouted solo, "Good Christ! This is our 'master' assassin and he can only tell a story in one piece like a string of phlegm? This one isn't smart enough to be framed for the Reichstag fire! No . . . that is untrue, he is smart enough; in fact he's the smartest idiot I've ever encountered. Is identification positive?"

"Yes and you did it," said Nolte.

Nebe rubbed his face as though it were the only way he could change expression. It seemed his face had been locked in a rigid grimace for hours. He got a smile going then ran his knuckles down the tops of his thighs.

"No," said Nebe. "No, take it up from where you were, but skip the family problems."

"Oh . . . well . . . Then I was packing my equipment into the double-bottomed wooden chest. The explosives were already in my suitcase, wrapped in my shirts and underwear. Anna-Sophie watched me as I packed, I kept my face adverted. There was nothing to say but I wanted to say it anyway, to put it into words so I could leave her with something, but the words wouldn't come.

"She asked me why it had a double bottom and it was a relief to have something to say at last. 'For my most valuable tools, so they won't get stolen.' I opened a trunk and took out three clock movements, wound them in rags and put them on top of the tools. The clocks had been left over from my three months work in Switzerland. The company had gone bankrupt and couldn't pay, so they'd given me the clockworks instead. From the corner of my eye, I could see her looking worried and scared. It's hard to keep a secret from a woman who knows you that well. 'They're for making cuckoo clocks.' I tried a smile but she was still wary.

'I know.' Anna-Sophie was almost whispering. 'But why are you taking them now?'

I replied casually, 'Oh, it may take months to find a job. Maybe I can make the little houses for the clocks and sell them while I'm searching.' She looked more worried. Then I saw that it would be easier than I had thought because she wanted to be lied to, she was determined to believe whatever I said. 'Yeah, I'm worried too. Talent just isn't enough these days.' I took a brown paper package from under the workbench where I had hidden it, I couldn't remember when. I cut the string to unwrap a rosewood box, inlaid with ebony and mother of pearl, the kind of things that used to be made in Damascus before they started faking it. I'd made it for some girl, I couldn't remember which one, but luckily the affair had broken off before I could give it to her. I gave it to my sister and that changed the subject neatly. She held it in front of her making happy Christmas morning noises. 'It's beautiful!' She was almost singing. Seeing my ability from a distance brought on a strange melancholy. 'Yes. I know it is.' She laughed at my seriousness at first but then looked frightened. . . ."

"Who cares?" asked Nolte.

"I do," said Brandt.

Nolte and Nebe turned their heads, creakingly, to look at him but there were no signals. He really seemed to mean it.

"OK, I care too," said Nebe. "You had no future and no past worth remembering. You knew you'd never see her again so you wanted to leave her with something and your skill was the only precious thing you had."

"Yes, sir," said Georg and his voice cracked.

Nebe seemed pleased by that. "I understand," he said. "I understand why it was important for you to tell me. But, let's skip ahead. What did you do about the bomb?"

"I had tracked down Ulrich and we were walking to the railroad station. I no longer used the crutches but my foot was still in a walking cast and I had a decided limp. Ulrich was gallantly carrying my bags for me. He was wearing his Reicharbeitdienst uniform and it hung loosely on him. He'd lost weight, too much weight. The streets around the station were still cobble stoned and wet with late summer rain; they bounced twinkled reflections, filling the air with ambient light. It made Ulrich look as blue-gray as a corpse, but for once his features were working together in a coherent expression, eyes narrowed and lips compressed. He seemed to be clamping down on reality and it was finally penetrating his self-absorption.

"Ulrich was there because I needed him to be, not to carry my bags, just to keep me alive. I was short, poor and limping—I could have easily been taken for the leftovers of a Gestapo raid. With my foot in the cast I wouldn't have been able to run from the crowd that would have assembled to finish me off. It would have been an inexcusable gamble when I was leaving left nothing else to chance. The preparation was complete and what remained was so straightforward it felt like it had already happened. I couldn't stop running through my memory what was yet to happen.

"I smiled at Ulrich, his brown uniform was our passport through the street, identifying me by association as an injured worker, incompetent or unlucky but racially pure. He grudgingly smiled back. The corners of his mouth jerked up, more a signal than a smile. He was satisfied to be there and that was strange because it wouldn't leave him with a story that he would ever be able to tell. Ulrich could be relied on not to endanger his life, even for a story as good as what I was about to do.

93

"A thin, cold breeze caught my attention. I decided that it was a beautiful night, then we turned a corner and there was Hannah, leaning against a building with her back and palms pressed flat against the wall, leaning back as if to let something pass.

"'Don't go,' she said.

"'Hannah, what are you doing here?' I had tried to sound casual and surprised and pleased. Ulrich looked up at the sky, frowning belligerently at one star after another as though one of them had pissed on him.

"'Don't go,' she said.

"'I'll be back when I get the cast off,' I lied of course, 'and I can work again.'

"'Don't go,' she said it again so it wasn't much of a conversation.

"'I can take care of myself, I have to.' I thought it made sense but she wouldn't hear of it.

"'My God! No you can't.' Hannah had her hands to her head and was tearing her hair like they did in old movies.

"I observed her sadly. 'Well, I'll listen to an argument.'

"'The way I feel, that's my argument. I haven't asked you for anything else.' She was passionate about it.

"I glanced at Ulrich who was staring straight up then back to Hannah. 'How can I possibly have any idea how you feel? I have no idea how *I* feel! All you do is ask me to do things—ask, desire, need, demand . . . marry you . . . take you away!'

"Ulrich drew his eyes back to the planet earth. 'I think I should meet you at the station,' he said.

"'You stay right here. We're leaving together!' I snapped at him and Ulrich started inspecting the sky again.

"'Please?' said Hannah.

"I spoke slowly and lightly with my charm on full. 'I'm visiting my sister at Lake Konstanz.'

"'With a suitcase full of dynamite,' she said it in a way that wasn't exactly a question. So Ulrich put down the suitcase and the tool chest and swallowed a mouth full of saliva. 'What else does she know?' he said, though that wasn't really a question either.

"'Why are you doing this?' she asked. I thought hard for a moment and the words came.

"'There are 40,000 Swiss francs waiting for me in Switzerland,' I said. 'I'll send for you when I get to Geneva.' I kissed her lightly on the mouth and then jerked away from her. I hobbled off fast toward the railroad station. Ulrich picked up the bags and followed me cursing.

"'You son of a bitch! Is that true?' asked Ulrich but I gave him a shy smile. 'Of course not. . . . But you must have seen that I had to give her a reason she could accept. Now she's dreaming of opening her own dental clinic in Geneva, and most importantly she won't talk.'

"'No, I don't think she will,' Ulrich seemed to be mulling something over and we walked in silence the rest of the way to the station. The platform was empty and the thick yellow light was so saturated it had a brownish tint. Ulrich put down the bags and turned around to face me, resuming the conversation of 20 minutes before.

"'You also gave me a reason I'd accept. What's the real reason? Why are we killing the Führer?'

"I was embarrassed and tried to laugh, which didn't help. I tried to think up another reason that Ulrich could accept. 'No one else will.'

As Elser paused for breath Nebe, Nolte, and Brandt were staring at him in something between disbelief, fury, and self-righteous indignation. Brandt was actually the first to react.

"Two accomplices! He actually named them, we have to bring them in!" his fervor was contagious.

"We torture the girlfriend! That might inspire him to tell us who promised the 40,000 Francs." Nolte was being practical. Brandt was scandalized.

"Why should she pay for his crimes?"

Nolte sneered, "If she was stupid enough to get involved with this bum again she deserves whatever she gets."

Nebe suddenly stood up and paced around his desk, stopping to glare down at Georg, who seemed genuinely alarmed at their reactions. Turning his fiery gaze toward his colleagues Nebe bellowed, "Have you two dolts been paying any attention at all?" The question achieved its desired effect and shut them up, at least temporarily, while they tried to realize what they might have missed. He turned back to Elser and leaned over him heavily, he hoped menacingly, his forehead nearly pressing against Georg's and his eyes boring into his, which stared back into Nebe's like those of an opossum caught on the road. Nebe roared in exasperation before returning to his chair. All three men stared back at him in solemn silence, waiting for some revelation.

Nebe turned slowly to Brandt, "How much of that did you type?"

Brandt gazed down at his typewriter as if seeing it for the first time, "Uh . . . just to the part about the suitcase full of dynamite."

"Good." Nebe nodded as if checking things off a mental list, "Shred it."

"What!" Both men shouted in unison but Nebe held up both palms as if to hold them in their seats.

"I really don't know whether our boy Elser here is actually some sort of evil genius, or just the most naive son of a bitch on the planet. Either way he is a fucking hazard to our health, gentlemen, so wake up! How many times have we been over the fact that, whatever the infuriating reality may be, it is officially politically impossible for an Aryan German worker to want to kill the Führer? Here he just blithely tosses out the fact that not one, but THREE Aryan German workers were in on it and you two morons start shouting 'Stop the presses!' He tells us the fabrication of a fabrication, that conveniently parallels the sort of rubbish we've been trying to get him to tell us since the beginning and you two get all emotional. Snap out of it and pay attention." He turned to Elser, "As for you, focus, Georg, and stick to what happened after you got off the train in Munich."

Georg nodded and you could almost see the gears turning as he wound his memory forward to his arrival. Brandt dutifully pulled the last sheets from the typewriter and carefully placed a fresh carbon between two fresh sheets of paper and fed them in. Nolte snatched up those Brandt had removed and proceeded to methodically tear them into pea-sized pieces.

Georg carried on, "The Nazis had an information booth set up in the railroad station. With all the flags and eagles and poster-sized photographs of the Party leaders, it reminded me weirdly of a booth at a craft fair. There was a huge sign over it, signs in all directions that announced: 'ROOMS FOUND FOR TOURISTS TO MUNICH: CAPITOL OF THE MOVEMENT.'

"There was a rat-like little man in the booth, clad in the oily brown Nazi Party uniform. He had many gold teeth. I walked up and Heil Hitlered casually. 'I need a room.'

"The ratlike man seemed unimpressed. 'Why?'

"I drew a blank on that, I hadn't thought I would need a reason.

"The little man went on, 'I hold party membership number 763.' That was supposed to make him sound important but he had to have been a total loser to be stuck with a job like this while having a party number that low.

"I clicked my heels to attention anyway and said, 'I am honored.' That was expected, and then I nodded and hummed in awe.

"The rat-man was sufficiently appeased. 'I take jobs like this sometimes because it helps me stay in touch with the mood of the people.'

"'Very shrewd.' I kept nodding and scanning my surroundings with my peripheral vision.

"When he returned to his original question I was prepared. 'Purpose of visit?'

"I pointed to the sign that said 'Capitol of the Movement.' Rat-man, looking oh so proud of his job, spun through a large roller card index. He wrote down an address and handed it over with an evil smirk that made strange sense that night. 'I hope you find these accommodations comfortable.'

"I walked off with the address in hand. It had to have been September 2nd or perhaps 3rd as there were placards on a newsstand to announce that Germany had just invaded Poland to liberate East Prussia. . . .

"I thought that booth was only for overnight visitors," said Nolte.

"I'm getting to that." Georg said it with irritation and all three detectives nodded. At last, an emotional response!

Nebe urged him on with almost motherly approval. "Where were we?"

"I was limping through Munich looking for Franz's place, that embittered drunken carpenter Ulrich and I used to drink with back in Heidenheim. I was lugging my tool chest and my extremely heavy suitcase and set them down at every corner to check the street signs against the return address on an envelope I carried in my pocket, then picked them up and kept hobbling. There was a sick lead-gray in the colors of the street as though one was see-ing everything from a great distance. The slightly blue gray-black of slate, the slightly brown-black of trees, the pearl-gray bowlers and the grayed-out walls and eyes and overcoats. Only the metallic colors came through clear: steel and chrome and glass; they were clear but not quite real. The street had the glassed-in look of a street where people no longer lived, as if it existed only in somebody's memory, a figment of the past even if it hadn't happened yet. A broken umbrella hanging out of a garbage can caught my attention. I put down my bags, picked it up, and broke off the bent ribs. I managed to get it closed and hung it on my wrist in a most dapper fashion. I picked up the suitcase with the thirty kilos of explosives and the tool case with 25 kilos of sappers' tools and kept walking.

"Franz had his own shop. He never did say how he'd managed to raise the money and I didn't intend to ask. The two-room store was almost bare and some tattered bunting clung to the lintel of the front window. The opening had obviously been recent.

"He wasn't necessarily happy to see me, yet he didn't seem surprised either. I had considered writing to him first, to be polite, but was pretty sure it would be harder for him to refuse in person. I congratulated him ceremoniously on his independence but Franz said nothing and just looked at me with affectionate helplessness. 'I could help you out with some joinery work.' I volunteered and the idea genuinely appealed to me, a pleasant diversion from my task, but Franz shrugged sadly. 'Not enough work for one man.'

"I couldn't help but smile. 'I'm not asking for a job.' And then he was suddenly happy to see me. 'Thank God for that!'

"I elaborated. 'I could work in return for some space.' Franz was still listening so I elaborated a bit more. 'I'm working on an invention. I need a place to build the model.' Franz looked like he would have liked to find something wrong with that but couldn't.

"'Well, yes, I guess that would be alright.' He pointed to an unused work bench in the back. I marched up to it and sat down, opened my tool chest and placed the umbrella on the table as though it were a patient etherized for surgery. I clipped the ribs and tacked back the fabric so that it was shaped like a boat when open. I removed the umbrella shaft and threaded it to the base, replacing it so that it could be unscrewed. Franz had nothing better to do than sit down and watch. What he saw didn't make sense but he didn't dither; the seriousness of the work was beyond question. I was even beginning to sweat.

"'I guess I shouldn't ask what kind of invention, at least not until you get the patent.' Even Franz had admirable qualities. He walked away.

"The work ahead of me was boring and repetitive, long over prepared. From memory, the work of that following month could be collapsed into a single action. But I could never forget that landlady. She told me she had once been in the chorus at the Wagner Festival at Bayreuth. Well, she certainly had the Brunhilde build for it or at least she had had it, once upon a time. She was fortyish and now too fat to be called luxurious. She could still be attractive though—at 4:00 a.m. when one was dead drunk and entirely sure that no one else would ever know. She led me up the stairs, keeping her shoulders back and her chin high. Discrete little rolls of fat squished out the top of her corset and the tops of her silk stockings. It all showed through her dress. I had to look away. Her living room held two large paintings: one showed the apotheosis of Franz Josef, who was being frog marched into heaven by three huge Brunhilde angels, and the other Mussolini leaning out of the sky to bring order to the Italian railroad system. Crossed spears hung on the wall. There was a bookshelf, even a Nietzsche title, *The Birth of Tragedy from the Spirit of Music*, but somehow I didn't feel compelled. I would have to find an opportunity to peruse the thin-spined, cheaply printed plays and periodicals that showed more promise, and I was somehow sure such opportunities would be plentiful. There were gigantic dark-wood throne chairs that looked as if they had actually been stolen from the Bayreuth Festival, accompanied by lamp shades that were made out of horned brass helmets.

"'The room is twelve marks a week. Can you pay it?' she said it over her shoulder as she led me up the stairs. I knew she was trying for dramatic effect so I played along. 'Yes.' But my tone of voice inferred that I probably wouldn't be able to for long. She paused on the landing and turned to appraise me, her eyes lingered on my hands and forearms, 'A carpenter?'

"I smiled. 'Cabinet maker.'

"Her voice was taking on an operatic lilt. 'It will take some time to find a job.'

"I began to relax. 'I had expected as much.' My tone was warm, encouraging. She stopped at an empty room and led me in. The place was small and worn, the wallpaper bulging and peeling. The bed spread had been mended too many times and washed until it had acquired the fragility of smoke. But at least the room looked clean. She gazed at me over her shoulder again, 'Don't squash bugs on the wallpaper.' She warned and I appeared appropriately scandalized.

"'Oh, I'd never do anything like that.'

"Her tone became almost motherly. 'Put them in an ash tray and burn them with a match.'

"I looked at her with eager attention. 'Of course.'

"There was a silence then she sighed and straightened her shoulders again. Her corset creaked and moaned. 'If you want to cut down your expenses, there may be a few things for you to do around the house.'

"I gave her my most gracious and enthusiastic smile. 'I'm sure there will be. I'm Georg, by the way.'

"She actually blushed. 'My name is Margit. Welcome Georg . . .' and she closed the door with the sweetest of proprietary smiles.

"An hour later, I was in the bathtub washing myself with indecent pleasure, running the water through my fingers like a silver necklace. 'Don't use up all the hot water!' Margit had shouted through the door. 'Think of the other borders!' There were two other borders, both men, both fat and bald with lumpy heads. They were completely different but they looked alike because each of them was going bald in an odd way. One had hair just on top and the other just over one ear.

"'It was a long train trip,' I shouted back and slid down into the water until only my mouth and nose were sticking out."

"So much for ideological purity," said Nolte. "Your landlady must have gone through your things?"

Georg appeared completely guileless. "I kept my case locked."

Nolte chortled evilly. "Like that would have stopped her! She had to know something."

Nebe reined Nolte in. "I hate to interrupt but we skipped something. I'm losing the story in all these details. Can we get back to the reason why you had to kill so many people? This is not the usual assassination situation where you kill a man and he is immediately replaced by another man who is effectively his duplicate. The Führer is irreplaceable."

"The Führer is brilliant," said Brandt.

Nebe sighed. "Thank you. The Führer has divided up power between the Army, the Party, the police, and the SS. We all have overlapping and contradictory fields of authority. None of these organizations have the power base to replace him. The Führer has reduced us all to a kind of feudal ineffectuality."

"It must be wonderful to have gone to college." Nolte frowned. It was the one expression he did well.

Nebe shot him a withering stare. "You could wake up and find yourself directing traffic."

Nolte perked up at once. "I'll take the job. I'll take it right now."

Nebe diligently returned to the task at hand. "Why didn't you place the bomb in the podium under his feet? What was it doing on the balcony?"

Georg looked surprised that the man hadn't realized the obvious. "To blow out the pillar so the roof would fall in. I had to kill all of them: Hitler, Himmler, and Goring. Himmler would have declared martial law. He'd have owned the country in an hour."

Nebe wondered if Georg would really believe he was stupid. "But he doesn't have popularity."

Georg was adamant. "He'd have had it in a week."

Nebe considered the possibility. "Perhaps . . ." There was nothing else to say.

"You really shouldn't argue with him; he just might be smarter than you are." Nolte was behaving like an embittered fiancé. "You know I love that Prussian thing you do, squinting then widening your eyes to show that you're angry."

Brandt had a sudden burst of curiosity. "Was Himmler really there?"

Nolte felt he was being one-upped. "What are you suggesting?"

Brandt seemed hurt by his tone. "Not suggesting anything, it just hadn't been mentioned before."

Nebe was quite suddenly revived; he shot another glance from Georg to Nolte. "So, was Himmler there? And Goring?"

Nolte despised having to confirm information; he considered it beneath him and yet that was his fate. "Yes? I think so."

Nebe stood up with a sadistic grin. "Well then, the rest of us will have a break until you know so!"

Nolte snapped to attention as Nebe shouted down the corridor for the turn keys. Brandt stretched in wide-eyed wonder. As the small headed giants dutifully snatched Georg up Nebe gave him an almost fatherly reprimand. "Stick to the meat Georg, ignore Nolte, he doesn't even mean well."

As they all filed out, Nebe rubbed his hands together in anticipation. The way things were going he would soon have nothing; he decided to treat himself to another prostitute while he still had the rank and the means to get him in the door.

NOVEMBER 15TH, 1939

BRANDT HAD JUST PLACED A very ominous looking cup of coffee in front of Nebe when Nolte charged in and Heil Hitlered with renewed vigor. "They were there!"

A clearly more relaxed Nebe gave him a sardonic smile. "Of course they were. Now go have them bring Elser in." Brandt stifled a chuckle and Nebe's eyes flashed at him. "Remind me at which point of his mind-numbing tale we left off."

Brandt glanced quickly through his typing. "The umbrella boat and the fat landlady's bathtub." Nebe tried to take a swig of the coffee but had to spit it back in the cup. Brandt shrugged apologetically as Georg and his body-guards entered followed by Nolte.

Nebe seemed full of youthful vigor, "feeling his oats" as the Americans would say. "So you shaved and bathed, Georg. When did you plant the bomb?"

"The following evening I walked into the BürgerBräuKeller carrying the umbrella and my tool case. There was nothing unusual about that, a number of tradesmen got off work and stopped for dinner on their way home. The waiters were all tall, big-bellied men, but professionally light on their feet. Their beaked faces glided by, almost a foot over my head because I'm only 5'4". A Viking prow of a face loomed over me. 'We close in half an hour, sir,' he said it in a voice you'd use when talking to a dullard. I smiled, nodded, and kept walking through the ranks of dining rooms. The table cloths looked as crisp and tight as the clothes on a sculpture.

"The ballroom was empty and lit only by what light leaked in from the hall and the street. I slipped in and took the stairs to the second-floor balcony then walked along it, checking every room. Most were unlocked but with the look of constant use, full of canned goods and barrels of sauerkraut, table wear and busboy trolleys. Three quarters of the way around the balcony there was a knob with a broken latch, the knob wouldn't turn but when I released it the door sprung open a crack. When I placed my palm against it, the door eased open with a satisfying squeak of disuse. The room was empty except for a painters' drop cloth, two saw horses, and some dried-out cans of paint. The peeling wallpaper looked prehensile. I walked in and closed the door. There was the smell of cockroaches, the stale smell of old newspapers and the sweetish smell of old age in the darkness. I lit a candle and wedged the sawhorses against the door, then pulled the drop cloth over myself like a blanket, blew out the candle and went to sleep.

"When I woke up and checked my watch, it was 1:35 a.m. I picked up my equipment and walked out to the balcony. The ballroom had huge French windows. A light might have been seen from the street but two street lamps gave me enough illumination to work. I sat down in front of the right-hand pillar and laid out the tools. The first night was to be the most difficult but also the most interesting. I had to cut out a section of the paneling and hinge it so that when closed, the join would be undetectable. For a talented cabinet maker under normal circumstances it was a pitifully easy test, but there it had to be done in semi-darkness, in the few hours before dawn. It would have been suicidal to leave it incomplete, with the cuts visible in the wood.

"It went slowly, at first. Fortunately, the pillars were painted white and, if I had to, I could putty the cracks closed with old paint from the storeroom, until the next day. The columns were mock Roman so I made the vertical cuts along the edge of the fluting. That was no problem; it was the horizontal cuts that could be problematic. The lower one could be made where the pillar joined the base and that too would be invisible since it followed the natural lines of the pillar. The first three sides were straight forward in construction and required only ordinary skill. But the top edge of the door had to be hidden in plain sight and that required magic. At 3:00 a.m. I went back to the storeroom and scooped up a chisel load of rubbery white paint from a discarded can and plugged the cracks with it. It looked fine, so I could conceal my work if I had to. The sky was still reassuringly black so I took out the doll house hinges and began to hang the door. I was now working entirely by touch because I couldn't trust my vision in the faint light. To avoid distractions I closed my eyes. The work seemed to go more quickly that way, even though I knew it made me move more slowly.

"When I opened my eyes, it was 4:17 a.m. The door into the pillar was fitted and hung and stood wide open. I touched it gently with minimal pressure, almost cajoling it shut. When the door was closed I couldn't see its outline against the wood. I couldn't risk a candle but I moved to an angle where the light from a street lamp fell full across the pillar. The door was invisible. I ran my hand across the wood until my finger nails found the join, then eased the door open again and leaned it back. I opened my boat-shaped umbrella and fitted the flat side to the pillar so it would catch the debris, tacking the fabric to the inside of the paneling and unscrewing the handle. The pillar itself was brick. With a hammer and chisel I began to chip away at the mortar. I started sitting down but found it ineffective; I needed leverage so I switched to my knees. I'd gotten one brick loose and the umbrella full of concrete flakes when the sky began to gray. I repacked my tools and looked around. Sawdust wouldn't show in the darkness so I wiped the floor around the pillar with a damp rag to be sure before I went back to the storeroom.

"When I next lit a match and checked my watch, it was 6:00 a.m. I walked out along the balcony and stooped in front of the pillar. When I brushed the floor with my fingers they came up clean. The door was still undetectable; following the lines of the moulding on three sides and the top edge looked like a random scratch in the paint. The ballroom door had been unlocked and the place was technically open but a dismaying quiet came from the outer rooms. Regretfully, I had to return to the storeroom until noon when the restaurant was too crowded and rushed for the staff to notice me arriving from an odd direction.

"At 11:50 a.m., I threaded my way out through the horizontal stack of dining rooms and sat down in a room just off the central hall. I suddenly remembered that I had forgotten to eat for the last two days and hunger swept through me like an anthem. I grinned at the waiter as he walked over and handed me the menu. The waiter half smiled in acknowledgment. 'I'm sorry, sir,' said the waiter as he pulled out his book, 'I didn't see you come in.' I was still conscious of the limits of my finances in correlation with the time this endeavor was going to take. I would have preferred my favorite Jäger Schnitzel, but the Bratkatoffeln potato casserole with bacon and onion was more in budget. Despite the two baskets of bread, after two beers I was abruptly the drunkest I had ever been in my life. I had to walk carefully the twenty feet to the cashier, watching my feet all the way. I tried to keep my face expressionless and managed a mask of whimsical euphoria.

"'You must be in love,' said the cashier as she handed me the change. I compressed my lips and nodded then turned away and walked out the back door of the BürgerBräuKeller and through the deserted brewery yards. I was carrying my reassembled umbrella and the tool case. Every so often I opened the umbrella and dumped a few handfuls of concrete chips and sawdust on a pile of miscellaneous debris. I added a brick from my tool case and swaggered off singing. It was a song that I had made up on the spot and it didn't make any sense so I forgot it immediately after. I walked back toward the rooming house and Margit. I was very tired, too exhausted for one night's sleep to leave me fresh. But a hard day's work makes a man make love all the better and, besides, she wasn't about to accept any excuses. I knew her that well after only one afternoon.

"I passed a church and entered knowing that I had something to do there. It was a Catholic church and I was Lutheran, as my family had been for four hundred years, but that was the least of my problems. I knelt, which seemed to be the thing to do, and winced as my knees touched the rail. They were raw already and that, too, was comforting. I clasped my hands in front of me, wet my lips, and prepared to address God. Problem was I had nothing to say. I wouldn't pray for success, there was no reason for the lieber Gott to prefer one side to the other; he was on all sides at once. There was nothing to explain, the Good Lord knew everything already. I couldn't ask for forgiveness. If I were right, there was nothing to forgive and, if I was wrong, forgiveness would be impossible. I turned my head from side to side, looking for a cue from the pulpit or the statues.

"The Good Lord was waiting and I thought hard about what I had meant to say. I couldn't ask for understanding, I already understood more than I could handle. In fact, I seemed to be the only one who understood, but that didn't help. It was entirely my own decision. I knew that much and it was torturous enough for it to be unfair to ask anyone else to share the guilt, not even the Good Lord. Still, there was something that had to be said. I tried my face in different positions, trying to think of what the words might be.

Then the answer came to me. I clasped my hands in front of me and recited the Lord's Prayer, only once, but I was surprisingly comforted by it.

"Mercifully I managed to leave Margit panting and wide-eyed after only an hour and got to the carpentry shop by the middle of the afternoon. I was working on the design for a trigger mechanism and doing some careful arithmetic. Franz was watching over my shoulder showing no recognition of what the design meant and saying nothing. I looked up quickly and our eyes met. Then we both looked at the design. Franz showed no suspicion, only a quiet, slightly resentful admiration. The draftsmanship was impeccable. I was brooding about a problem.

"'I need some parts that I can't make myself. Can you recommend a machinist?'

"Franz rummaged in a drawer and came out with a solid business card. 'You can say it's for me, for the shop. He'll give you a discount or he won't charge you at all,' Franz said it but looked unhappy; he thought he was going to have to give me a job after all. He managed to find a safe target for his annoyance. His fourteen-year-old apprentice had been doing some hand sanding but was watching us over his shoulder. Franz saw him watching and the apprentice quickly looked away. Franz came up behind him and swatted him mightily alongside the head. 'Now, maybe you'll learn to mind your own business if you can't learn anything else,' said Franz, doing his Führer imitation as I walked out.

"I did get the machine parts for free. Franz had made a double cradle for the machinist's twin daughters and that small charity had taken the sting out of having two women to marry off. The master machinist was eternally grateful; he said so repeatedly and lathed the parts out of surgical steel, something his apprentices weren't competent to do. I watched and waited. Franz hadn't acted out of charity. Working for free was better than not working at all; at least you might generate some trade. But the machinist suspected nothing, not even though Franz had carved his name and the address of his shop in five centimeters high letters into the kick board of the cradle, just an artist signing his work.

"Finally, the parts were done and the master machinist handed them across, standing back and waiting for flattery. Instead, I offered to make a rocking horse for his daughters, a twin rocking horse. The Machinist had tears in his eyes and spoke of the new comradeship and solidarity created by the Party and the imminence of war. The words had been badly chosen, they had communist overtones, but I just smiled and nodded, which was always the appropriate reply when someone was talking to himself. I bowed my way out and that was appropriate too, since I was only a journeyman, and I went out into the street admiring the miniature pivots, levers and hammers I held in my hand, my mouth pursed in a small O of wonder. The store next door had a cracked plate-glass window with a paper banner pasted diagonally across it. The banner read: TRUE ARYANS DON'T PATRONIZE STORES OWNED BY JEWS. It meant nothing to me. Generally, I thought Nazi posters were like medieval art, some very advanced techniques were used but the things they were saying were so simple, it was like looking at a comic book. Simple, directed at the lowest and most primitive emotions, but there is nothing wrong with enjoying your lowest and most primitive emotions. I stopped thinking, slid the parts back into their envelope, put them in my pocket and went back to Margit . . . home sweet home.

"The days took on a blurring regularity. I spent the nights napping in the storeroom, scraping and chipping away at the concrete through to the early morning. I worked on my knees. After the first night, I knelt on a pillow but the damage had been done.

"While dumping another umbrella load of concrete chips, I realized that a week had passed and there was a fairly large pile building up. There were even nine bricks. I counted them several times with satisfaction. I walked out of the brewery yards around the block to Rosenheimer Platz. The Sausage Maker's Guild was having a parade. They were wearing lederhosen and Alpine hats and carrying pikes and cleavers. They had the maudlin baffled meanness of halberd bearers in a Breughel painting. They were carrying a sausage two blocks long. The parade was led by a Mark I panzer. The tank commander was wearing a suit of armor with rear-view mirrors welded to the sides of the helmet, angled forwards at 45 degrees, like a bug's antennas. I tried to think about that but nothing came.

"I was sitting on the bed, bandaging my knees when Margit opened the door without knocking and walked in as operatically triumphant as she'd ever been on the stage. 'What happened to your knees?'

"I sought the appropriate expression of martyrdom. 'Scrubbing floors, what does it look like? And don't tell me I don't need the money.'

"But Margit gave me a childlike and conspiratorial smile. 'You mean, cracking a safe. And yes, we both need the money. I saw the dynamite.'

"I laughed with relief because she thought I was a common criminal. I put my arms around her, no easy task, and pulled her onto the bed. Afterward, I lost consciousness and slept for 36 hours. When I woke up, I decided to change the schedule, working only three hours a night in the BürgerBräuKeller and spending the afternoon at the carpentry shop.

"It took two weeks to get the device half built, incorporating the clock mechanisms. The axle of the hour hand winding up a length of wire until the detonator clicked. This was a more elaborate version of the device I'd tested in my sister's garden, this one used two clocks and two detonators since one might fail. I took the time out to build the double-hobby horse for my new friend, the machinist. I helped Franz with the joinery work on a cabinet for a massive Telefunken radio, the first important commission for the shop. The joins were so perfect that the cabinet looked carved out of a solid block of wood. Franz offered to pay and when I refused he almost kissed me. But this was Holy. Even Margit wasn't too bad once I could trick myself into getting started. The bomb itself was going almost too well. I lined the trap door with tin in case a waiter drove nails into the pillar to hang party bunting. I lined the tin with cork so the pillar wouldn't sound hollow if someone rapped on it. Once all the preparation had been done and the routine had become settled, the work began to go quickly."

"And you never wondered why the ballroom was unguarded?" asked Nebe.

Georg may have been very tired. He could have only been doped on Nebe's orders and this story was already insane enough without adding any narcotic aberration.

"There was no problem so I had nothing to wonder about," said Georg.

"What a Nazi you would have made!" Nebe said that admiringly while Brandt and Nolte made faces of warm encouragement then, the telephone rang.

As Nebe lifted the receiver the hysterical shouts of the caller got everyone's attention. He listened, trying to retain the objective distance toward everything that he had regained on his most recent visit to the brothel. He grunted at appropriate intervals until the shrieking on the other end came to an abrupt halt. Nebe went on stoically. "Seems there has been a procedural disagreement between SS-Brigade Führer Christian Weber, they found him after all, and our friend the Munich Prasident of Police, Karl von Eberstein. My presence has been requested. Can you be trusted to entertain Herr Elser in an appropriate manner until I return?" It was a general question but it was to Nolte that he gave the most meaningful look. "I thought so; it is such a comfort to have competent colleagues."

Munich Party HQ was in an ancient office building of the utmost respectability and poorest maintenance. They'd stripped it bare. The Party had to be uncluttered and efficient but the five-meter ceiling had oppressed them. It made the rooms look unoccupied, almost as though they were squatters and transients. As such, they had filled the office with Scandinavian Art Nouveau, Viking Art Deco, thick-legged desks, and straight-backed chairs that would support a hippopotamus made in slabs of exotic wood that had been hand polished and glowed, entrapping the light under ten layers of buffed lacquer. As Nebe took it all in yet again, it appeared to him like the set from Kriemhilde's *Revenge*, the last bounce of the Siegfried Cycle. He kept walking until he reached the end of the foyer, then cringed and then straightened himself before knocking on the massive door. Even the four-inch-thick hardwood couldn't muffle the shrill voices emanating from within.

You could always tell the difference between the cops and the Party even without their costumes. The Police were in plain clothes and looked like cops anywhere: tired, bored, and dangerous. The Nazis were in Party uniforms or expensive suits and posturing with the histrionics of men convinced that they could get away with anything, which was perfectly true. Von Eberstein was caught in the guff, somewhere in between. He was an appointee, in other words he wielded political clout, yet refused to go Gestapo, suspiciously altruistic.

As Nebe entered von Eberstein had just completed a phone call and was waving the phone at Weber for emphasis. "Your negligence endangered the

Führer! You are an anarchist and very possibly a Jew!" He was shouting, trying to catch the mood.

"Then let's examine the evidence!" Weber shouted back and began to
unbutton his fly. Von Eberstein raised his hands in a prohibitive gesture, low-
ering his voice several decibels, which was still too loud considering that they
were standing nose to nose.

"I meant politically!"

"What you mean to say," said Weber as he tried to re-button his pants,
"is that I'm a threat to your authority! You value your career more than the
safety of the Führer. You'd rather lose a war than your job! Like the men who
stabbed him in the back in 1918!"

Polizei Prasident von Eberstein shook his head incredulously, stage whispering now, trying to entrain Weber into calmness. "You do have tremendous
sincerity, but it is now plainly obvious that you lack technical competence."

Weber replied in a voice more suitable to a bayonet charge, "Every minor
bureaucrat tries to protect his job by the claim that it requires some special
skill that they've learned from years of mindless routine! The functionaries of
bureaucracy claim to be a priesthood that demands that all bow before their
mysteries! To protect the Führer all that is required is the will." The Nazis
cheered and von Eberstein threw his hands in the air.

"Does this fool not realize he is a dead man? The will of God, may He
help us all," von Eberstein said, drowned out by the applause. Only Nebe
caught it, half reading his lips. For a second, Nebe almost liked him. He was
simply trying to do his job and that was a shock. The other Nazis were still
shouting "Sieg Heil" to each other when Nebe noticed that von Eberstein
was fingering a rosary. Despite everything and to his own amazement, Nebe
patted von Eberstein reassuringly on the back.

When Nebe finally returned to his own office he found Georg with a
series of intricate sketches laid out before him pointing out important points
to his eager audience of Brandt and Nolte.

Nebe called them to attention. "It seems, Georg, that several factors were
working in your favor that you, alas, were totally unaware of. The squabble, as
most these days, was about who was ultimately responsible for your successful failure. It went something like this: Adolf had decided, and I quote: 'Here
in this gathering, I will be protected by my Old Fighters led by Christian

Weber; police authority ends at the entrances. Overall responsibility for the event at the BürgerBräuKeller, for receiving the Führer and the guests of honor, for control of the participants, for security inside, and for the arrangements of seating: SS Brigadeführer Christian Weber!' So you see Georg? He was actually your enabler. Had von Eberstein been allowed to organize security you would have found no room at the inn. You owe your failed success to one Christian Weber." Nebe sat back and waited for Georg to speak.

"What's going to happen to him?" asked Georg.

Nebe looked at a note on his desk. "That is really of no consequence to your case one way or the other. Maybe nothing, he'll probably just disappear, like so many others, and some clever Party people will start the rumor that he turned out to be a Jew after all." As he talked Nolte was frantically scribbling a note, looking up at him between each word to make sure he had his attention. Nebe stopped and waited for Nolte to finish. There was an empty silence and Georg could hear the insect-like scratch of graphite on paper for a painfully long time. Nolte handed the note across. Nebe sneered politely and showed the note to Georg. Georg couldn't make sense out of it and looked to Nebe for a translation. "It says: 'YOU ARE BREAKING THE FIRST RULE OF INTERROGATION.' See, I'm not supposed to tell you anything you don't already know," Nebe said gently as he turned to Nolte. "Don't go handing me notes like that. It kicks the hell out of trust." Then he returned to Georg with his eyebrows semaphoring paternal encouragement. "You think you might have had a more difficult time if we had been in charge?"

Georg didn't want to hurt his feelings so he waited longer than usual to answer, but he just couldn't find another way to say it. "No, not really. No difference. If there's a standard procedure, then there's always a way of getting around it."

"Strike that!" said Nebe.

Brandt seemed frozen in place. "I didn't type it."

"Thank you," said Nebe. He looked at Georg with affection. "The speech had been cancelled. You had to have known that, so you couldn't have been plotting to kill the Führer because he wasn't going to be there. Who was it you were trying to kill?"

Georg was baffled. "But it did happen. He was there."

Nebe was calmly persistent. "In the end he was. But you had no way of knowing that. The Führer wasn't supposed to be there."

"Really?" asked Georg and a vague memory came back to him. He had dumped an umbrella load of concrete chips and walked out of the yards into the street. When he passed a newsstand, there was a headline on the Volkischer Beobachter: the Führer had cancelled his speech at the BürgerBräuKeller. "I remember seeing something, but I didn't believe it. All the previous papers, since 1935, had written that it had to be the same every year. Exactly . . ."

"I'll explain," said Nebe. The way he related the tale he had learned from the horse's ass himself played like a cartoon with animated mice: FührerBrigadeFührer Christian Weber had just put down the phone. Four other Nazis were positioned around him, twitching their noses, ears working up and down in anticipation. Weber announced, "Adolf isn't coming, cancel the canapés and the champagne. It's Rhine wine for the first round and beer after that."

One Nazi picked up the phone across the room. Another Nazi pushed it back into the cradle. They wrestled back and forth like a Fitzliputzli show.

"Hold it, so what did he actually say?" asked a third.

"He's busy designing his war. There will be some extension of the war effort. Hess will speak instead."

"This has to be a political move," said the one who was holding down the phone with both hands, "because everything is. He's saying that we're no longer important." There was heartbreak in his voice. "That means Heydrich can do what he likes with us."

"He can't have meant that," said Weber.

"But that's what it will mean to Heydrich and Dietrich and any of those young punks surrounding him. It's a death warrant!" said the one who was tugging on the phone.

Weber froze and somebody shouted, "Call him back and tell him that it is essential for the unity of the Party that he speaks at the beer hall."

"You tell him!" Weber pointed to the phone on his desk.

The Nazi who'd been tugging at the extension dove for the phone. The one who'd been holding it down jumped him and they fell out of sight behind the side of the desk.

They were all so terrified that they finally found a safe compromise. It was Weber's idea. "If we write him a letter, a careful letter, explaining that we are heartbroken and desolate, that we were counting the days until we see him again, he'd have to come, just have to!" It was like a squabble among nightclub waiters.

Brandt, Nolte, even Georg fidgeted with nothing to say. They all smiled faintly at Nebe.

"I didn't know," said Georg. "You told the story well," he added trying to be supportive.

"It improves with each retelling," Nolte said through his teeth.

"Thank you," said Nebe. "The nice thing about this quasi-feudal system is that you can always get the perpetrator to agree on a common set of enemies: the bureaucrats, the SS, or the Gestapo. It's a four-sided war with no partnerships."

"True," said Georg, again trying to comfort him.

"But something's wrong here," said Nebe. "You're not really confessing, you're writing your memoirs. The purpose of confession is to objectify guilt, to turn it into a solid object that can be grasped like a chess piece. I have to admit that you're doing everything you're supposed to, but nothing is happening because your attitude is wrong. You killed a bunch of people, yet you don't feel guilty and you're not crazy. That's most irritating."

"I'm sorry," said Georg. "I'm trying."

Nebe groaned. He pulled out a cigarette and stuck it in the corner of his mouth. He pulled it out and looked at it as if he wondered how it got there. He wanted to put it back, but that would undermine his authority even further. He offered it to Georg who accepted it with a grateful smile. Nebe lit it for him. Georg inhaled and closed his eyes in dreamy ecstasy. Nebe urged him on.

"You were saying?"

"I had managed to build a metal box, lined it with cork, put a ticking clock mechanism inside, and closed the lid. When I leaned my cheek against the side of the box the sound of the clock couldn't be heard.

"The next day I was sitting on the bed in my shorts. My knees had gone septic. They were purple-red with infection. In the middle of each was a black spider shape that gave off the sickly sweet odor of rotting meat. I heated a putty knife red hot in the flame of a kerosene lamp and cauterized my knees. I couldn't feel the pain at first, they were that far gone. It took three tries to burn off the rot. When I finally felt the pain I grinned with relief. I covered the burns with machine oil: that would deprive infectious microbes of oxygen and keep the scab dissolved. I'd burned the skin off most of the knee cap, in one place a white spot of bone showed through. The scab would break again whenever I knelt, but the oil would lessen the pain. I re-bandaged my knees thickly but it didn't make much difference.

"Most of the time I'd spent kneeling in front of the pillar the pain was continual so I just stopped thinking about it. The time to worry would be when the pain stopped because that would mean gangrene. I was chiseling away, slowly and lovingly, when suddenly there was a sound, like a key turning in a heavy lock or a weapon being cocked. I froze and put down my tools in slow motion with a grace that surprised me. I worked my way around the pillar away from the light. There was the sound of heavy footsteps, leather heels that rang on the polished wood of the ballroom floor. The steps went round but nothing happened. Finally, whoever it was left and closed the door. I waited a long time, suspecting a trap, suspecting that the door had been locked from the inside and that my visitor was still there. I waited. Half an hour of anonymous alertness then I snake bellied my way to the other end of the balcony. From there, the entire ballroom was illuminated by the moon. The ballroom was empty. I got up slowly and walked back. I took a final look around and cautiously resumed work. I quit early that night and couldn't sleep. I left at 7:00 a.m. with the breakfast crowd and walked out the front door.

"It happened the following night. I'd been in the storeroom, napping. When I lit a match to check my watch and started out the door, I was met by the blinding white of a flashlight being aimed straight into my eyes. Courteously, the holder of the flashlight turned it to one side so that the light bounced off the walls and I could see his face. It was the manager and he didn't look angry, just ordinarily annoyed at a breach of routine. I felt a rush of hope. He looked me over stoically. "I knew you were here," he said wearily.

"I tried to seem like a respectable bum and told him, 'I'm out of work. I have no place to go.'

"The manager had wheezed, 'I know, just stay out of sight and stop making so much noise.' He left me standing there and walked out. I heard the ballroom door close and the latch click shut. I waited an hour, checking my watch repeatedly, before I went back to work.

"The door to the pillar was open and I had slid in the sheet metal box holding the explosives. It fit a little too snugly and I had to jiggle it patiently before it slid down to the base of the pillar. It never occurred to me at all that the floor boards under it would turn into shrapnel with the force of the blast, that half the ceiling would lose its support and, pivoting on one end, would scythe down through the Führer's audience, decapitating them, smashing them together, killing them by hitting them against each other. The stamped tin ceiling would make the world's largest guillotine. I kept my eyes on the pillar. There was a separate cavity for the detonator, three bricks high by three bricks deep and five bricks wide. Being of sound mind, I was keeping the detonator away from the explosives until I was ready to use the bomb. I measured the detonator cavity with a carpenter's folding rule. I checked the measurements against the numbers on a pad. My body relaxed and I gave a wan smile of satisfaction. I was just going to make it by the narrowest of margins.

"I slept past noon and left with my digging tools in my coat pockets. When I got to the dining room it was almost three in the afternoon so I skipped lunch and had three desserts.

"'What's her name?' the waiter had asked with more than polite interest, but I just grinned and shook the question off. I was goofy and half in shock from the quantity of sugar I'd eaten. I walked out the front door and down Tal to Isartorplatz into Zweibrückenstrasse to Steindorfstrass and a railing walk along the Isar River. It was a gray day. The wind was causing the water to bristle into spikes, but the air was full of fog. It leached the colors out of everything. The day was as gray and black as an English movie about having an affair with a married woman. I always wondered why that was supposed to be romantic. I'd had a married woman, a rich one with a telephone. Every time her husband answered, I had had to pretend to be a faggot hairdresser, indignant that she'd missed an appointment. It was demeaning.

"I pulled the bent chisels I'd used as digging tools out of my pocket and arced them into the water, one by one, as slowly as I could and still make them fly, making the moment last. Each was a piece of my past and I was suddenly tossing them away and leaving it behind. My past didn't matter anymore because it didn't affect what was going to happen next. All the sad, dead-end, unskilled, or menial jobs, the worn out determinedly dignified rooming houses, and the cunning fat landladies, they were all behind me. I was young again, almost a virgin, and felt very optimistic probably for the first time in my life. I strutted into the fog, leaving the umbrella hanging over the railing in front of the river. A sharp-nosed man in a gray gabardine overcoat scurried up and surreptitiously stole it. He minced off rapidly and then opened the umbrella with a great flourish. Through an oversight, it was still full of debris and a fist-sized piece of jagged concrete caught him on top of the head at the junction of the four sutures of the skull. The sharp-nosed man dropped to his knees in an attitude of prayer.

"I found myself laughing and that didn't make sense. I had no morals, my poverty had made them an unaffordable luxury, but I did have ethics, spiky and incomplete and played so much to myself that they felt almost like a moral code: you kept your word when it was the only equity you had. As such, you used it carefully. There was a dumb, blind loyalty to my friends, when I'd had friends. And there was something in it about hating cruelty and that was a gut response indistinguishable from moral outrage. But I was laughing and that didn't make sense, the contradiction could not be resolved so I forgot it. I went home to Margit. Now that I wouldn't need to see her again, ethics demanded that I muster some faint affection for her. I couldn't feel anything and that worried me as well. I allowed myself to drift slowly to sleep, and napped until 9:00 p.m. I got to the BürgerBräuKeller just before closing and worked my way through the maze of dining rooms with the weary ease of routine.

"The ballroom door was locked. I started to force my way in then stopped, realizing that it would be a decisive mistake. I lacked the tools to slip the lock. There was no way to force the lock that wouldn't leave marks and, if I did it, that would be the end of the adventure. Suddenly the detonator in the suitcase was very heavy. There was nothing to do but go back the way I had come. A waiter shouted, 'Just closing, sir.' But I ignored him. I reached the main hall and the cashier widened her eyes inquiringly.

"'I guess I'm too late,' I said and walked outside. I walked to the English Gardens and back, repeatedly starting and stopping the same thoughts. When I came back, the beer hall was closed and the street was empty. I inspected the French windows to the ballroom and hoisted myself up two meters to the ledge. The windows were locked, thin glass in a wrought iron frame. There was no procedure to open them that didn't leave the cracked glass and scratched metal that would explain itself as a forced entry and that would mean I wouldn't be able to come back; they'd be waiting.

"I turned back and stopped again. I could have finished the work then and there, and not come back, but if I broke in a week before the Führer's speech the ballroom would be searched; any serious search would find the bomb. I got down off the ledge and picked up my suitcase, standing there in the moonlight like a gravy spot on a lace doily. Then I trudged off back to the rooming house on Leopoldstrasse. I allowed myself to worry; it was too late to do anything else. I had to finish it. There was no way back and nothing to go back to. I thought of Margit. I'd have to deal with her one more time and the fondness I'd faked in the afternoon was an obsolete weapon. Just maybe, she would know where to find a lock picker. She seemed like the type. I looked back once. The windows gleamed as impenetrable as mirrors in the fuzzy glare of the street lamps and the silvery moon.

"Margit was asleep when I got back and out the next day when I woke up, that was a blessing; I thought maybe my luck was changing. I sat on the bed and waited, constantly checking the clock but it was still early afternoon. I did something strange, used my keys to Margit's apartment. I finally had an opportunity to peruse her space at my leisure, and that violation of her privacy almost made me want her again. I took the bottle of brandy from where she'd hidden it under the sink, poured myself a glass and began to rifle through her bookshelf, or should I say play shelf. It was almost touching seeing her unrequited ambitions there, neatly lined up in a row. Of course I passed on the dark Scandinavians and Russians, but that operetta was actually entertaining. I chuckled as I slipped Hannah's *Der Blaue Engel/ Professor Unrat* in its place; I guess Margit's theatrical background just made it somehow appropriate. I took her play—only slightly uncomfortable about the fact that it had her name written inside the front cover—and the bottle of course, back to my room and got resolutely drunk, drunk and waiting. I started to masturbate to pass the time but couldn't do that either. Margit would be coming home to be serviced and I would need all the appetite I could muster to handle it. I don't know why but that evening I spanked her, and she responded like I was the only man who had ever understood her.

"I finally escaped, got to the BürgerBräuKeller early. There was nowhere else to go. It was 8:00 p.m. and the dining rooms were still busy. I walked through carrying my suitcase, overcoat buttoned up, trying hard to be non-chalant. Music and party noises grew louder as I got closer to the ballroom. When I arrived at the door I found that a dance was in progress. I bought a ticket and went up to the balcony. I spent several hours watching the dancers and waiting for them to leave. They were all young, dancing waltzes out of an operetta, or in small groups plotting their next intrigue at the top of their lungs. They all looked rigidly cheerful. I didn't know if they were happy, but they were very alive and made the night seem crisp and clear. I looked over the girls, finding the flaws in their features or the cheapness of a dress, but then I stopped myself.

"I suddenly felt old, which was silly too. Thirty-six isn't old; it isn't young either but statistically only women get old, while men on the other hand just get more interesting. Ulrich had said that, but he must have heard it some-where else. The memories the situation called up weren't pleasant; my mind skipped back fifteen years. I'd played the zither very competently but without adding flourishes or trying to show off. I tried to remember the music. It had been mostly folk songs, all with the same stomping beat and almost the same melody. I couldn't remember any of them, only the sound of feet pounding out the rhythm on the floor. I felt very tired.

"The dance was breaking up, the dancers leaving, the girls chattering and the boys grunting reassurances. The musicians were packing up, some of them leaving their instruments on the bandstand. I suddenly wanted to handle the bass. Perhaps, in the middle of the night, I could come down and play for a while. It had been such a stupid idea that I began to giggle. I lin-gered another moment in silence with a lonely smile watching the girls leave, and then went back to the storeroom to wait. The door to the ballroom was unlocked. I thought about that, but nothing happened. More information was needed but I was too tired to worry, too tired to feel fear. I sat down resting my elbows on my knees; seemed like I could feel them beginning to heal. I waited. There was nothing to think about and nothing I wanted to remember. I fondled myself through my pants, a childish vice but I'd grown up too fast so I figured I deserved indemnity; while I wondered if I'd ever actually been young, I fell asleep without realizing it.

"When I woke up it was almost 4:00 a.m. I grabbed the suitcase and rushed out to the balcony. Sitting down in front of the pillar I clawed the door open, opened the suitcase, and took out the detonators. That moment I switched into slow motion. I carefully fit them into depressions in the explosives and taped them in position. I lifted the metal box containing the clock works. The trip wires dangled from it and I swept them back over my shoulder until the box was in position and I could connect them to the detonators. I adjusted my position, switching to my knees and guided the box forward into the cavity. It wouldn't fit. I eased it in at a slight angle working it from side to side between my hands, but it still wouldn't fit. The box was a fraction of a millimeter too big, horizontally and vertically. I put the box down and wanted to curse but when I opened my mouth the only sound that came out was the hoarse raging scream of a trapped animal. I tried to modulate it into words, to control it, but my voice tore away from me in a vast open-mouthed groan. Then I leaned my head against the pillar and cried like a baby.

"In the end it wasn't as bad as I had thought. When I left in the noon crush I checked and re-checked the date below the headline at a newsstand. It was only November 6th. I still had nearly two whole days.

"I arrived at the carpentry shop and immediately set to work at the rear table, cutting the joints of the box deeper with a pair of borrowed tin snips, bending it into shape and trimming it down. Luckily there had been enough play in the dimensions that I didn't need to find a way to reduce the contents as well. Franz didn't ask any questions, as I said he had his admirable qualities; he wasn't stupid however, though he was almost everything else, and he had suddenly passed the point of suspicion to the realm of real terror. Anything he might be told would involve him further so, of course, Franz said nothing and asked nothing. I worked quickly and it took less than two hours so there'd been nothing to worry about after all.

"That night when I pushed the box into the hollowed section of the pillar, it fit perfectly. I removed it again and opened the lid to get at the clocks. I took the neatly folded clipping from my wallet and read it one more time. It said that the Führer always started to speak at 20:10 and finished at 22:20.

I subtracted 20:10 form 22:20 and got 130 minutes. I divided 130 by two to get sixty-five. Sixty-five minutes after 20:10 made detonation time 21:15. It was 02:45 on the morning of November 7th; I quickly did the math. Had the box fit the previous night then the trip wires would not have been long enough; I would have had to come back anyway. I quickly made the necessary adjustments: in forty-two-point-five hours the bomb would detonate.

"I closed the lid. I picked up the apparatus and slid it back into its scabbard in the pillar. I connected the trip wires to the detonators and fit them into the explosives, it was suddenly absolutely and totally real, the only reality I knew and I looked at it hungrily, fingers twitching, but there was nothing left to do. I closed the trapdoor with slow-motion grace and studied the result. The edges of the door were still invisible, hidden among the corrugations and fluting of the pillar. There was nothing left to do and that was painful at first but it gradually turned into something else. I stood up, stretched my arms in a Y toward the ceiling and bent my head back waiting for ecstasy. It was a pagan gesture, something totally unheard of for my theretofore very Lutheran self. It was a gesture I had never seen or even imagined before but it seemed quite natural. The ecstasy came and turned into a rapture that made thought impossible, it felt like talking to the angels and, had I concentrated more, they might have even answered me."

"Why three clocks?" Nolte's anal interjection was like a bucket of cold swill heaved in his face.

Georg gazed around him, trying to get his bearings after his reverie. "One might have failed, or even two. I thought I had said that."

"What did you do then, Georg?" asked Nebe, reasserting the fact that he was actually in charge of the interrogation.

Elser looked up at him with doe eyes. "I left, what else was there to do?"

"And that was on . . . ?" A prissy question but predictable.

Georg seemed confident. "November 7th, it had to be."

Nolte couldn't restrain himself. "And you had no way of knowing that the Führer wasn't coming?"

Georg looked from one to the other with suddenly growing uncertainty. "No, I didn't know he wasn't coming, or rather wasn't supposed to come. Can anyone finally tell me what actually happened?"

Nebe signaled to Brandt to stop typing. "His old fighters had written him that letter," said Nebe, "saying that it was a change in fundamental procedure and, for that reason, it would be taken to mean a basic change in the status of the Party. And saying that, they were sure he would agree that this kind of internal confusion was an undesirable distraction at a time when the war effort was being extended, or something to that effect. There were also expressions of personal loss and a disordered collection of arguments that gave the impression of hysteria, which was the primary reason why he finally came in the end. He didn't want them to be a nuisance while he was busy invading England. The invasion had been postponed because of the rain. You can't have an invasion without air support and the cloud cover was too thick for the pilots to see the ground. Of course they didn't know anything about that in Munich, they simply knew that the weather was bad. They had expected that to work to their advantage. They had even hoped that the Führer might stay overnight for the parade, but that wasn't the way it happened."

"And how do you know all that?" asked Nolte, indignant as always.

Nebe savored his colleague's discomfort a moment. "It's my job after all. I do still have a few friends in Berlin."

"Fascinating," Georg said supportively.

"Thank you," said Nebe. "But let us return to your saga. You say you ran. Munich is only sixty kilometers from the Swiss border. So where exactly did you run to?"

Georg lowered his eyes in shame. "My sister's house."

"Oh for Christ's sake!" Nolte made to lunge for him but Nebe raised his fist so Nolte turned and kicked a chair instead.

Brandt looked desperate. "Can we stop?"

Nebe nodded and gestured to Nolte to fetch the guards. Nobody had the courage to say another word and Georg was left to gaze around anxiously until his bearers whisked him back to his cell.

NOVEMBER 16TH, 1939

NOLTE AND BRANDT STRODE DOWN the corridor toward the office, Nolte testing yet another theory. "Maybe their relationship was incestuous?"

Brandt stared at him. "What kind of sick family did you come from?"

Nolte ignored the jibe. "It would explain why she was repeatedly willing to put up with his freeloading."

Brandt was not convinced. "They are Aryan Lutherans!"

Nolte simply shrugged and Brandt shook his head hopelessly.

As they entered the office they stopped short. Nebe was already there drinking coffee with Georg, there was a chessboard set up between them. It meant nothing to Brandt but Nolte bit down on his lip; Nebe's King was in repose. Nebe addressed them stoically, "Places, gentlemen." He nodded to Georg to begin.

"So it was the late afternoon of the 7th. I walked through my sister's yard carrying my tool case and suitcase, full of my underwear, socks and old sweaters. It would be a respectable gesture after all of her hospitality and I had no use for them. It wasn't that I expected to get caught, getting rid of old things just felt right, part of the ceremony of leaving myself behind. Werner and son were out at some rally and it was Anna-Sophie who answered the door.

"'Georg, what are you doing here?' She was past the suspicion stage and simply alarmed to see me. It might have had something to do with Werner.

"'Anna-Sophie . . .' I eased through the door sideways and she stepped back a little to let me pass. 'I'm leaving you whatever clothes I don't want to have to lug around as well as what's left of my tools.'

"She was terrified. 'What will you do? How can you find a job without your tools?'

"I smiled at her, and it was an honest smile it really expressed what I thought I was feeling at the time. 'It's too difficult to care for them moving around. Besides, the way things are going I'm sure I'll just have to retrain again in another skill anyway.'

"She leaned back against the wall. 'Georg, what have you done?' She sounded like she was crying and trying to sing at the same time.

"Her question suddenly reminded me of my son and the answer came to me in a flash, 'Got a girl in trouble.' I watched for the reaction and saw that my choice had been exactly the right reply.

"There was no more anger but also no more doubt. 'This time will you marry her?' Her stout resolution was admirable, or at least would have been under other circumstances.

"I was resolute in my own way. 'No.' I didn't explain. She was convinced that men were by nature irrational, so I really didn't need reasons.

"'Don't tell me it was that nice girl you brought out here?' I couldn't even remember when or who that had been, seemed like a past life.

"'No, someone you don't know.' She tried to slap me but I blocked her arm. 'I'm going to need some money. I'm down to my last ten Reich marks.'

"She stared at me as though she didn't recognize me and was trying to remember who I was. Then she jumped from in front of me and ran through the house crying, stumbling up the stairs, covering her face with her hands, and keening. I picked up my cases and followed her. She ran into the bedroom and knelt down by the bed. At first I thought she was praying, but actually she was pulling out a box she had hidden under it, obviously a family trait. She opened it and grabbed out a fistful of money and thrust it at me. She closed her eyes and resorted to self-conscious theatrics so the worst was over. I made no move to take the money so she looked up and started counting the bills in her hand. 'Is thirty marks enough?'

"'Plenty.' I took it and wadded it into my pocket. We stayed like that, me standing and her kneeling, watching each other and waiting for one to think of something to say.

"'When will you be home again?' she asked.

"I kissed her forehead tenderly. 'This isn't my home, it's yours; but I thank you.'

"That seemed to upset her even more. 'When will you be back then?' The cords under her neck were tightening again. I didn't really know so I couldn't answer. 'Never?' she said. That might have been a relief, perhaps the only words that would have made her happy.

"'Yes, I suppose it has to be never.' There was another silence but that was finished too. I did an about-face and walked out of the house.

"I caught the last train from Stuttgart to Konstanz, then walked the two miles to the border. The moon was waning but still bright, running behind high narrow clouds, it seemed to flash on and off as the clouds riffled by in front of it perfect weather for sneaking across a border. The light was off for about three seconds at a time, just long enough for a person to move from one clutch of trees to the next, even if the border was being watched, and it would be better if it was, the guards would say that they'd been watching the crossing continuously and that no one had gotten through. I saw that school house 100 meters from the border and detoured to pass in front of it. I'd hoped that the customs guards would be looking over my head at the border crossing and as such would not see me.

"The building shut up for the night. The windows and shutters were closed. It seemed to be some kind of government home for children; I looked around but there were no other buildings except for the one behind me. The guards might have been hiding behind the trees but there really seemed to be no reason for them to be doing that, it was a cold night. I walked straight toward the border. There was no logical way they could stop me. If I had heard shouting, I'd have started to run. It would have taken an expert marksman to bring me down, zigzagging among the trees in the erratic moonlight, not to mention that every expert marksman in the Reich was being put to use elsewhere. I figured it was a pretty safe bet.

"There were no shouts. I walked up to the border and stopped. Suddenly there was no rush. I wondered if I had forgotten something. Once in Switzerland I wouldn't be able to make myself turn back. That moment there on the border was my one chance to think it all through from the beginning, sped up by internal simulation, but I had forgotten nothing. Or had I?

"I realized right then that I had made one oversight. The escape had never been part of the master plan. It had always appeared easy so there had been no reason to dedicate any thought to it. When I used to live in Konstanz I had crossed the border so many times that it seemed almost impossible not to be able to cross the border; ergo, there was nothing to plan. That was my mistake. I'd created a future I couldn't actually imagine, but I was carried forward into it step-by-step by the process of preparation. There I was with the future behind me and there was nothing to do but wait. It was like waiting for combat orders, nobody ever gets used to it, just scared.

"My life had been at stake all along but that was different. The danger was point blank, hard edged, in front of me. It would be comparatively easy to handle because there would have been something to do about it. There would still have been a next step in the plot to carry me forward and out of it. Suddenly there was nothing to do but wait. I thought of the thirty something hours ahead and time lost its continuity. It split into a sequence of identical empty moments of nothing to do but wait. A repetition that changed so little it seemed to be happening in progressively slower motion. It ended in a fixed wax museum pose, staring into the knowing smirk of my next fat, cunning landlady. My stomach knotted and the taste of sauerkraut came up into my mouth. I gulped it back down and blinked. The moonlight was smooth and steady because even the clouds had stopped moving. There had to be something that I could recheck.

"I didn't cross the border. I walked back to the railroad station in Konstanz. The ticket seller was asleep and I banged on the window until he woke up. 'One ticket to Munich, roundtrip.'

"The next train wasn't till morning so I sat on a bench outside and waited for dawn. That was alright because I was used to staying up all night and allowed me to think about the future for the first time. I would mail back a detailed plan of the bomb so that no one else would be blamed for it. I would look for a job in a clock factory and do menial labor until I could find one. The future promised to be exactly like the past. I took out the play, no better way to kill time than making someone else's life seem like your own.

"I reached Munich at 9:00 a.m. and the BürgerBräuKeller half an hour later. The breakfast rush was over and the waiters were waiting for something to do. They all saw me come in and smiled at me, the cashier whispered behind my shoulder and it carried clearly in the silence.

"'He's one of the plain clothes men sent to protect the Führer,' she said. 'He's been here almost every night.'

"I walked into the ballroom in broad daylight, knowing that my perfectionism had gone too far, it was making me careless, but that thought was thin and far away. The room was vacant. I glanced through the door to check that the hall was empty, but that was my only precaution. I squatted in front of the pillar and removed the timer. I had it out and clear of the door when a slight tug warned me. I stopped and closed my eyes then gently replaced the box between the bricks. I had forgotten to disconnect the trip wires from the detonators. I lit a cigarette and waited for my hands to stop trembling. I unscrewed the lock nuts that held down the wires and removed the timer box, opened the lid, and checked the clocks against my wristwatch. They hadn't gained or lost a second; it was working perfectly and I felt an irrational disappointment. I replaced the timer in the brick cavity and reconnected the trip wires. I closed the door in the paneling. It had been stupid to come back, an insane mistake. I'd lost a day and almost blown myself up. But, finally, it was over."

"The problem," said Nebe, "was that the invasion couldn't be delayed more than 36 hours, otherwise the schedule would have broken down. Continuous alert couldn't be maintained any longer."

Nolte leapt to his feet. "Why are you telling him this?"

"If he understands it all, it will be easier for him to talk about. You want to play tricks and games? Then you stop being his friend. He can't be honest unless he trusts us."

Nolte clicked his tongue but Nebe went on, "The weather could break anytime. He had to be back in Berlin that night. The airport remained closed so he had to take the train. There hadn't been sufficient time to change the railroad timetable, it would have had to be recomputed to keep the trains from running into each other and that would have taken days. That was why the Führer had his private railroad car attached to the back of the Munich train which returning would execute the 21:30 express route, the last train to Berlin that night. For once, he had to cut a speech short. The streets had been cleared along the way but it would still take fifteen minutes to reach the station. He had to leave the beer hall by 21:10 in order to reach Berlin that same night. The report stated that he actually left at 21:07, at least according to the watch of an Alte Kampfer who followed Hitler's party out. As I recall, your bomb detonated 21:20, just thirteen minutes later."

Georg stared straight ahead, how could he have possibly imagined that Hitler would cut a speaking engagement short?

"21:20! But I had set it for 21:15!"

Nebe shook his head in amazement. "Maybe the old man's watch was fast."

Georg was inconsolable. "I should have set it earlier. To come so close . . ." He crumpled his face morosely.

"No, Georg, you made the only logical assumption. A speech is far more likely to start late than end early. It was a good honest try. You didn't lose by incompetence; it was the luck of the dice. Just think, he wasn't even supposed to be there in the first place."

"Yes," Georg gazed at Nebe as if overcome by inspiration. "You should have been a teacher, you explain things so well. Maybe, if I'd had a teacher like you . . ."

Nebe beamed. Georg was actually sucking up to him; that was something new. He was finally beginning to act like a criminal. If they had achieved nothing else thus far in this parody of an interrogation at least they were teaching him how criminals were expected to act. If he could only learn to lie a little more convincingly, the situation might yet be saved.

"But," said Georg, "I can't understand why he changed his mind so many times, doesn't that make a bad impression?"

Nebe smiled at his innocence. "The Führer believes that the only defense against assassination is to be totally unpredictable. Of course that can't work so well against a man like you who doesn't pay attention. He reversed himself one too many times and ended up precisely where you had expected him to be."

"I think you have given three theories about that thus far," Nolte said, "and they all contradict each other."

Nebe was deadpan. "We always have to enumerate the possibilities. At least one of them has to be true."

Nolte seemed to think it wise to change the subject. "Georg, we're going to have to bring in your mother and your sister."

"What for?" Georg was alarmed and confused.

"You wanted to play the game. You have to play it by the rules. The rules are that we have to confront you with your family." Nolte looked to Nebe for confirmation.

Nebe nodded and pressed a buzzer on his desk. Then he continued to talk. "It doesn't have to happen, Georg."

Georg was now even more confused. "I thought you just said it did?"

Nebe gave him an indulgent look. "It's up to you. We can keep them out of it. Even arrange a small pension. All you have to do is tell us who was in on the plot with you. That's all we have ever wanted to know right from the beginning."

Georg sagged forward and dropped his head; he seemed to shrink inside his clothes. "There is no one else . . .," said the voice out of the lowered head.

Two Anwarters entered with atrophied expressions of hauteur. Nebe made a renaissance gesture, raising his right forefinger a fraction of an inch. The Anwarters stayed in the door way.

"Then lie," Nolte suggested. And Georg looked up in alarm. "Make it up. Say the English put you up to it. Your family is at stake."

Georg nodded emphatically. "The English put me up to it!" he parroted obediently. The detectives looked at each other.

"One more try," said Nolte. "There was that girl. Helga? Hannah?"

"There were too many of them," Georg said it as though it had all happened a long time ago.

"OK. How about this one?" Nolte said and pulled Hannah's photo out of the dossier.

Georg laughed and made faces. "Her! Why would I ever want anyone to know I went with a girl that ugly?"

"Thank you, Georg," said Nebe. He raised his eyebrows at the Anwarters, pointed to Georg and made a flicking motion with his hand. The Anwarters quickly marched forward, laid hands on Georg, and heel-and-toed out fast. The door closed gently.

The detectives stretched and writhed themselves awake. "That was entertaining, yet not quite satisfying." Nolte was inordinately smug; Brandt simply shrugged. "Maybe it's all a trick to make us lose interest." To his mind at least Nolte's cleverness had reached its expiration date.

Nebe deliberately forced his shoulders back to take the kink out of his spine. He started packing his briefcase. "Don't look for subtleties where there aren't any, you'll drive yourself crazy. In any case, bring in his mother. You tell her that we're going to torture him horribly if he doesn't talk. She begs him to talk and then we torture him horribly."

"Think he'll talk?" Brandt appeared hopeful.

"No." Nolte had rummaged through the dossier and came out with a form filled in with tiny copper-plate script. "Or rather yes, all he does is talk but he never actually says anything. Here's the medical report: his heart is sound enough, so he should be able to live though it. But, isn't it a little soon?"

"We do this by the book," Nebe announced then braced one foot against the desk and pulled up his silk knee sock where it had peeled back from his thick patrolman's calf. He adjusted the other but in the act of bending his belt slid down and his belly popped out. He pulled his pants back up over it.

Nolte watched, waiting for him to say something more but apparently the subject was closed. "You mean to say it's already over and we're just going through the motions."

"I wouldn't take that from him!" Brandt advised.

Nebe gave Brandt the benevolent smile one gives a loyal hound dog, then buttoned his coat, picked up his briefcase, zipped it shut, and then put it down. "Why won't he save his life?" he said. A nice thing about being a senior officer was that your rhetorical questions got answered.

"I really don't know," said Brandt on cue.

Nebe took a chance. "His accomplices are in England by now, so what difference can it make?" If he said it confidently enough, maybe, just maybe, he could make himself and the others believe it, and that would be halfway to making it a truth.

"Yes," said Nolte.

Nebe picked up his briefcase again and shivered. Nolte and Brandt looked away politely. "If only he were a real intellectual," said Nebe. "They feel obliged to have an explanation for everything." But they were all out of "real" intellectuals; erudite carpenters were probably the best they could hope for from here on out.

"Want to bring in his girlfriend?" asked Nolte. He got up also and was spinning the brass knuckles from finger to finger in a game of long practice. "He tried to protect her, sounds like a vulnerable point."

Nebe stared at him in amazement, enunciating clearly. "Are you insane? Remember what he told us, about leaving for Munich? If she confirms his statement . . . that means more German workers plotting against the Führer." He looked back at the desk and did a double take. "There was a roll of masking tape there, what happened to it?"

"He must have taken it. I'll go get him." Nolte was always looking for an excuse.

"Forget it. What can he do with a roll of masking tape? Let's get out of here." He twitched his head at Brandt, who rushed to open the door for him. "I'm half tempted to let him escape just to follow him and see where he goes."

"Don't say that, even as a joke," Nolte protested.

"But of course, that kind of inventiveness would be a sign of desperation." Nebe said and walked out to the hall with his two assistants following at a respectful two steps behind. Beyond the window, the sky was black. He checked his watch, but again he'd forgotten to wind it.

"Sorry, I have to . . .," said Brandt gesturing towards the toilet at the end of the hall. "Heil Hitler and goodnight!"

"Heil Hitler!" cried Nolte and saluted, Nebe noticed that the brass knuckles were hanging from his pinky.

"Why do you carry those?"

Nolte slid the weapon back into his pocket with his practiced gesture. "I'm too old to carry a teddy bear."

"Think I'll get some too," said Nebe as they headed for the stairs.

The hall was over lit, as nightmarish as if the light were the spirit of inquiry itself. When they reached the street floor, Nolte paused, pulled out his notebook, flipped back through the pages and began to read. "He said he had dinner at the beer hall and then went to the storeroom. Something doesn't make sense. He had three alternatives: he could have paid his check and then walked back to the ballroom instead of walking out, but that would have attracted attention. He could have hidden in the storeroom and paid his check the next morning, but if they had any kind of accounting system at all they'd know he paid the next morning for a check from the night before and would know that he had stayed over. So, what did he do?" Nebe stopped walking to listen courteously, so Nolte talked faster. "If he didn't pay the check at all, the second or third time he tried it, they'd be waiting for him. So, he didn't do that. On the other hand, it would be a hard place to get out of without paying a check. So, he didn't have dinner. He went straight to the ballroom and had breakfast the next morning and paid before he left. That's what I have." Nolte's face jerked at him, point blank.

Nebe took out his own notebook and checked. "You are forgetting one very significant detail: the staff had come to believe that he was part of the Führer's plain clothes security detail."

Nolte was indignant. "That is what Elser wants us to believe."

Nebe gave his most pontifical smile. "It makes sense that not even the wait staff at the beer hall could imagine Weber was such an idiot as to have left the ballroom totally unguarded. That would give them plenty of reasons to overlook a variety of irregularities, would it not?"

"Shit." Nolte hated being caught out.

"The place to start is always the small contradictions." Nebe stretched his patience a bit further. "Suppose then that you have it right and I have it wrong, then what?"

Nolte's expression brightened. "That would prove that he was lying."

"We already know he's lying, or at least for official reasons he has to be." Nebe realized that his tone had become seismic because the desk sergeant looked up at them in alarm. "I have read the manual too. Who remembers every exact detail unless they're lying, simply repeating a memorized script like a satyr play? Explanations of motives are usually fantasy. If a man appears rational you expect a rational motive, but real motives are rarely rational. Our contradictions contradict the contradictions of our contradictions. No man is sane enough to follow a rational motive with any consistency." He stopped to gulp a breath and saw that the desk sergeant was signaling to him. He wound up the lecture. "The small contradictions prove he's telling the truth. Big contradictions would have proven he was lying, but, much to our chagrin, there aren't any."

"Herr Oberst." The desk sergeant was frantic. "Reich Minister Goebbels was on the line, but said not to interrupt you if you were interrogating."

"Always the gentleman," said Nebe. "Well? Get him back on the line!"

The desk sergeant literally galloped down the stairs and unlocked the door to the day captain's office. Nebe followed, and was followed by Nolte who was followed by Brandt, who had just caught up with them. Nebe turned on the lights, which were mercifully dim, and sat down behind the desk. The day captain's family stared at him carnivorously from out of a framed photograph. Nebe picked it up and put it face down and then talked to Berlin.

"Do you know what time it is?" Goebbels was accustomed to conducting the orchestra.

Nebe however was possessed of a fatalistic disregard for hierarchy, if they wanted him dead they would find an excuse no matter what, so no cause for worry. He was a condemned man one way or the other. "I'm returning your call, Herr Reich Minister."

"That was five hours ago! Anyway, tell me what is happening, and I don't give a crap about the psychobabble. We are in the business of creating myth, Herr Nebe, what can you tell me about that?"

"I couldn't agree with you more . . .," said Nebe.

"All myths are dramatic narratives because that is the most natural form for the depiction of conflict. War is the ultimate reality exactly because all things are born of conflict."

Nebe was wary; he had to intervene before Goebbels could work himself into a fury. Nebe said, "Remarkable how well you express that."

Magically the Minister's tone softened to a mild lector's pitch. "The Law itself is a myth. Suppose there actually was such a thing as the 'Law,' what properties would it have to have?"

Nebe would have answered the rhetorical question, but, of course, was not given the chance.

"The Law must be 'Just but Merciful'— morally logical yet economically efficient. It must be completely unambiguous, however open to a range of interpretations. These contradictions cannot be resolved, but are an essential part of the definition of the Law itself: that it must be free from contradiction. Therefore, the Law does not and cannot actually exist."

Nebe genuflected. "I am honored that you should deem to enlighten me so, Herr Minister."

"The Law is a myth. Its function is to comfort the petty bourgeoisie, creating the illusion that there are limits imposed on the strength of the strong, but the only true Law is the Will!"

He's not crazy, thought Nebe. He has to know that he's full of shit. He has to know that I know he's full of shit and now he's daring me to say it. Ergo, I am in extreme danger. "You are an inspiration," said Nebe.

"You are welcome."

"Herr Reich Minister, if you would provide us with a transcript of exactly what you want him to say, we can wrap this up in a few hours." There was dead silence on the other end of the phone for what seemed a very long time. Nebe crossed himself.

"That bad?" said Goebbels in a suddenly sane voice.

"I'm afraid so. It seems likely that he had introduced a few friends and colleagues into the plot but, if we uncover them, we have a conspiracy of German workers against the Reich, so the problem would be multiplied. There don't appear to be any foreign connections. We're going to try torture next but we've already threatened his family, and he'll say anything we want and is more than willing to die, but he can't provide any detail. I was counting on you." There was another silence.

"No," said Goebbels, "that would be a mistake. You don't want to manufacture evidence. You would be placing yourself in competition with the Gestapo and the RuSHA." The Racial Resettlement Office, aka the night-and-fog boys. "You don't want to do that. Even worse, if any facts did happen to emerge later on then that would look like a cover-up."

"We are aware of that Reich Minister, but If we don't find a resolution to the case then the police will be discredited."

"No," said Goebbels. "It would be disappointing perhaps. A number of prominent people would probably lose interest in you; however, since their interests are in conflict, that could even be to your advantage in the end."

"Thank you, Herr Reich Minister." Nebe would have clicked his heels, but he had kicked off his shoes. He squatted fast and grabbed them from under the desk and, holding them under his chin, he clapped the heels together in front of the phone. Goebbels chuckled and hung up. Nebe put down his shoes and then the phone. He rested his fingertips on the desk and stared in front of him.

"What did he say?" asked Nolte.

Nebe let out a long breath and smiled. "He said to relax because we're fucked no matter what we do." He slipped into his shoes. "So, let's go home."

DECEMBER 24TH, 1939

IN THE DAYS THAT HAD followed Nebe's conversation with Goebbels Georg was placed under strict solitary confinement. None of them cared for waiting but that was all there was to do until the Reich Minister meticulously orchestrated the diffusion of the situation. Solitary could be justified as interrogation technique, some of Nebe's colleagues even considered it "ingenious cruelly," the calm before the storm of family confrontation and torture. Nebe was really only interested in buying time to review every aspect of the confession thus far and to insulate he and his immediate colleagues from Elser, a respite to gain perspective. He knew Georg would hate it, he even felt bad about it, although of course he mentioned that to no one. His particular variety of sadism was more of a niche fetishism that a general aberration of character, as such that type of torment offered him no pleasure.

After Hitler and Stalin had summarily divided up Poland, giving the French and English a pretext to declare war on Germany without actually having to do anything at the time, there was intense debate among Hitler's advisors as to what the next step should be. That internal uncertainty defused to some extent the immediate pressure of what to do about Georg. Goebbels's propaganda machine through calculated manipulation of the press had successfully diminished the attempt to the status of an unfortunate accident. That meant for all intents and purposes that ground for Elser's disappearance had already been laid. The interrogation had officially been relegated to going through the motions: because there was a book they were obliged to go by it.

The mere thought of the process of bringing in the family and then pointlessly torturing the man had set Nebe's teeth on edge. Certainly any skills he actually possessed would have been better applied anywhere else but the situation had passed into the realm of absurdity, beyond hope of return. Nebe was standing outside his office with Nolte waiting for the situation to unfold. It was almost noon and they were both clanking with tension. Then Brandt went by with Elser's mother, the wreck of a once pretty woman. The frown lines were cut so deep at the corners of her mouth it resembled the hinged jaw of a marionette. Georg's sister followed with a dizzy dignity, looking off in odd directions and smiling inappropriately. Brandt opened the door to where Georg waited between a brace of Wachtmeisters. Georg and his mother fell toward each other, throwing their arms about each other, holding each other up.

Georg was saying, "Mama, I'm sorry," over and over and his mother was saying, "It's alright, baby, my sweet baby . . ." over and over. It was a two-part fugue.

Nebe lurched away and nearly ran for the toilet. Nolte turned back from the door and started to follow him, but Nebe made an about-face and put a hand against his chest. "No, you stay here in case he cracks."

By the time he threw open the door, he was running with his mouth full of bile. He made it to a stall and threw up with a great green gush into the toilet. He leaned over it, inspecting the spiderweb cracks in the porcelain bowl then looked around for toilet paper. There wasn't any and he used his handkerchief to wipe up the flecks of vomit that had splashed out to speckle the walls and floor. He looked at it and threw it away, cursing. He walked to the sink and splashed cold water on his face and neck, letting it trickle down his back. He looked at himself in the mirror. He looked like a criminal. The man he had been interrogating for nearly seven weeks still didn't look like a criminal but he, the officer in charge of the investigation, could easily be mistaken for a vagrant or a gambler down on his luck. He leaned against the wall and held out his hand to see if it were trembling. It wasn't and he abruptly felt better. He lit a cigarette. It tasted harsh, but somehow that was reassuring. He thought about it. It was a question of motive. The guy hadn't done it for fame or love or money and that's all there is. There was satisfaction in his craftsmanship, but couldn't he have gotten that by building another cuckoo clock? He apparently took no pleasure in killing and was genuinely shocked to discover that people had been killed by what he'd done. He had known it on some level, of course, but he hadn't thought about it.

So, what was his motive? He claimed that he was trying to stop the war, but what was in it for him? The problem was that the attempt appeared to be an altruistic act and that was intolerable.

Since antiquity philosophers had been able to detect only one altruistic act in all of nature: dolphins pushing exhausted swimmers back to shore. Even that had come under question because many maintained that dolphins simply enjoy pushing things, so the only swimmers heard from were those pushed back toward shore. Even dolphins were easy to frame on circumstantial evidence.

Gibbon had written *The Decline and Fall of the Roman Empire* covering 1,500 years of history without once finding it necessary to suspect anyone of a decent motive. But, in the case of Elser, a bad motive didn't fit the facts; there was simply nowhere to put it. It was intolerable and, worse, it would never be believed. The Gestapo would say that they were trying to turn the man into a hero, a plaster saint, and Nebe himself would inevitably be killed. He had to find a lie that would be believed and that was possible only by a selective suppression of the facts that would not look like a cover-up. He leaned his forehead against the cool tile and was comforted by it.

He thought wistfully of Maurice Bauvard, that Swiss theology student on vacation from a seminary in Alsace Lorraine. He had also come to Munich to kill the Führer. He'd bought a 7.65 automatic in Basel, a typical amateur with a little shit pistol who had stalked the Führer around until his money ran out. He was caught on a train without a ticket and the police found the gun on him. He immediately confessed that he intended to kill the Führer. Like a typical amateur, he didn't really want to hurt anyone, he just wanted to attract attention. The Gestapo would have never known about the intended assassination if he hadn't thrust his confession upon them. Nonetheless the Gestapo obligingly took him off the train, executed a perfunctory "investigation," then cut his head off, another success story. No one ever asked about his motives, no one was even vaguely interested. Even so, it would have been easy to spin that into a Catholic conspiracy, masterminded by the Pope, and that would have been fun and useful too. Why did they have to build a conspiracy on such poor material as Georg Elser? Nebe thought, and then he knew the answer: Elser had almost succeeded. That demanded an explanation, a theory at least if not a full-blown conspiracy.

Nebe ground out his third cigarette and walked back to his office. He could see through the glass that Elser was alone with Brandt. The women were gone. Nolte was outside the door, arms crossed and leaning against the wall.

"Well?" said Nebe, but Nolte simply shook his head and opened the door. Nebe walked in with Nolte behind him. Elser and Brandt were both smiling at him. They seemed glad to see him. Brandt had just finished typing Georg's confession. He rolled it out of the typewriter and walked it over, oaring it with the gesture of a head waiter offering a menu. Georg automatically reached for a pen.

"No," said Nebe, "read it first." It was a one-page summary and Georg took a few minutes, read it then re-read it, his lips moving in time with his eyes. Nebe thought longingly about the bottle of schnapps in the bottom drawer of his desk. Finally, Georg stood up and turned his face questioningly from one detective to another. He's trying to act stupid, thought Nebe. Did that prove conspiracy? No, either he is stupid or it proves that he thinks we're stupid.

"Something wrong?" asked Nebe.

Georg looked up at him in astonishment. "It says at the bottom that I set the clocks for 3:00 p.m."

Nebe was nonchalant. "So? Change it and put your initials next to it. To prove the change was made with your approval of course."

Georg suddenly had an idea. You could almost hear the wheels go round. He smiled. "You put in that mistake deliberately," said Georg, "so I'd catch it. So you could prove I had read it."

Nebe smiled at him. "You have put in a few deliberate mistakes yourself, Georg. We know you're a British agent. We just need to hear you say it. Then it would be over. It's purely a formality."

"I'm a British agent!"

"That's not quite enough. It was a one-man job so there was no reason to involve anyone else once it started. But you didn't start alone. How did the British contact you?"

Georg jiggled his head and shrugged and flapped his hands, all in different directions. He was sure Nebe had gone insane, though he hadn't seemed that crazy to start with. That's the way it happens sometimes, one moment they were here and suddenly they were gone and unreachable. He couldn't follow Nebe up and down the winding staircases of his delusions. It was obvious there was no way to satisfy him. "No one! There was no one!"

"You would never make a decision like that by yourself," said Nolte, leaning into it. "You're sane enough not to trust your own judgment. You'd have to talk it over with someone else, a close friend maybe? It's only natural."

Nebe was waving his hands back and forth like the signal at a railway crossing, flagging Nolte to stop. Nolte looked puzzled, or at least tried to.

"No," said Georg and Nebe let out a wheezy sigh.

"Georg," said Nebe, "I dislike torture, for a lot of reasons. It works perfectly if you know exactly what it is you want a man to say. But as a means of extracting information, well, it's unreliable at best. If there's no way to double check a man's story, it's completely pointless."

"Yes," said Georg but Nebe kept talking, patiently explaining.

"It is standard European police procedure for extracting the names of accomplices after confession. Did you know that?"

"Actually, no," said Georg.

"No, of course you wouldn't," said Nebe. "Do you want to change your story in any way? You can't undo the harm you've done, but you can stop your friends from doing any more. That would be a service to the Reich. It would be . . .," he paused visibly trying to think of a believable promise, "taken into consideration." He offered, "You want to tell us their names."

Georg thought he sounded more troubled than concern for his career would explain, almost afraid. He looked at Nolte, who seemed afraid too, he was making faces of approval.

"You know I did it alone," said Georg. "Why do you keep asking the same stupid questions?"

"Because it's my job," said Nebe, "and if we don't uncover a conspiracy," he paused again, "we might be seriously inconvenienced." Georg shook his head, baffled, or trying to act like it. Brandt and Nolte stood up. Georg looked from one to the other then Nebe pressed a buzzer underneath his desk.

They took Georg downstairs for a very long time to a subbasement and into a windowless, soundproofed room. They strapped him into a heavy wooden chair with an elaborate leather harness that left only his mouth free to move.

Two uniformed Wachtmeisters entered and with utmost efficiency methodically beat on his shins with night sticks. The beating was supposed to alternate with questions, with promises and fake arguments about whether the beating had gone too far or not far enough, anything to keep him uncertain what was going to happen next. That was the only effective use of fear. Predictability led to stupor and indifference or, worst of all, to courage.

But the Wachtmeisters beat on and on with a slow steady rhythm. They took no pleasure in the work, which was one of the qualifications for the job. It kept things from getting out of hand. Occasionally, they looked to Nebe, but he kept gesturing for them to continue, as though he were waiting for Georg to scream 'Stop, I'll tell you everything.' But Georg just screamed.

As interrogation, it made as little sense as trying to seduce a girl by throwing snowballs at her. But Nebe didn't expect it to work; he simply did it so he couldn't be accused of having left anything undone. Stupor and indifference were overcoming the interrogators. Nebe was startled to find himself wondering if von Eberstein might not have been right after all. Could Georg actually have been completely innocent? Yet another confession made by an innocent man desperate to save his family.

No, he knew too much; in essence no one else could have done what he had done. Had they told him? Fed him his confession and had him repeat it back. Nebe couldn't remember. He began to wonder how crazy he really was, because this whole situation was certainly not sanity. Then one of the Unterwachtmeisters swung high and caught the inside of the knee cap and consciousness went out like a blown candle. Georg slumped in his straps. The inquisitors dumped a bucket of water on him, just like in the movies, thought Nebe, and held ice to the back of his neck, but Georg stayed out. Nebe wondered why he had to be here and then he remembered. He had to be present or it wasn't an interrogation, it was just frustration, and that was contrary to regulations.

One of the Wachtmeisters dug his wristwatch out of his pocket. You do not beat a man while wearing a wristwatch; he took Georg's pulse. "One hundred and forty-eight," he said. "His heart's burning out. You want to call the doctor and give him a shot?"

"Let him sleep it off," said Nebe, "or pretend to, or whatever it is he's doing. Maybe he'll go comatose or die of an aneurism. . . ."

"And if he dies under interrogation . . ." Nolte was mortified; they'd all be out directing traffic in Warsaw in the rain.

"Call the doctor."

The Wachtmeisters tilted the chair on its back to prevent shock, then Nolte and Nebe went out into the corridor. Nebe stuck a cigarette in his mouth and lit a match, holding it two handed as though there was a wind.

"Why can't we smoke in there?" asked Nolte.

Nebe took a deep drag and blew the smoke at Nolte. "That'd be 'Undermining the Majesty of the Law.'"

Nolte pulled out a cigarette as well but paused. Nebe thought he was waiting to have it lit; outrageous impertinence to a superior officer, but Nolte was staring at Nebe's hands.

"You're trembling," observed Nolte. There was amazement in his voice and a touch of delight.

"Shut up," said Nebe and with difficulty steered a lit match to the end of Nolte's cigarette.

"He's telling the truth," said Nolte, but that wasn't really a change of subject.

"Of course he is. To get through a beating like that . . ." he shook the memory off. "If he'd known what was coming he'd have been scared."

"Maybe he was," said Nolte, almost supportively.

"No," said Nebe. He was staring at the floor and getting smoke in his eyes. He rubbed them. "They sweat, their eyes get flat and shiny like they had tinfoil behind them; you can't control that. He was trusting as a dog." And Nebe managed to stop talking. If his voice had cracked, Nolte pretended not to notice.

"What now?" Nolte asked in a dead voice.

"We could take him to the Dornier works at Friedrichshafen, sew him in a sack and leave him in the wind tunnel. Or hang him on the Bolger swing. They're doing marvelous things with electric shock these days."

"A man can't even remember his own name after that," said Nolte.

"I know that," said Nebe, "but it's new, untested technology. We wouldn't be entirely responsible." Strangely, anger helped him to stop shaking. He held out his hand and it was satisfactorily steady, but Nolte had carefully averted his eyes. They walked down the hall. It was as humiliating as Napoleon's retreat from Moscow.

"None of this makes sense," said Nolte.

Nebe sighed yet again. "Why should it? It doesn't have to because it has already happened."

Nolte was agitated. "You going to say that in the report?"

Nebe paused and drew himself up into a stance suitable for reviewing troops or waiting in front of a firing squad. "I'm going to say that he appears to have acted alone and that there is no evidence of contact with any foreign government or underground group."

Nolte was looking at him as though he had never seen him before. "We were told to find a conspiracy," said Nolte. "Specific orders."

Nebe smiled. "Exactly, so let's call Berlin and get it over with." They went back to Nebe's office. Nebe looked a little happier as soon as he was back sitting behind his desk.

"Who are you going to call?" asked Nolte.

"Does it really matter?" said Nebe. "They're all on the line." He called SS-Reichsführer Heinrich Himmler. He talked for a long time with no apparent reply. Then Nolte heard the Reichsführer say something loud enough for the noise to be heard across the room. It ended on a high note. It was a question. "Yes, he acted alone," Nolte heard Nebe say into the phone. The voice at the other end was screaming unintelligibly a man who had never before needed to raise his voice. "I understand all that," Nebe said into the phone, "but it seems to be the truth."

"What do you mean 'seems' to be?" Even Nolte heard the Reichsführer's shrill voice clearly, all the way from Berlin.

"To the best of our ability," said Nebe and the voice on the phone screeched a series of remarks about that. "We did," said Nebe, "of course we did. If we go any further, he'll die under interrogation. What do you want us to say he said?" The Reichsführer was screaming again. Nolte heard a reference to betrayal and the treaty of Versailles. "Yes," said Nebe, "we will at once." He kept holding the phone long after the Reichsführer had hung up.

When Nebe clanged open the door to his cell Georg slowly gave him his full attention then jumped around on the metal shelf of the bunk in a frantic and dissipating search for a position in which he could not be surprised. He gave up, panting.

"I'm sorry, Georg," said Nebe, "but the Führer doesn't believe us. You're going to have to go through all of this again. We're moving you to Gestapo HQ in Berlin."

Georg was quite naked. He had been savagely beaten and his legs were purple and black splotched with red. Below the knee, most of the skin had burst and peeled back from the swollen red meat underneath. Nebe couldn't think of anything except that they'd have to put him under full anesthesia even to get his pants on. He called the doctor to shoot him full of cocaine and Georg got very happy. He began singing something inane from *The Student Prince*. It was Christmas. Nebe wanted to say Merry Christmas, but was afraid that he'd start crying and kissing Georg all over. Only Reinhard Heydrich could get away with interrogation methods like that.

Cultural Musings

Fascism and art: Anouilh's version of Antigone was first performed in Paris in 1942 during the Nazi occupation. A plot summary makes it sound like a plea for resistance, but not the way he tells it. In Anouilh's version, Antigone's motives don't make sense even to herself, it's a blind compulsion, and her real motive is to get herself killed doing something romantic because she can't face the banality of getting married and raising children. Creon is the hero in this play because he deals with the world as it is and makes the necessary compromises. The Nazis loved it.

To be fair, no nation can be at its cultural best under foreign occupation and all of the French plays of the time are morally subversive in a very sinister way. The most famous example is *The Madwoman of Chaillot*, which argues that the solution to the world's problems is the mass extermination of all unpleasant people. It argues further that only a madwoman would be capable of this, but the kind of madness necessary is really a higher form of sanity because there is no other solution. Giradoux had the tact to die in 1944, before the liberation. If he had survived the war, he would have gone to the guillotine for Collaborationist Art. This may seem a little severe but the one nice thing about the French is that they take Art seriously.

This Antigone went further. It had language even in its costumes. In the play police uniforms were represented by having someone wear a dark-blue trench coat over a white dinner jacket. Certainly this play is a sedative, apology for all forms of authority, still it is possible to see in this something of the French attitude of elegance as authority and, perhaps, something of the national character itself.

Hegel said there were three kinds of tragedy:

Tragedy of character is where the hero is laid low by a single flaw of personality. There are many examples, but even Shakespeare couldn't always make it work. Desdemona didn't have to drop that handkerchief at precisely the wrong moment. Romeo didn't have to drink the poison quite so quickly. Edgar could have arrived at the Tower five minutes sooner and saved Cordelia's life. That was melodrama not really tragedy.

Tragedy of fate, like Oedipus or Macbeth, is where you're screwed no matter what you do and by trying to escape your fate you run smack into it. That's called dramatic irony. That works, but those were the only two examples he could proffer. How could he have imagined a situation such as that Nebe and his colleagues were facing?

Then there was perfect tragedy: the conflict between public and private loyalties. Both sides, being perfectly/utterly right are of course incapable of backing down, catastrophe is inevitable. Hegel knew of only one example: Antigone. Elser came later and had the misfortune of having inconvenienced the Third Reich so they would make sure his story faded away.

The German theatricality of the police was embodied by the Gestapo. Its full name was the Geheime Staatspolizei—the Secret State Police. It was, supposedly, a plain clothes organization, but in the absence of uniforms, they took to costumes. Black leather raincoats and chocolate Tyrolean hats with a green feather were especially popular. Even their headquarters had the quality of stage sets. They were all reconverted office buildings and security was impossible. Escapes were common, not that there was anywhere to go. Certainly, there was no real police work, no investigation since they relied entirely on informants rather than the assembling of evidence. Accusation was enough.

As theater, the Gestapo could be compared to the games of the late coliseum where Greek tragedies were re-enacted with real killings: an Antigone who was really hung, an Oedipus who really had his eyes gouged out. Dramatically, it was very effective. The Gestapo, occasionally, did hire an experienced police officer but almost in the same way as a movie director might hire him; as a technical advisor to provide some realistic detail.

Artur Nebe was perfect for that job. He had never taken anything very seriously and had been most successful at it for the entirety of his adult life. He had changed sides many times but always just before his faction began to lose popularity. It had begun to look as though his defection was an omen if not a deciding factor. It created the illusion of almost supernatural power, indistinguishable from the real thing because it was never challenged. He had done the equivalent of tossing a coin and having it come up heads ten times in a row. By that point, if the coin came up tails, there were enough men to stare it down and say: it looks like tails but it must be heads because that man said so.

Most men, knowing that they were standing on thin air, would have given in to panic, or a belief in their own magic, which would have killed them even faster. But Nebe's cynicism saved him time and again. He believed that he would only be a Nazi for a few months longer. He was confident that the war against France would be a disaster, that is, unless Hitler's generals managed to kill the Führer first, but Nebe hoped they wouldn't. He'd had enough and was looking forward to working with the French army occupation. He spoke fluent French and so would be recognised as a civilized man. All he had to do was get Georg's perfect tragedy off his back and bide his time.

January 1st, 1940

Nebe and Nolte were smoking in the men's toilet. Nolte, always the straight man, asked, "Do we really have to smoke in the toilet? I feel like I'm back in school again." The decor was actually more like a whorehouse. That particular toilet had been the executive washroom of whatever civilian organization has used the building previously. The faucets were gold plated, the sinks were shaped like seashells and the window and mirrors were framed with thick burgundy velvet.

"Führer's orders," said Nebe. "No smoking, even at a book burning." Nolte believed him. Nebe dropped his cigarette and stamped it out on the carpeted floor as Brandt walked in and quickly picked it up and threw it away.

"I still can't believe it," said Brandt, "a German worker trying to kill the Führer."

But Nebe had come to consider it totally sensible. There were hundreds, probably thousands of German workers who would be delighted to kill the Führer if only they could find someone to order them to do it. There were plenty of foreigners as well such as General Oster who was in the habit of carrying a pistol in his pocket to shoot the Führer just in case he gave the order for the attack on France. There was Colonel MacFarlane, the British military attaché to Berlin. His apartment was less than three hundred yards from the reviewing stand for all major parades. He could have potted Hitler out of the window at any time. For a big game hunter like the colonel, it was an easy shot but he wouldn't make the decision by himself. He wrote to the foreign office, begging for orders, but no one in the foreign office would take the responsibility either, so the Führer lived on.

But Elser hadn't needed marching orders and there was nothing mystical about that, it was just bad luck. Nebe had once been interested in small-unit tactics and had read the field manuals of all the major armies. They were fascinating, especially those of the Americans. They were extremely well written by the best technical writers but, unfortunately, they were paid by the word so they went on and on about even the simplest points.

Nebe remembered the advice on the selection of platoon sniper: "He must be intelligent; the predator must always be smarter than his prey. He must be a loner, not a sulking adolescent, but the real thing: the one man who doesn't need or even want the emotional support of the people around him. He must be a man with no pleasures but delight in his own precision. Men like that," the manual said, "are one or two out of a hundred." Usually they had cowboy jobs like long-distance trucker, so they slipped through life unnoticed. When you found one, you made him a sniper. It was the only thing he was good for and he was perfect for the job.

Elser had the sniper mentality. Of course, it took more than that. It took a man with nothing better to do and nothing to lose. Men like that were common enough but almost none of them were opposed to the war precisely because they had nothing to lose. The social upheaval that accompanied every war might get them back in the game for one more long-shot last chance. A man like that, opposed to the war and with nothing to lose, they were one in ten at most. And when it came to a man with Elser's skills, his quirks and opportunities, a born killer who was also a skilled clockmaker with easy access to high explosives, then an easy calculation with very few assumptions showed that men like that would be fewer than one in 200 million. If there were 20 million men in Germany between the ages of 18 and 60, the odds were ten-to-one against there being even one. But there was one. Georg Elser was just an unlucky roll of the dice. Q.E.D.

And yet . . .

Those were only remote, enabling causes; they made it easy but they did not in themselves prompt him to action. They were perhaps necessary but not sufficient. Something more was required. Well, there was more. He made cuckoo clocks, an embarrassing occupation at the best of times. But now his art was obsolete and unemployable; it could do nothing to affect the forces acting on the people he cared about, which wouldn't be that serious if the result was simply beautiful but its value was unclear even on its own terms. It was the only thing he was good at; to do anything else at all would be a total sacrifice benefiting no one. He had the craftsman's itch, that lurking dark desire to create and his art no longer made sense. The prompt to action came built in. He had to save his world but he could only do it with a cuckoo clock. And he had almost succeeded. Q.E.D.

And yet . . .

The theory of probability could be applied only to repeated events, like rolling dice or tossing a coin. Applied to unique events its terms were undefined and you generated paradoxes very quickly. The textbook example was: what is the probability that Antony and Cleopatra kissed on their first date? If it had already happened then the probability of it happening was one. If it didn't happen the probability was zero, otherwise "probability" was undefined. John Maynard Keynes had tried to evade the problem by considering unique events representative of some larger sample class. If instead of "Anthony and Cleopatra" you said "a heavy-duty seductress and an over-the-hill general doing the middle-aged crazies," the probability that they kissed on their first date would be rather high. But you couldn't assign a number to it. And the purpose of mathematics was to go into a problem and come out with a number that, in some sense, represented the solution. Anyone who told you anything else was full of shit. But you could assign a number to it, any number you wanted, it would be in the way you chose the sample class. So that was out.

And yet . . .

Being German was not a unique event; there were certainly enough of them for random sampling. But Elser was unique. The argument would hold only if it could be proved that the assemblage of Elser's qualities were necessary for the assassination, if there were no other way it could have been done. And that was ridiculous, the armored glass on the Führer's limo was only twenty-five millimeters thick, it might have stopped a small caliber bullet but a soldier's rifle could have blown him away at any time. So, where were all the others? The English, Jews, and Communists all had clear and acceptable motives for an assassination and the resources of entire nations behind them. Why hadn't they tried to kill the Führer? Obviously, they were insane; another way of saying that there was no rational explanation, which in itself was not an explanation.

And yet . . .

He didn't have to explain the Jews, the English, and the Communists. He only had to explain Georg Elser, and that was an event as random and unpredictable as the decay of the radium atom. Elser was just an unlucky roll of the dice.

But, the Gestapo didn't believe in the sovereignty of chance and so they felt surrounded by intrigue. They weren't mathematicians and so, to Nebe, they were lower than beasts. "It's so stupid, I can't even get angry," said the beast next to him, looking at a scar on his knuckle, "it's just sad and dumb."

"The slave mentality," Nebe said dutifully. "We're finally beginning to win and he can't handle it. He thinks it must be a mistake."

The second beast hissed through his teeth, "Wish he were a Jew."

"Well, he is a Communist." Brandt had the look of a man having the same practical joke played on him for the third time.

Nebe elaborated, "He voted communist in 1933."

"Well," said Brandt, "shouldn't that wrap it up?"

"How else was a worker supposed to vote?" Nebe gazed at Georg intently, as if waiting for him to finally get it and start to play along. "You do what's expected of you. That way there's nothing to think about and it gets to be habit. But the attempt was unexpected because you don't usually try to solve your problems by killing people. It's not a habit, so you stopped to think about it. What did you think?"

"The Führer must die," replied George.

"Why?"

"I've told you that."

"Tell us again."

Gestapo inspectors and police detectives were as much alike as chess pieces from two different sets. It made sense. If you were the Gruppenführer, you would choose your assistants so that they couldn't possibly replace you. One would be a little stupid and very physical, preferably handsome since you wanted all forms of authority working for you at once, and the other to do your thinking for you, as smart as possible but with a real dislike for making decisions. Nolte was the smart one without leadership ability. Brandt was the beef.

Georg couldn't find a reply. Nebe regarded the ceiling. Angels blowing trumpets had been spooned out of the plaster moldings that were layered on like cake frosting. Nebe lurched back and slapped the arms of his chair.

"He might change his story the second time but not the tenth or the fiftieth. Give us all a break," said Nolte in a disinterested voice.

Nebe drew his automatic. It was an American .45 worn gangster style in a shoulder holster. He didn't trust the 9 mm. He fired a shot into the ceiling and skinny sharp-faced men, wearing pinched suits and fixed stares, erupted out of the stairwells, guns drawn and looking dedicated.

They took Georg downstairs to an auditorium and sat him between two uniformed guards. It was the gray army uniform with a metal garget hanging by a chain around the neck, signifying: Sicherheitsdienst—the Gestapo's competition.

When Nebe and Nolte entered an hour later with a girl stenographer, Georg was holding a clasp knife in one hand and a Walther P38 in the other, waving them at one of the guards. "Try this," Georg said in a triumphant voice.

Nebe and Nolte ponderously drew their guns and dove among the auditorium seats with all the exasperation of cops who had achieved desk jobs and never anticipated that they would have to move fast again. The guard grabbed his gun from Georg and swiveled it around wildly, not knowing which way to point it. Quite casually, Georg pocketed the clasp knife as though that were completely natural. Nothing happened. Still crouching behind a row of seats, Nebe and Nolte peeped over the top to find the explanation for the silence.

The stenographer was kneeling on a seat in the row in front of them, looking down at them with motherly concern. Both guards had their guns out and were looking to Nebe for instructions.

"What's wrong?" asked the first guard in a hurt tone.

"He had your gun!" screamed Nebe.

"Oh," said the guard, "he made me a custom grip for my pistol. Hand carved." And he held it aloft like a trophy to display a hand-carved custom grip that would flatter an Olympic match pistol.

"I want one too," said the second guard insistently, like a sibling jealous at another's being favored.

Nebe stood up very slowly. He stuck his pistol back in his armpit, adjusted his tie, and buttoned his jacket. He and Nolte walked single file out of the row seats, holding themselves rigidly erect and stiffly showing their profiles. They waved off the guards and sat down on either side of Georg.

"Georg," Nebe said reflectively, "I'm afraid you're becoming a morale problem."

"I'm sorry. I don't mean to be."

"I know. I know you don't. That's what makes it a problem." Nebe sighed with a wheeze. "We want to show you something, a movie. You like movies, don't you, Georg?"

"Yes, very much."

Nebe checked that the stenographer was in place in the first seat on the aisle and the guards were standing by the only door. Then he signaled to the projectionist at the rear of the auditorium. The lights went out and the movie began. "It's the funeral of that sixteen-year-old waitress you killed at the BürgerBräuKeller. Just one of the many people your bomb killed."

Funerals followed one another in a morbid procession: all with wailing relatives and majestically expressionless ministers and bureaucrats. Bund Deutscher Mädchen were marching beside the coffin in their black uniforms and pilgrim collars, taking little high-kneed steps. They looked awful. Then the movie was over and the lights came on.

Georg had been crying, not sobbing; just water running down his face. "I didn't want this," Georg said.

"You care about the people you killed?" asked Nebe.

Georg looked up at him, his sincerity was infuriating. "I care very much."

"Of course he does!" the first guard yelled fondling his new pistol grip.

"Yeah!" the second guard shouted from the door.

"You hear that? He cares, very much. So what would you do if, right at this moment, you were set free?" Nebe scrutinized his face, Georg was unflinching.

"I'd find a job. I'd help support the families of those . . ."

Nebe leaned in for emphasis. "Innocent people you killed?"

Georg took a deep breath then swallowed hard. "Yes. I'd like to help them. I'd like to be part of my country again."

Nebe raised an eyebrow. "Would you be able to do that?"

Georg continued eagerly, "Yes. I know now that it was a mistake. I shouldn't have done it."

Nebe shook his head slowly. "You say that because you have been arrested?"

Georg grew insistent. "No. If my plan had been correct, it would have succeeded. Since it did not succeed, I am convinced that my understanding was wrong."

"Very Hegelian!" said Nebe.

"What did you say?" the typist at the end of the aisle asked.

Nebe chuckled. "I said, 'Now we're getting somewhere.'"

Georg's cell was a remodeled office like every other room in the building. It had a steel door and bars on the windows but the walls looked like plaster board. The two guards were supposed to be watching him but they were playing chess at the end of the corridor and making the ceremonial noises chess players make to cheer themselves up. Georg let his mind wander. Shiny pictures of shiny women hung in his imagination like Christmas tree ornaments. He had been enlightened by *Vogue* as a young man in 1920. He was in a news agent's and was looking at the magazine rack. He saw the cover of one of the first issues of French *Vogue* and thought: *Wait a minute! So that's what they're supposed to look like, not the shapeless baggy creatures with faces like shelled walnuts that had surrounded him since he was born.* It had explained everything and substantially raised his expectations.

He thought of one of his women, that blonde milliner's assistant, Ingrid. A milliner's assistant wasn't quite fashion so it wasn't quite glamour, but it had been as close to it as he was ever going to get. It may have had something to do with his taste for oral sex and that certainly had something to do with a lack of confidence. But he liked the feeling of power: they screamed, they passed out, or suddenly they didn't know where they were or what was happening. One girl had told him it had felt like she was being kissed by God. Hannah had told him that she had finally found something she didn't want to live without.

He thought of Hannah. He thought of Ingrid. He had a quick impossible daydream: Hannah running a dental clinic in Geneva with Ingrid as the receptionist and then suddenly, he knew that he was going to escape. These people were impossible. They couldn't accept a simple explanation.

It had to be complicated or they couldn't be detectives. You don't get pro-moted for solving a simple problem so it had to be excruciatingly compli-cated. There was a story everyone knew about the German revolution of 1848. The revolutionaries had studied the French version and knew that they were supposed to heave up the paving stones to form barricades. But Germany was very advanced and many of the streets were already paved with concrete. There were big holes in the barricades so the revolutionaries put up signs saying EINTRITT VERBOTEN—ENTRY PROHIBITED. The troops marched up, saw EINTRITT VERBOTEN, turned around, and marched away. It was a kind of blindness and that was a reason for hope.

Out of simple boredom he cut a panel out of the plaster board with the clasp knife he had stolen. There was another wall a few inches behind the first. This one was ragged plaster and soiled, peeling paint. It had been sim-pler to build a plasterboard room inside the office than to repair the walls. He reached through the opening and the plaster crumbled at his touch. He clawed at it and the plaster came away in clumps. The outer wall was brick and concrete with a plaster face. He thought about that. He had several inches of masking tape secured to the raised arches on the undersides of his shoes. He peeled it off lovingly and used it to make a hinged door out of the plasterboard panel. He tested the door several times. He had worked fast. When the panel was closed the seams were clearly visible. He opened the door and scratched out a hand full of crumbled plaster from the outer wall then closed the panel and used the grayish caked dust to wad up the cracks which outlined the door stand. They had given him a chair and it wasn't bolted down. He placed the chair in front of the escape hatch and then sat down on the bed to think it over. He could leave the debris in the space between the two walls. It was that easy.

He was startled out of his calculations by one of the guards. "You want coffee, Georg?" asked the guard with the new pistol grip.

Georg smiled at the thoughtfulness of the gesture. "No, thank you."

His smile was contagious, the guard was practically beaming. "Alright, see you in a couple of hours."

Georg heard the outer door close and dove for the wall. The work was easier this time. It took an hour to remove the first brick. Watery-gray day-light showed through. He was outside. There was another wall in front of him. No one would see the hole. The next wall looked about three feet away. He could rappel his way to the ground. Painfully, but it could be done. It came into consciousness that he was actually going to escape. He thought madly that it might get him into trouble and then, when he realized that it didn't matter, he felt shame. Then he felt guilty that he would be leaving without saying goodbye but decided, sensibly, that that didn't matter either.

After all he doubted they would blame him.

January 15th, 1940

He heard the click of the hall door. He closed the panel, moved the chair in front of it and skipped across the room to the wash basin. The guard opened the cell door. He smiled at Georg. It was time for more charades.

Nebe and company were waiting for him and as he was led into the room and Nebe immediately picked up on something. Georg had changed, tangibly changed, but he couldn't put his finger on how yet. He eyed Georg curiously, "So you know why we're all here, get on with it. You were saying."

"I've said everything there possibly is to say. I've told you my reasons plenty of times."

"Oh, go on Georg." Nolte and Brandt looked from Georg to Nebe then at each other. They too sensed that something had changed but weren't about to bring attention to themselves by asking what it was. Nebe was obviously enjoying Georg's exasperation and the job offered so few pleasures anymore.

Georg regarded his captive audience with a sigh of resignation before pressing on. "Well, there's the Hitler youth. I don't like what they've done to the children, making them spy on their parents. He has no right to do that it's unnatural."

"The young understand quicker," said Nebe. "At least that is the rationale behind it. What else?"

Georg thought a moment. "And I don't like the way Jews are being treated."

"The Arabs have a saying: When you see a blind man, kick him. Why should you be kinder than God?" Nolte was showing off again so Nebe indulged in a display of anger.

"Do you have doubts or something? Why are you being so defensive? Go on, Georg."

Later, much later.

Georg now had a light of determination in his eye. "And the workers are furious at the Party."

Nebe was the only other person in the room that wasn't on the verge of coma. "I didn't know that."

Georg was almost passionate. "This was supposed to be a workers' revolution. I made less money at the munitions plant than I did ten years before and taxes tripled."

Nebe raised his eyebrows again. "Workers complaining? Can you remember a specific instance?"

Georg scoffed. "They're too frightened to complain openly."

Brandt had woken up a little. "Then how do you know they're dissatisfied?"

Georg repeated for emphasis, "Because they're making less than they did ten years ago and taxes . . ."

Nebe cut in, staring at Brandt, "You keep talking about money, but you pay child support for your son, anything over twenty-four marks, it even says so in your file. What's his name?"

Georg sighed, "Manfred."

Nebe thought about that. "Like von Richtoffen?"

Georg shook his head. "Like the opera by Beethoven."

Nebe considered that then returned to his original tack. "A fine name; but still everything you make over twenty-four marks a week goes to him the ruling of the court. You'll never make more than twenty-four marks no matter who's in power Georg; you are full of shit!"

Georg turned his palms upward and gazed at the ceiling like a Renaissance Jesus. "I wasn't thinking of myself."

It was Nebe's turn to sigh. "Of course you weren't."

Nolte groaned.

Later, much, much later.

Georg seemed possessed of an almost-superhuman ability to endure insanity. "And it is unethical to bring the churches into your politics."

Brandt was nodding. "It's true, it's very true."

Nebe was dying for a drink. "Georg, can't you just say: I. Am. Angry."

Nolte interjected, "That's descriptive not expressive. He would have to put himself at a distance from it to describe it. You're asking him to talk like a bystander."

Nebe feigned patience. "He is a bystander. It's an English plot, remember?"

Nolte never knew when to shut up. "Then he doesn't need to be angry."

Georg was becoming confused again. "Angry about what?"

Nebe rolled his eyes. "The workers are angry at the Party."

Georg was trying to follow. "Yes, I said that."

"And you are a worker."

"Yes."

"Therefore, you are angry at the Party."

"Yes."

"Say it. Say: I am angry at the Party."

"I am angry at the Party."

Nolte couldn't take any more. "For Christ's sake! The man blew up a building and killed people; we already know he's angry."

Nebe resigned himself to the fact that if the situation continued, his men would snap. "Let's get out of here," said Nebe. "Let's go out for a drink. Would you like that, Georg?"

Georg didn't understand.

"He can't go out like that," complained Brandt, "he's been sleeping in his clothes for ten weeks."

"Then get him some clothes," Nebe said patiently.

Nolte took out a flip notebook and his fountain pen. "Georg, tell me your suit and collar size," he said.

Later that evening, the three inspectors were sitting at a table against a wall with Georg wedged in among them. The restaurant was old, cold glitz with waiters that looked like retired college deans, creamy-white walls and chandeliers like upside-down glass Christmas trees. The table cloths were so fiercely white that Georg kept his hands in his lap.

"This isn't my kind of place," he said.

"Mine either," agreed Nebe. "You have to be tremendously cold to feel at ease in a place like this."

"If none of us like it, why are we here?" Georg asked.

"Oh, there's no back door," said Nebe. "Security is easy. We always use it." He looked Georg up and down. "Suit fit alright?"

"Lovely," said Georg, "Thank you. But how will you justify the expense?"

"You can wear it at the trial too. It's no problem," said Nebe. The waiter arrived and looked them over contemptuously.

"Beer?" he inquired with infinite sarcasm.

"No," said Nebe. "Schnapps. The best you have Swiss!" The waiter jerked back as if slapped and went to get it from the bar.

"Those two thousand people that disappeared in 1936," said Georg. "What happened to them?"

Nebe shrugged. It was in the worst possible taste to even bring that up. "I imagine that you mean to ask: 'How were they killed?' Well it is said that they had used a meat packing plant. An assembly line hanging. On meat hooks sliding down a rail past the execution team. They could hang 400 an hour but it took another hour to get their clients to calm down. There wasn't time for niceties like tying their hands with the result that they were all trying to climb on top of each other to take the weight off their necks. It took an hour before the hanged could begin to relax and be sensible about it."

Nebe looked longingly at the bar.

Georg found it impossible to grasp. "Were they guilty?"

Nebe was matter-of-fact. "Of what?"

Georg's eyes grew wide. "How can you justify that?"

Nebe was stoic. "It was fantastic theater." Everyone jumped as though the table had just ridden over a bump so he clarified. "I don't justify it. I could if I had to though. I could justify it morally, aesthetically, legally, politically, practically. I could justify it anyway you liked, as long as you were to tell me what the rules were. It's a ceremonial game, it won't change anything. My father wanted me to be a lawyer. I studied mathematics instead, which turned out to be criminal law with an imaginary client. So, I ended up here." . . . A peculiar hell where the only reality was the meat hooks.

The waiter arrived with the schnapps and four glasses. Nebe poured a round. "You do drink, don't you, Georg?"

In reply, Georg gulped the schnapps and widened his eyes as the oily, fiery liquid exploded in his stomach and spider-webbed numbingly through his veins. He went white, then red.

"You want some water or something with that?"

Georg shook his head and held up his empty glass. Nebe refilled it. Georg spoke as soon as his breath returned. "Why do I have to be a British conspiracy?"

Nebe sighed again, it was almost becoming a reflex. "The party line is that the Führer has the support of every German worker, therefore, a German worker could not have possibly wanted to kill the Führer on his own."

Georg was incredulous. "But I'm the only one."

Nebe donned his school master's hat yet again. "You're missing the point, Georg. We find ourselves in the position of the virgin who said, yes, she did have a baby but it was only a small one. You wanted to stop the war. That's a purely altruistic act. That's unbelievable and it makes us look evil and we're not going to put up with it. But let's not talk business."

Nebe'd only had one drink and the Christ symbolism was creeping in already. That was bad. It was very bad indeed. Georg's glass was empty again. Georg held it out to remind him.

Nebe shook a finger. "Three's enough for now. Let's have some fun before the nerves go dead. There's a sporting house we maintain. I'd like to show it to you." Georg looked depressed. "I don't like paying for anything either," Nebe consoled him, "but this is departmental business. Heydrich had it built for his personal use but then he decided that it might be useful in interrogation, so he got the department to pay for it. The man is a genius." Nebe shuddered. "Look, Georg, this is all part of the interrogation." Georg was fidgeting, opening and closing his mouth. "Don't worry about it. I'll prove it to you later. Trust me a little."

The government-issued Mercedes pulled up in front of a very nondescript building and the motley crew emerged, careful to keep Georg in the middle. Nebe was playing the gracious host. "This is Obergruppenführer Heydrich's headquarters in Berlin." He said it by way of orientation.

Once inside, the waiting room didn't look like the Obergruppenführer's taste, but that man was full of surprises. The walls were covered with black velvet curtains that sported an abstract pattern of photographs demonstrating oriental positions. Instead of couches there were black and gold recamiers that looked like they were out of an ad for an overpriced perfume. The girls didn't swarm out and grab at you; they swaggered out one at a time like runway models. It didn't feel like a whorehouse, more like a fashion show where you got to sleep with the models. That's the way Heydrich liked it. As Nebe had mentioned, the man was a genius.

Nebe watched Georg out of the corner of his eye. He was crouched forward in his chair, rigid as a kitten that'd just seen its first mouse. Nebe smiled.

The first girl was a German expressionist hooker who looked like Jean Harlow with green hair, black lipstick, and a red satin dress glued to her skin. As she was about to exit, she bent her knees, stuck out her derrière and waggled it, sucking her thumb and looking over her shoulder at them in shy speculation.

"This is sociologically interesting," said Nolte.

"Isn't that a rather desperate attempt at detachment?" asked Nebe.

"Just trying to take an interest," said Nolte, spitting the words.

The next girl was, perhaps, eighteen and dressed in a long fluted dress and an expression of open innocence: impersonating a student about to set out on her Wandervogel year. Maybe she actually was, but that was of little interest to her audience.

The next girl was a tall red-headed woman in black leather fetish gear with a four-inch clitoris and a knowing smile. She noticed Nolte's expression and gave him a slow-motion grind of her hips that was, somehow, in the most scrupulous good taste.

"Oh my God," said Nolte. "This is it. I'm going to rush home to murder my wife."

"You're on duty," cautioned Nebe. The girl pirouetted and struck a few poses. Then half-squatted, hands on her knees, and opened her mouth to a soft wet O. Her tongue was in three separate positions at the same time.

"Fuck theory," said Nolte, "this is reality." The girl had turned around and was giving them a sample of what she could do with her derriere.

Nebe looked over at Georg who didn't look bored. "What is reality?" asked Nebe, loving the sound of it.

"The scene of the accident," answered Nolte, "that which is out of control."

"I thought that was passion," said Nebe. The girl had stopped in front of Nolte, imperiously pointing to the toe of her boot. She tapped it in impatience. She made a sickle-shaped feline lick of her tongue by way of explication.

"Passion is the only reality," said Nolte.

"Fear is good too," Brandt pointed out.

"Hate is better. It gives you a little backbone," said Nebe and waved the girl off. He turned to Georg. "You see anything you like, you just tell me."

"Oh, I will," said Georg.

"Nothing you like?" asked the Madame.

"We'd like to see them all," said Nebe, "if that is permitted."

She smiled indulgently. "Everything is permitted."

The next girl was tall and blonde, squelched into a shiny black corset strapped to black nylons and wearing black patent leather high heels. Her hair was ash-blonde, gray as cast tin, in an upswept hairdo lacquered hard as vulcanized rubber. Her forehead was high. The girl had been sweating and her face was unpowdered and full of highlights. Georg liked shiny things.

"I want that one," he said.

"Then proceed." Nebe directed with a magisterial gesture.

Georg stood up uncertainly. The girl took his hand and smiled in reassurance. "My name is Ingrid," she said.

"Yes, yes, it is." Georg said somewhat inappropriately but it was spontaneous, she fit right into his fantasy. They went off together.

"How bourgeois," complained Nolte.

Nebe raised an eyebrow at him. "What the hell did you expect?"

Nolte seemed genuinely disappointed. "Nothing. But I had hoped that he'd go off with a hard-edged Gypsy girl who did Flamenco on the table top."

Brandt was astounded. "Whose side are you on, anyway?"

"Just trying to find fulfillment in my job," said Nolte.

"That's always a mistake," said Nebe and shook his head.

Nolte was sitting huddled and miserable. The man's sexuality was troubled and uncertain, but at least he was fighting it, so you couldn't hold it against him. He had compulsive fantasies about cutting open a woman's belly and holding sexual congress in the wound. He was far too responsible to do anything about it but, sooner or later, you do whatever you have to do to get off, so there was a continuing risk of his becoming an embarrassment.

Nebe had arranged for him to watch surgery at the SS-Krankenhaus. His receiving oral sex while watching an appendectomy had seemed to be the solution to his and, therefore, Nebe's problem. The problem with the solution was that Nolte was insulted and indignant. You would think that, desperate as he was, he would be anxious to make any kind of a deal but, perhaps, he wasn't that desperate and, therefore, it wasn't that much of a problem. Meanwhile, Nolte continued to maintain the fiction that he had a wife and he was still talking.

"So trite, so superficial. I had real hopes for this one," said Nolte.

Perhaps if Nebe raised the conversation to a philosophical level he could get Nolte bored enough to snap out of it. "Male sexuality doesn't respond to messages, it responds to signals. And the hornier you are, the more blurred the signals can become. They show that with pigeons. He starts off humping a stuffed pigeon and then a block of wood and finally he's doing his mating dance to a shadow cast on a wall. I think we've all done that one."

"I'm going to do that one right now," said Nolte and went after Georg and Ingrid up the stairs. Brandt looked worried, the one expression he did well.

Ingrid's bush was blonde too and that was comforting. Georg wanted to use his hands on her, but she said she didn't like back rubs. He kissed her, starting at her knees. He did her slowly. Her eyes were closed and her mouth was pursed in concentration, but there was no sign of rapture. She held him in her fingertips and moved his head a fraction this way and that. That was sweet and he knew she was paying attention, but no rapture. He didn't want to enter her until she was close to coming, but it didn't look like it was going to happen. He entered her and it was unbelievably comfortable.

He labored with concentration, but still no rapture and finally he came. Usually, his orgasms were near the tip, but this was two inches behind the base. It was an explosion of light that exited his body in all directions, but it seemed that light was really the darkest half of the sphere. He was entirely convinced that he could move, if he wanted to, but he couldn't think of any reason why he should. He moved his arm to his surprise and opened his eyes. Ingrid smiled benignly and said, "Take as long as you like. It's all paid for."

Georg and Ingrid had finished for the moment. She lay back on the bed with a smirk of proud accomplishment. The bed spread was a non-secular blue-green with a pattern of gold oak leaves like an epaulette. Georg was sitting on the edge of the bed, naked, with his hands between his knees and watching her with incredulity. "You're fantastic," he said finally.

"You mean, we're good together," Ingrid said with natural courtesy. "We're fantastic."

"I never knew it could be like that," Georg was still saying. "Not even when I was twelve and thinking about it, before I knew what it was like." Ingrid laughed and reached, competently, for the inside of his thigh. Georg admired competence above all things.

Nolte was watching Georg and Ingrid through a two-way mirror. He had a movie camera, which was working and a wire recorder, which had jammed. He watched with detached interest, too detached, there was something spooky about it and he knew it. He worried about that, absently. Georg and Ingrid mimed silently behind the glass.

They finished a second round and were sitting there looking at each other. Georg didn't know what to say. "You make me feel shy."

Ingrid was surprised. "Well, you certainly didn't act shy before." She sounded indignant.

"Well," said Georg, "before, I knew exactly what I had to do and how to go about it."

"Had to?" she asked, genuinely touched.

"I don't express myself very well," Georg admitted and averted his face. The room was the same deep non-secular blue-green as the bed spread a soothing color. The girl was blazing white in the middle of the bed and she reached for him.

"You can learn," she said. "It doesn't have to be the last time."

"No." But Georg knew that it was.

"You can learn to talk," she said. "If the politicians can do it anybody can." Georg made a sudden decision. "I'll send for you."

"From Hell?" The girl was laughing.

He smiled. "No. Heaven! Geneva." She started caressing him. He sat and stared at her for a moment, looking ashamed before reaching for her suddenly.

Once Nolte had rejoined Nebe and Brandt, they moved to the bar. Nebe looked Nolte over appraisingly. "Was it really that dull?"

Nolte scoffed. "Even worse than watching my parents."

Brandt seemed genuinely alarmed but Nebe just chuckled. The bar was Hansel and Gretel kitsch, but the beer flowed freely. After draining his first glass, Brandt excused himself; the man couldn't hold his liquids.

The minutes ticked by and Nebe peered around, then back at Nolte who was sitting across the table in the booth. He started to ask a question. His eyebrows and one forefinger were raised and his mouth was half open but then he knew the answer and froze, trying to find a question to go with the gestures. Nolte was raising his eyebrows in concert with him, tilting his head inquisitively, right then left, in theatrically attentive silence. So Nebe said it anyway. "What time is it?" asked Nebe, looking at his watch.

"It's two pitchers of beer since Brandt went to the toilet." Nolte's voice had an edge to it.

Nebe was more gregarious. "Maybe something happened to him."

Nolte's tone was hard and flat. "I'm sure it did. Is your fly open?"

Nebe checked. "No, why do you ask?"

This had the logic of a nightmare. He shrugged his shoulders experimentally and his shirt stuck to his back. He was sweating, had been sweating for minutes.

"Well," said Nolte, "there are some ferret-faced citizens at the bar who keep staring at us. I was wondering why."

Nebe looked over and recognized them. Gestapo costumes. . . "I don't believe it. This is ridiculous."

Nolte tried on cynicism. "You're perfectly right. It is. And, therefore, it can't be happening. And you're right not to believe it."

"I really don't like you," said Nebe, saying it slowly like a sentence that would instantly be carried out.

"So what?" said Nolte. "That isn't going to make a difference." The sense of unreality was complete now. Nebe felt himself moving back along a tunnel, inward from his eyes, until the pinpoint of consciousness in the center of his head was the only thing he believed in.

"If we can reach headquarters. . ." he heard himself say.

Nolte resumed, hard and flat, "We won't. They'll have the streets cordoned off. They always do. It's supposedly one of the things they do with competence."

Nebe braced his hands on the table and half stood up. The sharp-faced men at the bar turned toward him and unbuttoned their suit jackets. They were double-breasted suits and, unbuttoned, the long cross-over lapel flapped and drooped. It looked silly, thought Nebe; a man should never wear a double-breasted suit with a shoulder holster. Nebe sat down again. "I just don't understand, why now?"

Nolte was bitter. "Does it really make any difference? I doubt they're here to argue."

"I can take anything so long as I know why." Nebe was nearing the verge of hysteria but maintaining a plausible veneer and Nolte was realizing that his sarcasm wouldn't keep the situation at a distance. One way or the other he was running out of sarcasm.

Then Nebe had a sudden thought. "There's a chance, just a chance, that this is only surveillance."

Nolte was wary. "What about Brandt?"

But Nebe was actually clinging to that sliver of hope. "Maybe they thought he was trying to run. Maybe he did run, he's pretty alert, tactically. If we can get out of here, if we can get back to headquarters, we interview Elser's family at Konstanz, to investigate the location where he actually designed the bomb. It's sprinting distance from the border. We might as well try."

Nolte was skeptical. "What about our families?"

Nebe was incredulous. "Fuck 'em!"

"We could at least kill the two weasels at the bar." Nolte was having a fit of caution, so Nebe felt obliged to snap him out of it.

"That wouldn't change anything; the only chance is to brass it out." Good man in the crunch, thought Nebe, he'd get him a promotion, if they got out of this, once they joined the Swiss Police. There was always a need for experienced men, thought Nebe as he got up to go.

Just at that moment Brandt came back from the restroom buttoning his fly. "The girls had the bathroom staked out. They were in there for 45 minutes. I had to find the kitchen and piss in the sink."

Nebe laughed, perhaps a bit harder than appropriate.

Crisis averted, Nebe, Nolte and Brandt moved back to the waiting room of the whore house, smoking cigars and feeling like executives. Time passed.

Too much time passed. "What the hell is he doing up there?" Brandt complained. "It seems like hours."

Nebe shrugged. "Perhaps we underestimated him."

Nolte nearly choked on his cigar. "You're kidding! The way he fucks is just as colorless as everything else about him; he's probably bored the whore to death by now!"

"Won't he try to escape?" worried Brandt.

"Not for at least half an hour," Nebe said then thought again. "Besides, the building is surrounded."

"Oh?" said Brandt without enthusiasm.

"You did take care of that?" Nebe inquired.

"I thought they just always did that . . ." Brandt false started.

Nebe stared at him for a long menacing moment then shook his head. "Bah, he's not going to escape," he said. "It hasn't even occurred to him."

Brandt wasn't entirely convinced. "You sure this was a good idea?"

Nebe blew a smoke ring. "The best," he said. "Give him a taste of freedom. Remind him what it's like. That's the cruelest of all. Hope was the last scourge out of Pandora's Box. Men go on hoping when there's no reason for it. No reason at all." Brandt looked at him oddly but said nothing.

Nebe longed to scratch his head, but it would undermine his authority. He had severe dandruff and it was a secret pleasure. Just that morning he had torn off a piece of scalp the size of the nail on his little finger. It even had three hairs sticking out of it. He kept the head of a department store dummy in his bottom desk drawer, behind the files and his bottle of schnapps, a blandly pretty girl who should have been blonde, but her wig was missing. Nebe carefully glued the supersized dandruff flake to the crown of the mannequin's head. It was almost covered by pieces translucent brittle skin with hairs attached. He had sighed in complete satisfaction. Everyone over the age of five has something to hide.

They were back in the interrogation room at Gestapo HQ and starting on their sixth liter of schnapps, anemic light leaked into the room but it was impossible to say for sure what time it was. Nolte had progressed from crying to borderline suicidal. Brandt was staring at some imaginary horizon. Nebe had a hangover, but was still drunk. He had forgotten that was possible. It was the kind of hangover that made you drink liters of water without relieving your thirst.

"What was the girl's name?" asked Nolte. "The one at the whorehouse? The one I liked."

This time Nebe ignored him and Nolte began to cry again. "Georg, just shut up," said Nebe.

Georg stared at him. "I didn't say anything."

"The war is over," observed Nebe. "The British were just looking for a way to save face."

"That was the problem," Georg explained. "I kept waiting for them to do something and what did they do? They sent Chamberlain to Munich. Chamberlain! The kid who always got beat up coming home from school and they sent him to stop a war!"

"So then they sent you!" said Nebe and started to giggle, then scowled and pushed his glass across the table. Georg was watching with animal caution.

"A little more schnapps, Georg?" Brandt suddenly rejoined the here and now. He poured a double shot into Georg's glass. He held the bottle out to Nebe who shook his head. Then Nebe changed his mind and poured himself a triple. They looked inquiringly to Nolte, he made a face like a gargoyle then ignored them.

"The war is over," Nebe pointed out. "Secret negotiations are going on, right now, on the Dutch border."

"Georg's doing a better job of interrogating you!" snarled Nolte.

"Perhaps," said Nebe. It was what he always said when someone told him he was full of shit.

"Can you put it into words?" asked Brandt, resuming the conversation after a decent interval.

"No," Georg answered sorrowfully.

"Then you haven't thought it through thoroughly," Brandt argued.

"Something had to be done," said Georg. "I thought that through."

"Georg," said Nebe while trying to focus his eyes, "the war is over, so why did anything have to be done?"

"Not this phony war, the next one. I know they won't fight about this one." Georg drained his glass. Brandt refilled it. Georg continued. "Like the way a street fight starts: 'You took my place!' He'll keep on taking their places until we have all of them against us."

"All of them?!" squealed Nebe, his voice breaking and tweaking off into an upper register. "We're not fighting the Americans and Russians like last time. It's not a mistake we'd make twice."

Nolte slammed his glass down on the desk. "We make every mistake twice, trying to prove it wasn't a mistake the first time."

"Perhaps . . .," prompted Nebe.

Nolte stuck out his hands in a Christ-like pose. "We're going to end up like the Jews; intellectual whores to the world with no country of our own."

Nebe suddenly looked sober with no transition. "Where did that come from?" he demanded in a level voice.

"An interrogation in 19 . . . 36," answered Nolte and rested his forehead on the desk.

"That was a good year," Brandt confirmed wistfully. They stopped and zoned out contemplating their memories.

"We don't seem to be getting anywhere. Are we getting anywhere?" asked Nebe, suddenly wide awake.

"I'm having a good time," whispered Brandt and reached for the bottle.

"Oh, yeah," said Nolte still face down.

"Georg," Nebe started again, "if we have a war it's because we all want to. You're not going to stop it by killing one man."

"I had to try," said Georg. "Anyone else would have to be better. He's the worst. He's a pig-headed lunatic."

Nebe jumped to his feet. It was clear that he wasn't as sober as he seemed to think he was. He struck an oratorical pose.

"I know," agreed Nebe. "I know he is. But you don't understand. It's not the fanatics that cause all the trouble. It's the sane, sensible men like Chamberlain! With dirty little compromises that leave everyone feeling cheated, guaranteeing another war. This will be the last war one way or another!" He was screaming now, his voice breaking and clogging and clearing with a quick grating cough, just like the Führer, just like all the party hacks. "Anyone can sacrifice his life for his country!" he bellowed. "I'm willing to sacrifice my soul for my country."

Nolte picked his face up; his features seemed to be wandering at random over it. He suddenly picked up the typewriter and walked to the window. He opened the window and threw the typewriter out onto the cobblestones two stories below. Brandt gazed at him with an expression of hurt wonderment. It made a magnificent noise but it didn't attract attention, noises coming from Gestapo HQ never did.

"How are you going to explain that?" asked Nebe.

"You're in charge, you explain it," said Nolte. He walked away from the window and poured himself a drink then he sat down on the edge of the table close to Georg. "Georg . . .," he began.

"Yeah, play out your hand," said Nebe.

Nolte just glared at him. "Georg," Nolte began again, "looking at your face, I can tell you've won a fight once or twice in your life. You're not a coward."

Nebe nodded. "Yeah, that much we know."

Nolte ignored him continuing, "And some things are worth dying for." Nolte went on, "You of all people should understand that."

"Losing is certainly not worth dying for," Georg reflected.

"But you lost, Georg," Nebe reminded him, "and you are going to die for it. How do you feel about that?"

Georg held his glass out to be refilled. Brandt poured him a triple, which killed the bottle. He held it upside down over the glass. "How many drops do you think I can get out of this bottle?"

"Twenty six," guessed Nolte. They counted twenty three drops dripping into the glass and then watched Brandt holding the bottle upside down for a full minute with nothing happening.

"That was very worthwhile," groaned Nebe. Brandt opened the last bottle, it was brandy since they were out of schnapps, and poured another round.

"A toast?" asked Nolte.

"To Germany!" Georg said happily.

"That's dignified but a little dull," said Nolte, putting his arm around him. "Can't we do better than that?" he asked.

"Peace? Brotherhood? Love?" Brandt enumerated, waving his glass for emphasis, and managed to slop some on his pants.

Nolte dismissed the suggestions. "Even Clausewitz said: honor can be lost only once. So, I suppose, we might just as well relax. Come on, there must be something we can agree on."

Georg suddenly remembered something. "War is not merely a political act but also a political instrument!"

The three men turned and stared at Georg; Nebe actually guffawed. "I've got a better one: 'Many intelligence reports are contradictory; even more are false and almost all are uncertain. In short, most intelligence is bullshit!'"

Nolte was aghast. "Clausewitz couldn't have written that!"

Nebe couldn't repress his chuckle. "Maybe not exactly in those words, but believe me that was the message."

"To youth!" Georg said decisively. The three men stared at him again.

"Aha!" said Nolte and nodded approval. "To youth!"

"Yeah," conceded Brandt, "the children there's still hope for."

"Then I guess 'To youth' it is," decided Nebe and they gulped the raw acid brandy. Brandt swallowed the wrong way and choked and spat until he could catch his breath.

"We're all getting a little tired," said Nebe, courteously. "Let's all take a break." He then got up and stretched, signaling that the session was at an end.

Georg stood up, yawned, fell over stiff in one piece with every joint locked and banged his head, knocking himself unconscious on the corner of a chair.

"Oh, Christ," groaned Nebe. He bent over Georg and peeled back an eyelid. Sociably, the iris dilated. "No apparent brain damage. Get the guards to put him to bed." Dutifully, Brandt and Nolte drifted toward the door, bumping into each other and concentrating hard on their balance.

Georg was in bed semiconscious; his face wasn't swollen yet but his left eye was purple-black, the color branching out in bright red tributaries of blood lacing under the skin. Fritz was sitting on a stool next to the bed. "Georg, wake up," ordered Fritz.

Georg opened his eye and thought about what he saw. He was vaguely annoyed. "You're supposed to be dead," Georg pointed out.

"Oh, I am. I am." Fritz agreed. He looked healthier after death, people generally do. Georg had thought that was just the undertakers' art.

"I've finally gone crazy," Georg concluded. "It was that last knock on the head."

"No, Georg, in essence you're the only sane man on earth," said Fritz and patted him comfortingly on the arm. Georg looked at his arm then closed his good eye hard and then opened it again.

"This is a dream," Georg said, plausibly. "It was that last knock on the head."

Fritz wobbled his head in gentle reproach. "Aren't you trying to do to me what they're trying to do to you? You don't want to do that to an old friend, do you?"

"No, I suppose I don't. Look, Fritz, I am sorry." Georg sat up quickly, which was a mistake. He lay down again very slowly to avoid throwing up, even if it was a dream.

"It's alright. Really, it is alright," said Fritz, a little embarrassed. "You got a cigarette?"

"Sure." Georg gave Fritz a cigarette and lit it for him. Fritz let the smoke trickle out his nose. He was delighted by what he saw. He blew a smoke ring.

"They let you have cigarettes?" asked Fritz.

"Yeah," said Georg, holding his head again.

"They're deeply confused," Fritz evaluated. Some smoke began to leak out of the spot where the cleaver had made contact, but Fritz seemed happy nonetheless. "Beer too?"

Georg started to nod then thought better of it. "Behind the toilet. . . It's warm."

"That's fine," said Fritz and went for a beer. He came back and drained half of the bottle in one gulp. Some trickled out from the red ring of blood around his neck. Georg looked away in embarrassment, so Fritz pulled his head off his neck and poured the rest down his open throat. He replaced his head, fussing with it until he was satisfied with the fit.

"I had no right to get you killed, I feel like I sacrificed you." Georg was watching Fritz with his one eye and pressing the other back into its socket with the heel of his hand.

"Don't dwell on that now," cheered Fritz. "I was going to get sacrificed no matter what I did. I'm glad it was by an old friend."

"I should have asked you first," Georg sorrowed.

"You're talking shit." Fritz laughed. "I would never have had the guts for that. No, you did right. Mind if I . . .?" He asked, indicating the beer.

"No, go ahead."

Fritz came back with another beer.

"What's it like over there?" asked Georg, making it sound like a casual question.

"A little dull," Fritz acknowledged. "But exactly what I had expected. I think that's what you get. You know what you want better than anyone else, right? That's what you get."

"Yuck," Georg explained, touching his temple.

"You'll do better," Fritz said knowingly. "You've got more imagination. That's the only thing I know about you, really, a little too much imagination. Whatever happened to that typist? You know the one I liked?"

Georg searched his memory. "Oh, yeah, that blonde with the big mouth . . . She tried to give herself an abortion with a knitting needle and managed to kill herself. Poked a hole through the uterine wall and hemorrhaged."

Fritz regarded him sadly. "Were you responsible?"

Georg shrugged. "Honestly, I don't know."

Fritz laughed. "I wonder if you're really as different from Adolf as you like to believe."

Georg jerked into a sitting position and swung his legs onto the floor, still holding one hand over his eye. "I'm right and he's wrong," he shouted.

"That's true. But it's only an accident, a roll of the dice. You mind?" Fritz pointed to the beer.

"Help yourself."

Fritz came back with another.

"Look," said Georg, "I'm getting killed trying to save a lot of fat asses. I'm paying my dues."

"But you didn't do it to save anyone, Georg. You did it for yourself." Fritz had stopped smiling.

"What's wrong with that?" Georg inquired.

Fritz smiled again with his lips compressed. "Nothing really," Fritz admitted. "It feels like there should be but there isn't. I guess I'm a puritan."

"You always were an asshole," Georg reminisced.

"I never liked you either," said Fritz, "but that doesn't get in the way of friendship. That's strange." He got up to go and Georg called after him.

"What happens next?" George didn't sound curious.

Fritz smiled in embarrassment. "Oh, you're about to be killed, that's why you can see me."

Georg shook his head. He tried to blink his vision clear. Fritz was gone. So were the empty bottles. Georg passed out again.

Nebe and Nolte were smoking in the latrine, still drunk but getting rational fast. Brandt was there as the voice of the moral majority. "You've got to drink with him," cried Brandt. "And drink. And drink! And sober up with a hangover in the middle of the afternoon. And we still don't know shit."

"We know he's lying," Nebe said lightly.

"How's that?" Brandt grumbled.

"He has too many reasons," Nebe told him. "The war, the church, the children, the Jews, the pay, the taxes. When a man has that many reasons for doing something it means that none of them are true."

Nolte exhaled a billowing cloud of smoke. "You're drunk, or insane."

"So are you," Nebe argued. "It will make sense when you sober up. All the reasons are vague, they're not thought out."

"He's a carpenter." Brandt shrugged.

Nebe pursed his lips. "I don't mean in the sense of thinking well, I mean thinking at all. The reasons aren't . . .," he searched for a word, "elaborated in the way they would have been if he had lived with them for years."

"Months," Nolte protested.

"Months," agreed Nebe. "He planned and executed it for months but he never thought about the reasons."

Brandt had his drunken moment of extra dimensional clarity. "There's only one way that makes sense: He was following orders." He looked at Nebe wonderingly. "We got him."

Nebe smiled back wide-eyed and started to laugh. "I guess we do."

Nolte lit up like a kid on Christmas morning. "Fuck him; let's go get him." And they ambled out of the latrine, hangovers forgotten, delighted with themselves.

They had Georg back in the interrogation room and Nebe was speaking as gently as a lover. "We finally understand your motive. You were following orders. Just like us." Georg looked sad and shook his head. Nebe smiled like a dog. "You didn't do it for love, Georg. You're a pro; you get paid for what you do. As one whore to another, tell me: Who paid you to act out this fantasy? Tell me and you'll be in Switzerland tonight." Georg shook his head and Nebe tried again. "You're an embarrassment, Georg—alive or dead. We just want you to go away. Why won't you go away? Tell us who paid you and then go away."

"Oh, I'll leave," Georg said cheerfully.

"Who paid you?" Nebe demanded. Georg withdrew into himself, cold and sad. Nebe didn't let up. "Who told you that you had to die for reasons you didn't understand?"

Georg looked each of them in the face. "Hitler."

"Who else?" Nolte probed, then put his fingers to his forehead and rolled his eyes slowly. It didn't seem to help. He closed his eyes and stayed motionless. That didn't help either.

"No one else," said Georg.

"I have an authentic inspiration," said Nebe. "It's almost divine intervention. All the parts of the story have snapped together into a construction of crystalline sharpness. It's giving me a pain behind the eyes like you get from eating ice cream too fast. I know I should pace this out over an hour but, the way things are going, none of us will live that long. So, here goes. Georg," he said it tenderly, "you're lying and I think I can prove that to you. You snuck into the BürgerBräuKeller 35 nights in a row. The last time, you slipped past the Party, the police, and the Gestapo. You even outwitted the Führer, but as soon as you were on your own, you couldn't even sneak through a deserted border crossing. Can you explain that?"

"No," said Georg even though he knew it needed an explanation.

"I can explain it," said Nebe, hunching his shoulders and cocking his knees, ready to spring. "It proves that you couldn't have planned it by yourself."

Georg was puzzled. He didn't have anything to say. Brandt had been following the argument with rising joy. His face said that this was the kill. "No plans, no money, no papers, no luggage, no tools," Brandt elucidated. "You simply wandered off to the border, sleepwalking. The rest of it was planned so well. If you planned it yourself, why was your escape so totally unplanned?"

Georg shook his head, he was lost.

"Because you weren't thinking of yourself?" said Nebe.

"Yes," said Georg.

Nebe walked to the door and threw it open with an operatic gesture and shouted, "Guards!" They appeared instantly. "Get him out of here!"

The guards pounced on Georg, locked his arms behind his back and heaved him along to the door with his feet dragging. "I can walk," said Georg. "I'm not drunk anymore."

Nebe kicked the door shut. Brandt was completely lost. Nolte was mortified. "Why did you do that? You even gave him answers he couldn't think of himself. Why?"

Nebe sat down heavily and pulled out a comb. He ran it through the fringes of hair on either side of his naked skull. "To get it over with. I offered him his life if he'd tell us what we wanted to hear and he couldn't figure it out." Nolte was watching him closely with a look of almost sexual frankness. "Nolte, go to the office and get me the diabolical plot file for this week."

"I already have," said Nolte and handed him a blood-red file with a white skull and cross bones on the cover. Nebe was dewy-eyed with affection.

"You're a good man, Nolte. We like to get them bitter and disillusioned to start with, it avoids the rush later on," he said and looked through the file, checking dates. Brandt was looking from one to the other, upset and baffled.

Nolte explained, "We keep contacting foreign agents and trying to involve them in a plot against the Führer. If and when they show up, we swallow them."

Brandt had his mouth open. Joints creaked in the silence and Nebe glanced up from the file, talking in a lecturer's leisurely tone. "Every organization of the secret police must justify its existence by proving that there are plots against the government. If there aren't any, we have to manufacture them; it's all about job security." Brandt was outraged and gave the impression of being ready to do something about it. "Grow up, Brandt," Nebe said dismissively. "We tried it by the rules and it didn't work. So we match him up with one of our ready-made plots and the hell with it."

"Don't you care who's really behind it?" Brandt was close to tears.

"No one is behind it! He thinks he's the Bamberg Rider, the Nietzschian Superman, 'The Man above the Law.' When you're above the law, you don't need reasons. Nolte, I can't read your writing here." He handed the file back to him.

Brandt interrupted. "You can't say that! At least, you can't say that officially."

Nolte read from the file. "A Major Stevens and a Captain Bast captured November 9th in ... I can't read my writing either ... I think Holland. That's the closest date."

Nebe slapped the arms of his chair. "Fine, it happened on November 8th, they were there on the 9th to pay him off."

"But that was in Holland," begged Brandt. "He was caught trying to escape to Switzerland."

"Write me a memo," Nebe said through clenched teeth. "Right now let's go home."

Nebe, Brandt, and Nolte walked out of the building through the flags, swastikas, and eagles and into the black street. The sky was fogged over and held the reflections of the street lamps in gray suspension. There was a mild wind, barely more than a breeze, but there was a cold wet edge to it. Nebe clamped his briefcase under one arm and methodically buttoned his overcoat. Brandt was thinking hard but none of his conceptual equipment fit the problem. If he couldn't solve the problem though then it proved his intelligence that he recognized it as a trick question and the defeat was really a moral victory.

"History will prove that he was a British agent even if we couldn't," he said, showing Nebe his noble profile.

Nebe made a philosophical noise, halfway between a grunt and a sigh. "History has the time. We have to reach a verdict right now."

They walked in silence. "But we have all the facts right now," Nolte objected. "Or at least all the facts we can have, and there never will be any more, only fewer and fewer. Records get lost, witnesses die. How can history make sense out of it if we can't?" He had stopped walking and Nebe stopped too with a courtesy that didn't feel natural.

"I suppose they make it up as they go, sort of like we have been doing," said Nebe and started walking again.

Nolte caught up with him. "Then why talk about it?"

"Because it is what it is, it's over," Nebe explained. "It's their problem now. And history can't be changed because some cuddly nonentity wanted to change it. That's disorderly. It's fucking undignified."

Nebe had to stop, his fist clenched on the handle of his briefcase and his head was thrown back and snarling at the sky. Nolte and Brandt were cowed into silence. They stared at each other's faces, looked away, and started walking again. They walked in silence for a while.

"It has to be something simple, maybe he has a crush on Eva Braun," decided Nolte.

"Handsome woman," Nebe agreed and Brandt nodded. They walked in silence until Nolte stopped and cursed.

"All this brain power wasted on a case this asinine. You were right; we should have faked it from the beginning."

"Never too late to do that," Nebe pointed out, "and we did have to go through the motions, it's expected." They walked again in silence. Nebe kept them on the edges of his vision. His face flashed on and off in the lights of oncoming traffic in a series of pain-filled grimaces. Then Nolte stopped under a street lamp, demanding attention.

"Something has sunk into me slowly," he said. "We've been had. He's in the SS!"

"Really?" Nebe asked in a soothing voice.

"It's too perfect not to be true. The SS staged the whole thing so the Führer could have a miraculous escape and get rid of a few more of the Old Guard. Then hand us the case to discredit the police and the Gestapo and increase their own power at the same time."

Nebe patted him on the shoulder. "Get some sleep. We'll talk about it tomorrow."

Nolte grabbed hold of his arm. "I'll prove it to you. It's a plot to undermine our authority."

"Get some sleep," Nebe insisted, wearily but without reproach. He waited for Nolte to let go of his arm, nodded politely to Brandt, then walked off and left them standing there.

Nolte called after him, "How about a beer?"

"Get some sleep!"

Nolte watched him stride off; there was nothing else to say.

FEBRUARY 19TH, 1940

IT WAS THE MORNING AFTER Georg's last interrogation and the inspectors were back in Nebe's office. They hadn't been reassigned and there was basically nothing to do but shred documents and that could only take up so much time even if you shredded each document twice. It felt like Christmas dinner with your mother-in-law. Nolte was late. He had said that he was going to confession but any honest priest would have burnt him at the stake. Nebe was trying hard to look relaxed, doing mental exercises to unlock the tension in his shoulders. He had tried to adopt a bemused philosophical attitude, one he'd worn as a younger man, but could no longer fit himself into. "I got the report to Himmler. Hand delivered it early this morning. I was hoping to avoid him but he starts work at 06:30. Would you believe that? He was not entirely satisfied."

Brandt met his glance and there was something frantic in his attentiveness. "He was... dissatisfied?"

Nebe rolled his head from side to side. "His exact words were: 'Get this shit off my desk!'"

Brandt paled. "There goes my career."

"I don't know." Nebe smiled philosophically. "We got off light. There'll be no trial. A trial, now that would have been an embarrassment. The whole point of the exercise was to make him go away, so it won't have been a total failure."

Brandt checked his pistol, a Walther PPK. Point blank to the head, the weakly driven little 7.65 caliber bullet would be as deadly as anything else. He jacked a round into the chamber and tenderly lowered the hammer. "I'll go get him," he said in a pillow-talk whisper.

Nebe coughed up a laugh. "No. No. He can't die and leave unanswered questions. He has to gradually disappear. The night-and-fog boys have him now. As I said, we got off light."

Brandt sat down heavily, limp and uncoordinated. "This goes on our record."

Nebe stood. "But, it will be forgotten. It didn't happen. It couldn't have happened therefore, it didn't. He doesn't exist."

"You're just trying to cheer me up," said Brandt and smiled.

Nebe laughed. "Come on, let's close it out."

Brandt stood up in alarm. "I thought you said that Himmler gave him to the RuSHA."

Nebe slapped him on the back. "That's what we're going to do right now." They exited, arm in arm and laughing.

As they walked down the overly lit hall they spoke of whores as mature men do, without bitterness but with the exasperated affection of the exile who reports his trouble in dealing with the embassy of his own country in a strange land. Against all orders, a window was open. The sky was clear gray and very cold and pale. The air was tense as forming ice: perfect weather for an execution. The cold gave a cottony sound to the rap of their leather heels on the marble floor. Their voices seemed to grow higher in pitch as they receded. Then there was the buzzing clatter of hard shoes on the metal stairs.

In his cell Georg paused as he heard the footsteps. He gazed longingly out at the facing brick wall; the hole was now just large enough for him to slip through. He could do it, was dying to just slip away. As the footfalls faded he let out his breath. The light outside was growing in intensity, so to try it now would be as pointless as his failed border crossing. Sure he might make it down the wall unseen but his chances of slipping through the city unnoticed in broad daylight were less than minimal. He dutifully cleared the hole of debris stacking the dislodged bricks neatly in the gap to either side. He tenderly concealed the seams around his escape hatch with plaster dust as he had each previous morning. He washed up at the basin and placed the chair diligently in front of his little secret. Another nine hours. . .

Georg's face was almost serene as he lay there gazing up through the ceiling at Switzerland. Nolte entered, flanked by Georg's bearers. He smiled as they scooped him up from his bunk. They carried him out the door but instead of turning left as usual toward the interrogation room they carried him right toward the end of the corridor and the metal stairs. Georg was suddenly fully alert, "Where are you taking me now?"

Nolte regarded him in mild amusement. "How funny, you almost look as if you actually had other plans."

At the street-level entrance to the police headquarters, Nebe and Brandt were waiting with all the necessary paperwork. Georg looked urgently from one to the other. His desperation could have passed for sentiment. Nebe gazed at him in almost paternal fondness, like one would a son going off to serve his country. He was feeling expansive; the case was officially no longer his problem. "Yes, Georg, we are going to miss you too." Georg could only open and close his mouth like a fish out of water as they led him out the door.

At the curb a black car with tinted windows and no license plates awaited. The two guards from the Gestapo HQ emerged from the car. The one patted his custom pistol grip and smiled at Georg as he accepted the paperwork from Brandt while the other dutifully cuffed Georg's hands in front of him. "Nothing personal, it's just a formality."

Georg let out a deep sigh and practically beamed at the guards. As the one guard opened the back door for him, Georg turned to look at Nebe before climbing in. "Thank you."

Nebe was speechless and Nolte and Brandt's heads swiveled in unison to look at him. The car pulled away with smooth efficiency.

Nolte looked from the car back to Nebe. "What was that?"

Nebe rubbed his hands together almost as if performing ablutions. "Honestly? I now officially no longer give a great God damn. Come along gentlemen, it's time to clean house."

Brandt was insistent. "But what will happen to him?"

Nebe was almost touched by Brandt's concern. "Himmler has set up a charming little camp, just perfect for embarrassments like Georg. It's the Führer's holding tank for political prisoners he may have a use for later, show trials etc."

Nolte was wary. "And what is our position?"

Nebe glared at him in disbelief. "You silly *fotze, we* have no position. The man doesn't, didn't, nor will ever exist. He has moved to the shadow lands, as will we if we do not successfully erase every bit of evidence that this unfortunate debacle ever took place! Clear?" Nolte and Brandt bowed respectfully, not unlike the manner in which Georg had bowed to Fritz.

MAY 1942

GEORG'S "PHONEY WAR" DID COME to an end, and Nebe's hopes for any kind of French supremacy were not to be fulfilled. He found it truly extraordinary and bitterly disappointing that the French didn't put up a fight. The French caving in gave new fuel to Hitler's fire and meant that Nebe would have to find another way to be liberated. The next best choice would be the Americans; the big problem was how to approach them without seeming obvious. On the other hand it would actually be comforting to be arrested by them rather than have to face the collapsing German hierarchy, or the rage of the Russians. The question was how to make it happen without becoming a total whore.

The best possible approach would be the representatives of the British, if they were capable of putting their petty differences aside. Still, Nebe had no leverage, at that moment he had nothing meaningful to offer them as an incentive to hear him out, they certainly wouldn't be moved by his rather pathetic desire to save his own hide. It would have been convenient to implement his errand boys, but they weren't having any. Nolte, and even Brandt, had steadily and methodically distanced themselves from him and that should have been enough to toll the bell of doom, yet as previously stated that slut Pandora was an unscrupulous bitch. She never seemed to know when to let well enough alone. Or shall we say: she reveled in same . . . and shame.

For the Gestapo, setting Nebe up was probably a most pathetically easy assignment. For Nebe himself it was more or less the next inevitable step on a path of continuous contradiction. All of his futile attempts to make contact with the allies were at best predictable, an embarrassment to the Reich and

184

to himself. A man of truly noble spirit would have simply taken his own life, quietly and neatly. Nebe had however finally embraced the fact that the meaning of life was survival, his survival.

The day they came, he was almost relieved. Even had he never met Georg Elser, he now found it nearly impossible to continue a charade he could no longer even pretend to believe in. He would be taken to a place where all the thinking would be done for him—Nirvana—someone else would have to explain what had happened . . . bliss. As far as his family was concerned he no longer existed, as such they were finally on even ground.

September 1944

In the office of the Commandant a balding middle-aged man was putting the finishing touches on the massif mahogany desk when a young guard sporting a rifle with a custom carved butt came in looking concerned. "It's confirmed, you are being transferred."

The balding head turned and although considerably heavier there was no mistaking the smile and the comfortably innocuous gaze. Georg Elser looked up at the guard paternally. "Hardly a surprise now is it?"

The young man looked at him with apprehension. "Don't you know what that means?"

Georg took a deep breath. "For them? Or for me?"

The young guard seemed baffled, Georg's smile grew warmer. "For them it means that I can't be explained away, so they have given up trying to make me something that I wasn't. I'm pretty sure that is why I was brought here in the first place; they needed time to gradually erase the event, to diminish it to the banal and everyday and thus unworthy of further consideration. They needed time to generate appropriate pretexts for the destruction and or loss of previous accounts. . . . They may have gone so far as to print that I myself was killed in the blast, not as the perpetrator but rather just a poor schmuck carpenter who happened to be passing by outside on his way home from work when the bomb blew . . . I ceased to exist on the night of November 8th, 1939 one way or the other. Perhaps that sort of deed can only be carried out if there is an element of definitive finality to it. Perhaps that is why I never bothered to plan my escape—to do so would have meant foretelling a positive outcome, for me at least. For nearly five years I've been living on borrowed time and that is probably more than most people embroiled in a world war can possibly hope for."

The young guard smiled at Georg, even though he wasn't sure why. The only certainty was that something profound had been shared and that his limited experience had in no way prepared him to comprehend such things.

The following morning an unmarked truck was waiting and Georg dutifully took his place in the line. There weren't many prisoners left at that small camp by that time and they all had one discomforting common denominator, they were *persona non grata*: the next best thing to being dead. Having been already dead would have been much more sensible, not to mention more humane and convenient to all concerned, but you can't ask for everything. To think of all the resources wasted simply because in reality there was no longer any real chain of command and the country was swarming with eunuchs terrified of responsibility.

As Georg approached the truck he carefully observed the drill: each prisoner was shackled and then assisted into the truck. Eyes down, as docile as cattle, their spirits had passed on long before. Georg locked his wrists together and looked deeply into the young guard's eyes with a most understated smile. The young guard smiled back and helped Georg step up into the truck. It really was after all a form of blindness, and that was, after all, a reason for hope. Georg was the eleventh and final man to be helped into the back of the truck.

And yet, when the truck reached its destination several hours later that afternoon only ten men stepped down.

March 1945

When Nebe received the news that he was being sent to prison, he genuinely hadn't known how to react. It was simply so unimaginable that it was entirely beyond his repertoire. He had managed so competently theretofore to be yet one more innocuous force in the status quo, a more pivotal role was totally unthinkable! On the other hand he had been secretly flattered that he still mustered enough importance to register on the scale at all, otherwise he would have been summarily executed with neither pomp nor circumstance.

Power is, at best, a poor substitute for life force. When you realize that you actually wield some sort of power, albeit in a shadow play, it can evoke a giddy feeling. On the other hand, that personal giddiness can often be mistaken for enthusiasm and thus be taken advantage of by idiots. Nebe had been far from giddy for at least a decade, yet he still felt taken advantage of. He could have had so much more to offer, and yet . . .

Nebe, Artur, SS-Gruppenführer of the Kriminalpolizei, assumed he was awaiting execution and as one does in such situations was finding it difficult to decide on the correct attitude to adopt. As dilemmas go it could be compared to choosing evening attire for an official Party event—as inane as it may seem to you, at that time the results of such a choice could have had equally irrevocable impact on one's future. He would be executed by the Sicherheitsdienst, the security service of the SS. The fact that men of that rank were still technically his inferiors made the matter of adopting the correct attitude even more of a problem. He would attempt at least to hang on to his dignity.

"Dignity," he said aloud to himself. "Dignity consists of keeping a straight face while someone is pissing in your ear." The SS-Gruppenführer had a flair for aphorism, or at least he knew how to keep a straight face, which may actually have been the key to his survival throughout his career.

He thought abstractly of escape, but the sound of the artillery assured him that was a pointless fantasy. His cell had no windows and he suspected that it was underground, still the sound reached him: like thunder, but more organized, in five-minute continuous bursts. The artillery was less than ten miles away so the Russians themselves would be much closer. Possibly, he could reach American lines, but he put the thought down. He'd been trying to make a deal with them all along and their ultimately annoying self-righteousness had made it impossible. That was after all how his "patriotism" and "dedication to the Fatherland" had been called into question in the first place. Whatever his motive might have been, an out-of-shape middle-aged man on the run was pathetic and that was a feeling worth dying to avoid. Even though he had changed sides several times, becoming a fugitive would have been a betrayal of his entire life.

It was at this point that Artur Nebe realized that he was terrified. He deliberately remembered that he was a naturally courageous man. To prove it to himself he rifled through the files of his memory but apart from a few schoolyard fist fights there wasn't much to prop that idea up. He quickly realized that the exercise was doing nothing to improve his demeanor so he put the question from his mind.

There was a sexually metallic sound, like machine guns being cocked. It was actually the bolts of the metal door being slammed back, followed by the clash and clang of the cell door being shoved open. Two children in SS uniforms stared at Nebe; they were wearing the dress gray with black piping that signified the engineering corps. The SD could wear any uniform they chose and, with the Russians this close, certainly all of the medical corps' uniforms would have already been taken by senior officers. The engineering corps would have seemed an unhealthy second best. They couldn't have been more than 18 although their collars announced that they were Obersturmbannführer, lieutenants in the SS. Of course to Nebe anyone under forty looked like a child. Those kids had obviously assumed that officers would be treated better by the Russians, the kind of stupidity that comes from being raised in a classed society.

As Nebe stared them down he observed that the one was nondescript save for soulful eyes. The other bore a striking resemblance to Reinhard Heydrich: pure Aryan, handsome except for a nose like a potato grater and an extraordinarily feminine width of hip. The children didn't know what to say. He saved them the trouble and walked out between them, up the stairs and down the long central corridor of the prison barracks. A naked man was being led between two other guards and the door slammed behind them with a screech of bolts that made him clench his teeth.

One of the boys ordered Nebe to strip. He took off his clothes, folded them neatly and kept a straight face. He took his place in front of the door between the two children in their engineer costumes and waited. And waited ...

That was the military, thought Nebe, hurry up and wait; though that aphorism was hardly original. One of the children began checking his watch. Half an hour had passed, too long even for a hanging. Or was it? Thoughts of 1936 came pouring back. . . . If they were simply being hung on a hook without a drop to speed the process along, it could take up to an hour. The situation could get ugly. The child that resembled Heydrich held out a red pack of Russian cigarettes. "Smoke?"

Nebe accepted the offering. "Danke schön." Thank you, dear. That should have been funny too, yet he maintained his straight face. After he had pulled a long, thin cigarette out of the pack the child held out a lit match. Nebe inhaled deeply.

"Are you sorry?" asked the child as he extinguished the match. That wasn't funny at all, but Nebe found himself smiling. A sign of tension he observed clinically. He had been in the Rommel plot against the Führer and, in retrospect, he was surely sorry. "It wouldn't have changed anything even had we succeeded. We were dreaming of a separate peace with the West that would enable us to continue the war against Russia, but we waited too long. We couldn't have achieved it because they had no reason to make a deal with anyone, the war was already over, the dust just hadn't settled yet."

His regrets actually ran deeper than that, yet there seemed to be no point in analysis so late in the game. The entire Wehrmacht hadn't been able to come up with a bomb that could kill one man. There wasn't one man among them willing to sacrifice his life in order to guarantee the Führer's demise.

That was pathetic and humiliating. Not even that three-fingered twit von Stauffenberg who thought he was a Renaissance man with a profile like the Bamberg Rider. Rank offered no protection against incompetence. Then that other idiot, Canaris, who had kept a list of all the conspirators in his diary so that when he was finally caught, all of the others followed in quick succession. The man suffered from such an unbelievable lack of imagination that he had even kept the diary in his wall safe. He should have just given it to the Gestapo; that at least would have been original madness. *Schweinerei!*

Nebe wondered what history would make of this mess. They couldn't possibly be remembered as heroes because, above all, heroes were supposed to be competent. Just to be affiliated with such people was humiliating. Why couldn't he have been sensible enough to get killed by the Russians? Some naïve historian out there would have considered him a hero.

The child with the soulful eyes pulled him out of his reverie. "You were rats deserting a sinking ship."

Nebe thought that was true enough but what he said was, "A man uses a cliché like that when he's afraid of the experience he is having and is trying to attain distance from it. Are you afraid, Obersturmbannführer?"

The soulful eyes flashed. "No! Clichés are dismissive." Then the lieutenant dropped his eyes and looked even more childlike than before. The brat was educated and suddenly Nebe felt ashamed. He was bullying children, and failing even at that.

The door was then flung open with a mind shattering screech of bolts and the humming clang of iron on stone. They were finally ready for him. Nebe stepped out into the yard walking between his two adopted children. It was dawn and the artillery had abated, replaced by the sound of birds singing in jubilant ignorance. He scanned the perimeter of the prison yard, but there were no trees. Suddenly, he could hear the beating of his heart. He could feel the blood wriggling in his veins, the air going in and out of the little prickly things on the inside of his lungs. He smiled again; his body just didn't want to die.

"There was one attempt on the Führer, only one that might have made a difference." Nebe actually chuckled. "The only attempt that had been competently planned, even if by an amateur assassin."

The Heydrich look-alike turned in annoyance. "By whom?"

"The Übermensch of course!" Superman. Irony when facing death was in bad taste, it gave the appearance of having lost control, but Nebe simply no longer cared what anybody thought. "That holy fool who blew up the beer hall in 1939. But for a few minutes there wouldn't have been a war." It all seemed so dim now.

The children glared at him contemptuously; Heydrich junior practically spat. "We thought we were going to win. It was an honest mistake."

They suddenly stopped walking and Nebe's eyes widened as he realized that there was no firing squad, no gallows or chopping block. It was a most perplexing relief. There was, in fact, nothing but a wooden chair against the wall near the gate with a neatly folded pile of workman's clothes on it. They couldn't have belonged to the man taken out before him, he had been naked too, and Nebe had watched him go. A small object lay on top of the clothes, an obnoxious artificial red.

The children weren't moving, Nebe considered kicking one in the shin but that would have been undignified. He stood there stiffly erect, hoping the lads knew their job. Nothing happened and finally little Heydrich snapped at him, "Do get dressed. . . ." He was clearly disgusted at having to escort naked traitors. Nebe knew better than to turn around and got down to business.

As he stepped up to the chair he discovered that the orange-vermillion thing was actually a Vatican passport, beneath it a worker's identity card.

"I'm being allowed to escape?" Even as Nebe uttered the words he knew he shouldn't have, yet his responses had now become totally spontaneous. Hope was unendurable and thus had to be exorcised in no uncertain terms.

The soulful child shook his head. "Actually you are being kicked out, but it will be said that you were killed in an air raid to avoid pursuit."

Nebe proceeded to dress, wondering what the hell he was supposed to do with the rest of his life. "That is most gracious of you; after all there really is no greater insurance policy than death."

The children were unimpressed by his philosophic banter; they simply waved him on to dress more quickly.

As Nebe dressed he suddenly found himself wondering whatever had become of the savant cabinet maker. It then became brutally obvious that all of the finest love affairs are always totally one-sided.